Stick to the Recipe

A Second Chance, Brother's Best Friend Romance

R.S. Barry

RILEY PAWS PUBLISHING

ISBN 979-8-9901858-2-1 (Ebook Edition)

ISBN 979-8-9901858-3-8 (Paperback Edition)

Library of Congress Control Number: 2024915233

Cover Design by Lily Bear Design Co — www.lilybeardesignco.com

Interior Design by R. S. Barry

1st edition 2024

To all my fellow caregivers.

You get to live your own life, too. Go find your own happiness.

Author's Note

Your mental health matters. Please be aware that this novel contains the following themes.

- Language: Strong and Frequent - F-bombs away

- Death of parent: This is a recurring theme. A parent passes from cancer on the page—if this may be distressing, you may bypass Chapter 13 completely. Grief and mourning are openly explored themes throughout the book

- Mental Health: The MMC suffers from PTSD—he suffers from nightmares and has a couple of minor episodes

- Sex: Fully described on the page but more plot that spice—3/5 Peppers

- Violence: FMC suffers two moderately violent attacks on the page by an antagonist. Also, a situation that hints at the possibility of sexual assault, although it does not happen.

First Meeting

DAVID - AGE 9

W hy did we have to move to this stupid town? I liked my old friends and my old school. Mom says Dad stayed behind for work, but I'm not a baby anymore. I know things. Isabel Torres's dad went away on business, and never came back. My parents are definitely getting divorced. They just haven't gotten around to telling me yet. Now I'm stuck in this stupid house, in this stupid town.

A rock skitters under my ratty sneaker as I flop down on the front steps and glare at the sky. The yard is bare, but green. Paint peels off black shutters against siding that may have once been yellow but has faded to an off-white.

Guess it's nice to have space to run around, I didn't have that in the apartment. My room is bigger, too.

Nobody to play with, though. I'm so bored.

Mom works so much more now. I barely get to see her. As a nurse, she spends most nights at the hospital. During the days, she picks up shifts serving food at a local diner. I went with her a couple times, but she thought I'd have more fun at home.

Why did we need to move to stupid Hitchcock, Georgia?

With a grunt, I fall back onto the stoop and look up at the crooked gutter hanging off the roofline. The branches of the giant magnolia tree wave overhead.

My stomach grumbles. When was the last time I ate? Guess I could have some cereal. Again. Not like I know how to cook.

"Hello."

I jump in fright as large brown eyes burst into my line of sight. As my heart pounds, I catch my breath and look over at a little girl.

She's about my age. Blond pigtails hang down her back in braids with pink bows at the end. Her faded jean shorts and t-shirt look loose on her skinny frame. She smiles and a gap between her front teeth winks at me.

"My name's Annabel, but everyone calls me Bella. What's your name? Momma says you just moved here. I've lived here my whole life. What's it like other places? Are you from a big city? I've never been to a city before. Sometimes my father goes for work trips, but I get left behind with Momma and the boys."

Her face screws up like she's sucked on a lemon. Guess she doesn't like these "boys". I stare at her. I've never heard so many words come out of such a small mouth so fast. Does she breathe?

"Oh. I almost forgot, here." She shoves a plate towards me. I automatically reach out and take it, slowly lowering the paper plate to my lap. She pulls a can of cola out of the back pocket of her shorts and puts it between us as she sits on the top step with me.

My eyes dart from the plate in front of me back to her. It holds two sandwiches cut into triangles, and stringy cheese stretches between the halves. The rising steam smells oily and slightly sweet.

"Well, go on and eat it already! It's not poison or nothing." She reaches over and grabs one triangle for herself. Her eyes close as she bites into the gooey sandwich and gives a little hum.

Tentatively, I pick up a half for a bite. It's a grilled cheese, but there's something slightly sweet and crispy in between the layers. This has gotta be the best grilled cheese I've ever had! The rest of the triangle disappears in three bites.

Bella smiles as she hands me the Coke to share. I smile back and take a swig, wiping my face with the back of my hand.

"So, you didn't say your name," Bella says.

"I'm David."

She turns to me, her dark brown eyes full of excitement. "Can I call you Davy? Like that song my dad likes? Something about Davy, who's still in the Navy."

"Um, ok. I guess." This girl is something else. She's kind of weird, but at least I'm not bored anymore. The second half goes down as quickly as the first.

She takes a swig from the can and wipes her mouth with the back of her hand, mimicking my earlier action. "How old are you?"

"Nine. You?" I eye the last piece, my stomach not quite full.

"Eight." She breaks the last triangle in two, handing me one. "What grade are you going into?"

I shove the entire piece in my mouth. "Fourth. You?"

"Third." She sounds disappointed. "My brother is ten going into Fourth. Any siblings?"

"Naw, it's only me and Mom." I frown a little, realizing the truth of it.

"Lucky! I have three brothers." She sticks out her tongue and blows a raspberry. That explains who "the boys" are. "Momma's teaching me to cook. They don't want to learn, so I get her all to myself. I guess that's cool. I made that grilled cheese! It's my own recipe." She grins ear to ear, revealing another missing tooth. Her pride is clear on her face.

"It's great. Thanks for sharing."

"I only cut myself once too!" She holds up a finger wrapped in a Band-Aid. We chuckle together and share the rest of the Coke. "Will you be my friend?"

"Huh?" I ask.

"Well, you'll probably get along with my brother since you're in the same class, but I met you first, so will you be my friend?" Her eyes are wide and desperate. Not sure why, but this is very important to her.

It would be nice to have a friend here. Especially if there's food involved. "Ok. Does that mean I get more sandwiches?"

She turns to me. "If you promise to always like me more than my brothers, I'll keep feeding you."

"It's a deal," I say.

Bella lifts her hand, pinky extended. "Pinky promise!" Her little mouth screws up into a serious expression.

"Pinky promise." I smile as I wrap my bigger finger around hers. Maybe Hitchcock won't be so bad. I already made one friend, and she lives next door!

Chapter Two

Military Retreat

David - Now

My palms are sweating, for Christ's sake. I wipe them on my jeans, hoping the dark wash hides the wetness. This is the most nervous I've been in my entire life—and I've stood on an active land mine for thirty minutes while someone disabled it.

I look up at the building before me. I can't quite motivate myself to enter. The bright lettering says "POP" and the bold pink logo taunts me. Big scary Marine can't walk into a restaurant and talk to a girl.

But Annabel Bennet isn't just any girl, is she?

Buck up, Marine. This is the whole reason you moved to this town. You are not a nineteen-year-old idiot anymore. You served through two contracts, saw a lot of shit, saved a bunch of people.

Out of habit, I touch my back pocket, hoping the lucky charm in my wallet will lend me courage. With one more deep breath, I ready myself for war, and open the damn door.

My eyes squint as they adjust to the dimmer light. It's 1500, and the restaurant is empty. The lunch crowd has moved on with their lives and the happy hour partiers are still counting down the minutes at work.

I scan the room, looking for threats and my target. Some habits die hard.

Three exits—the one I entered, another to the rear by the bathrooms, and doors that likely lead to the kitchen. The walls and tables are monochrome and modern, with bright splashes of art dominating the space. The plaques hanging by the hostess stand boast to customers that this is the best restaurant in town, four years in a row. Glancing around, I can believe it.

My Bella's done good.

That thought sends a pang through my chest. My Bella.

She isn't really my *anything* anymore. I'm not sure if I deserve to be something to her, but it's my mission to try—and a Marine always completes his mission.

Turning back, I find my target standing behind the bar, wiping a glass. She doesn't look up as I approach, and I can study her uninterrupted. Her blond hair sits on top of her head. The chef coat she wears is crisp and clean. Bella appears deep in thought as she inspects the glass and hums along to the music playing over the speakers—off-tune, of course. Her face has lost the roundness of youth but those adorable freckles still dance across her nose. Somehow she's even more beautiful after ten years.

Great start to the plan. I'm staring at her like a creep.

I know I should say something, but it's impossible around the lump in my throat. This could go so many different ways, most of them badly. I take a painful breath through tight lungs and will my heart rate to slow as I approach the bar.

"Hey, Hell's Bells." My voice is low and gravely to my ears.

Her head jerks up and her gorgeous chocolate eyes widen. Wordless lips part as her grip on the cup falters. It plummets. The side of the glass hits the edge of the counter and smashes, the sound deafening in the silent room.

"Davy..."

I barely hear her whisper. We simply stand there. Staring into each other's eyes. A million emotions cross her face. I read them all. The time apart doesn't matter. I know this woman better than I know myself.

So far, so good. At least she didn't throw the glass at my head.

The doors by the bar swing open and a man strides out, heading for her. "Anna, love, are you ok? I heard a crash."

Pain slashes through me as I watch him wrap his arm around my Bella. The motion is intimate and caring. My gaze locks on him as I assess my enemy. Shorter than me, but tall for a man—roughly six feet. His dimples and green eyes are annoyingly attractive. Women probably go nuts for the accent too.

Bella—or maybe it's Anna now? That's what he called her—is frozen still, staring at me. He rubs her arm soothingly and the muscle in my jaw spasms. An annoying squeaking sound pierces my ear and I realize I'm grinding my molars.

The touch must snap her from the shock. Her brown eyes narrow, and I swear I can feel her anger build like an electrical current. "What are you doing here?"

He follows her gaze and jerks back slightly in surprise. Intelligent eyes sharpen as they assess me, before looking back at her to gauge the situation.

"Good to see you, Annabel." I tuck my hands in my pockets, unsure what to do with them.

"Why are you in my restaurant? Shouldn't you be off playing hero? Or back in Hitchcock?" The hellfire I named her for burns in her eyes.

"My contract ended last year. A buddy from the Corps and I started a security business nearby. I live here now."

Her mouth opens and closes, but no words come out. It isn't easy to make my Bella speechless—the girl was always chattier than a magpie in May. Somehow I've managed it, though. I'd be proud if I weren't so damn nervous.

The silence drones on uncomfortably until the pretty boy breaks it. "We haven't met. I'm Colin. How do you know our Anna?"

My gut drops at the casual possessiveness in his statement. He carefully steps around the broken glass to give my hand a firm pump before reclaiming his spot by her side.

"David. We grew up next door to each other back in Georgia." I nod my chin at her while I maintain eye contact with him.

"David is friends with my brother," her tone is all southern belle.

Ouch. That hurts. Guess all the pinky promises meant nothing.

Colin smiles, his eyes never leaving mine. "Well now, isn't that grand. What a nice reunion. You should come by the house."

"What?" Bella's head jerks towards him, and his arm tightens around her back.

He's immune to the daggers she's shooting at him. "My better half and I recently got back from a trip to Ireland and we're having friends over for a get-together this weekend. I think you'd call it a cookout?"

What the fuck? Is this a power play or is the guy just dense? I immediately don't like how he's ignoring her wishes—or the clear "shut the hell up" signals she's throwing. "That's a mighty kind offer, but I wouldn't want to intrude."

See, I can hide behind southern charm too.

"Nonsense. Any family friend of Anna's is a friend of mine. You should come by and meet some locals. Right, love?"

He turns to her and squeezes her tighter. I clench my fist as I see his fingers dig slightly into her bicep as he stares her down.

"Yea, sure. More the merrier." She sounds flat.

I hate it. I named her Hell's Bells because she was a tenacious wild-cat when we were kids. This woman in front of me feels like a stranger, and it's breaking what's left of my heart.

"Grand!" Colin releases his hold on Bella to grab a bar napkin and pen. He jots an address and time down and hands it to me. Woodenly, I reach out and take it, eyes still on the silent but fuming woman next to him. I mumble my thanks and goodbyes and hightail it the hell out of there.

It's my first retreat in my long military career, and it sucks.

My feet eat up the pavement as I trudge along sidewalks of downtown Friendship Springs, Florida. He called her "love." What's with that? Her brother, Ace, is still my best friend, and neither he or his girlfriend, Grace, had mentioned a boyfriend when I FaceTimed them last night. Only two blocks and I'm leaving the muggy early summer weather for the sweet air-conditioning of my new offices. Even these two-ton units can't cool the fire in my veins.

The black and gold painted words "Smith and Hawthorne Security" don't fill me with the usual pride. The floor-to-ceiling displays of cameras and alarm systems don't excite me. The large prints of Marines hard at work and families safe at home don't make me smile. The company slogan, "let us protect what matters the most" doesn't inspire me.

No, I'm blind to what we've built here, too busy burning with rage and helplessness.

On my way to my desk, I kick a trash can in my way, then slump low in my chair. My pulse races and darkness creeps into the edges of my vision. All I see is that pretty boy's hand on her arm.

Squeezing.

An empty paper cup hits me in the head, freeing me from my dark spiral. I jerk up and see my friend and business partner staring at me.

"Yo! David! What's up, man? Did you hear me?" He looks more amused than pissed, so he mustn't have been yelling for me long. Then again, Ronnie Smith is probably the most laid-back Marine I've ever met.

I swivel in my chair to face him head-on. "Sorry, stuck in my head. What did you say?"

Ronnie's eyebrow arches as he studies me. "Take it the errand didn't go well?"

Not trusting my ability to speak, I merely grunt and shake my head.

"Well, buddy, what did you expect? After ten years of no contact, you'd waltz in and she'd run into your arms?" He shakes his head as he looks at me.

"No, but I wasn't expecting some guy to have his hands all over her." I grip the sides of my chair, then flex my fingers and turn towards the screen to stare at emails.

Ronnie whistles. "Damn, brother. That's rough. Is he still alive?"

"What?" I jerk my head back up to him. "Of course he's alive, asshole."

"Still got all his teeth?"

"Yea, left him just as pretty as I found him," I mutter under my breath. Leaning to one side, I take the envelope out of my pocket and toss it into the nearby trashcan. The paper is dirty and worn, the writing barely legible at this point.

Guess I don't need that anymore.

With a chuckle, Ronnie comes closer to sit on my desk and clasp one dark, scarred hand on my shoulder. "So that's it? What did she say? Is it serious?"

"Serious enough that he invited me to some stupid cookout. Since I'm a friend of *his* Anna and all." I shove the wadded up napkin at him.

Another long whistle. "Woo-ey. This is that rich suburb too. So was he being a dick or completely clueless?"

"Not sure." I replay the brief interaction in my head again. Reviewing it like surveillance.

Ronnie reaches out and tucks the paper into my polo pocket. "Well, obviously, you are going."

My chair squeals as I wheel to face him. "Are you nuts? Why the hell would I want to go?"

"Dave, you moved here for the girl. You're not seriously giving up after one try? What happened to 'never give up, never surrender'?"

"Pretty sure that's from a movie. I definitely didn't learn that one in the Marines."

"Faith, trust, and pixie dust?"

I shake my head and turn back to my email, but I can't fight the slight curl of my lips.

Typical Ronnie.

When shit got dark overseas, Ronnie was there to crack a joke and keep us together. I may have come home with some scars and demons, but I don't know if I'd be here if it wasn't for him. I'm not talking Friendship Springs—I mean alive. Period.

Having him here helps with transitioning back to civilian life. He's like a guide rope, tying my old life to my new.

"You need to get laid, man." I shoot him a side-eye and let him see the small smile. All good.

"Oo-ra!" he cries with a fist pump.

That gets a chuckle out of me. "Closer."

"So, what's the plan for this shindig? How do we prepare?"

Email forgotten, I rock back in my chair. "I don't know, man. The last thing I want to do is fuck up her life. Honestly, I'm not sure I deserve to be a part of it anymore. I may have been a dumb kid, but I fucked up bad. What is torturing myself seeing her big beautiful house, with her stupidly attractive European boyfriend going to accomplish?"

He winces. "Hot and an accent? Ouch, man."

I groan and let my head fall back. "I'm lost here, Ronnie. What can I do?"

"Improvise. Adapt. Overcome." With a brotherly squeeze of my shoulder, he walks back to his desk and gets back to work.

He's right. Now isn't the time to run scared, I need to make a plan.

Treat it like a mission.

That's it! I'll use the cookout as reconnaissance. That grip on her arm and the way he spoke for her didn't sit right. I'll check things out—for Ace and their father, of course. If her life with pretty boy is amazing, I'll bow out.

I rub at the ache in my chest. Living in the same small town would suck, but at least she'd be somewhat in my life. Even with her eyes full of fire, those few minutes together felt like coming up from drowning.

Definitely could use some expert guidance, though. I pull out my phone and start punching out a text.

Me:

Hey Sunshine, I need your help…

CHAPTER THREE

Tenderizing Chicken

ANNABEL - NOW

Thwack, thwack. The metal tenderizer hits the cutting board with a satisfying sound. If only it was that... that... scoundrel's face instead of chicken. *Thwack!*

Ten freaking years! Ten years without a word and he shows up *now?* Well, buddy, you're about nine years too late. GAH!

"Uh... Chef? You ok?"

I whip my head around to glare at my sous chef. Tameka Depp has worked for me since we opened Pop. She's a great cook, and the only reason I don't work 24/7, but that doesn't stop me from snapping at her today. "I'm fine. Why ever wouldn't I be?"

Thwack, thwack!

Why did Colin invite him to the cookout? So much for loyalty! I went out of my way to help him win back my best friend last year. Now they are happily married up and I'm here stuck facing a viper in a freaking polo.

I groan a little as I picture him again. David had always been a good-looking boy, but it was a man that walked into my restaurant yesterday. The dark trimmed beard suited him, though I don't want to admit it. He'd packed on more muscle, too. That shirt molded to his chiseled torso and bulging biceps. Tattoos peeked out from the bottom of the sleeve, another on his lower forearm. Those tight jeans had hugged muscular buns and thighs.

Not that I was looking.

Since he barged back into my life, I've felt on edge. Don't get me started on the naughty dreams and memories he stirred up. Why did he have to look so good?

THWACK!

Why did he have to come here of all places?

THWACK!

I twitch as something wet hits my face.

"Uh... Chef... you got a little something..." I turn to Tameka, the mallet still raised in my hand. She swallows as she points to her cheek.

My hand touches something cold and slimy on my face. Gingerly, I pull it off and inspect a bit of pink meat dangling from my finger and thumb. Then I look down at the mutilated poultry on my workstation. "Son of biscuit!"

My saucier, Tony Carbone, wanders over and peeks over my shoulder. "Wow, boss. That chicken looks like Swiss cheese! Ow! What the hell, Meeka?"

I turn to find him rubbing his arm and Tameka shooting daggers at him. What is happening to me? I never mess up cooking?

"Tameka, can you have someone run this through the grinder? We'll feature buffalo chicken sliders as a special tonight. Tony, think you can whip up some different sauces for that? Vary up the heat level, though."

"Heck yea, Chef!" He gives a little fist pump. "I have this ghost pepper sauce I've been dying to use!"

"Ok, just make sure we have plenty of milk and bread. If anyone goes to the hospital, it's coming out of your paycheck. Tameka, you're in charge of the rest of prep. I'm going to go wash up."

I'm already pulling off my apron and unbuttoning my work coat to drop in the laundry as I move through the industrial kitchen. A chorus of "Yes, Chef" echoes behind me as I climb the stairs by the back door.

When we opened Pop five years ago, I'd picked this location partially for the apartment above. Sinking what little savings I had into this place had left little room for a security deposit. I am so lucky my two best friends agreed to join me on this crazy adventure and invested heavily in my dreams.

Time for a quick shower and to get my head on straight. It's Friday night and the dinner rush is always mad. We've enjoyed a steady stream of success since we opened, but our popularity skyrocketed after a viral speed dating incident last year. It had been part of my plan to get Colin and Brianna back together.

The massive uptick in business was simply a bonus.

I hurry through my routine, hoping the comforting scent of my shampoo soothes my frayed nerves. Magnolia. It always reminds me of home. The slight licorice and rose smell turns bitter, though, as memories of a dark-haired boy come to mind instead of my family. With a frustrated huff, I turn the water full cold to chase the ghosts away.

As I'm towel drying my hair, my phone rings on the nightstand. Seeing my brother's name on the screen, I swipe to answer the video call. "Hey, Atty, what's up?"

At thirty-one, Atticus and I are roughly a year apart. His friends call him Ace, but he'll always be Atty to me. Being so close in age, folks confuse us for twins. We often fight like cats and dogs, but when times get tough, we are a team.

"Bella Bug! We got news!" The image shifts in a nauseating rush of color. A pretty woman with curly red hair and blue eyes joins my brother's handsome face on my screen.

"Hey, Grace! Good news?"

She holds up her hand to the camera and a giant diamond sparkles in the light. "We're getting married!" Her smile shines brighter than the massive rock.

"Aw! Finally, you guys. I'm so happy." They've been together since high school and are just about the cutest darn couple there is.

"I wanted to wait until after my residency, so I could get her the ring of her dreams. Not to mention have time for a honeymoon." Atty waggles his eyebrows at me before planting a loud kiss on a beaming Grace.

"Gross."

"Grow up, baby sis."

I stick my tongue out at my big brother. "Have you set a date?" I ask.

"Day before Labor Day. Figured the long weekend would make it an event."

"Wow, that's only a few months away."

Grace's face grows a little more serious. "I wanted to ask you this in person, but I wasn't sure if I'd see you soon enough. Will you be my maid of honor?"

My eyes prickle with happy tears. Grace has been like a sister to me for half my life. "Of course! What do you need?"

"Nothing. We've been talking about this for a long time, so it's practically planned. Ceremony at the church and a small reception in the backyard."

"Let me know if I can do anything to help. Food, cake, just name it. I love you guys."

"I love you too, Bella! I have to go call the other bridesmaids. Here's Ace." With a quick air kiss, Grace is off and I'm left with my big brother.

"Listen, Bug. Don't get huffy, but I need you to do something for me." His usual good-ole-boy smile is conspicuously absent. He suddenly looks a lot like our dad. Atty runs his tongue over his teeth and narrows his eyes. "I need you to be nice to David."

What in the ever-loving hell is he going on about? "Atticus…"

"Don't 'Atticus' me, Annabel. I don't know what happened between you two, and frankly, I don't give a rat's ass. He is my best friend and my best man. Find a way to get along. If your bickering ruins this for Grace, I swear I won't talk to you again."

This time, my eyes burn with tears of a different emotion. "Atty…"

He wipes one tanned hand over his face. When he looks at the camera again, his baby blue eyes soften. "Bella, I'm sorry. You two are just so important to me. I don't have a childhood memory without the both of you in it. It was easy to ignore whatever feud the two of you have going on while he was deployed. But he's back for good now, and I need you to find a way to get along. I can't lose either of you. Please don't make me choose."

My nose twitches as I hold back tears. I've never really thought about how my brother might feel stuck in the middle. There'd been too much loss in our lives, I can't cause him any more. "Ok, Atty, I'll try harder. For you."

"Thanks, Bug. It's for him too, retiring hasn't been easy. He actually moved near you and he could use a friend."

My jaw aches as I clench my teeth. "He already came by the restaurant. A heads up would have been nice, by the way." My brother has the decency to look guilty. "He's got an invite to a cookout at my friend's tomorrow, though." I glue a fake smile on.

"That's great. Keep an eye on him for me. I'm worried about him." I nod, unsure what to say. "I love you, Bug. Come home soon."

"I love you, too, Atty."

The screen goes dark in my hand and I'm left in thought. Conflicted.

I'm nearly thirty, for Pete's sake. A fully grown adult with my own highly successful business. A team of loyal staff to lead and supervise. I deal with demanding customers on the regular, I should be able to just paste on a smile and be civil to David.

My eyes land on the Hitchcock High football sweatshirt in the back of my closet. My fingers stretch out to touch it, but I pull my hand away as if burned.

There is too much history. Too many feelings. I would do anything for my family, but this almost feels too much. Not that Atty knows exactly what he's asking of me. How deep that wound still runs.

I hang the towel up and quickly fix my damp hair into a long braid. Walking through the tidy apartment, I slip back into my work shoes by the door and lock up.

There's a reason I moved away from home. The official story was that a small country town like Hitchcock couldn't support the kind of restaurant I wanted to create. That I was moving with my two best friends from college to start the business together in this up-and-coming area surrounded by industrial parks, businesses, and tourist locations. It made sense.

Heck, that's even what my best friends and partners, Brianna and Nic, believe.

David and our past are my personal dark secret. One I didn't want to bring back into the light. I sigh.

It's for Atty and Grace. For them, I can slap on a smile and play nice.

Even if I'm dying inside.

Atty said David needed a friend. He didn't say it had to be *me*. That's it! I'll introduce him to some guys in my circle. Find a friend for him, satisfy my promise to Atty, then stay the heck away. It's a small city, but it's bigger than back home. How hard can this be?

Feeling better, I skip down the stairs and re-enter my domain—the kitchen of Pop. The gleaming stainless steel surfaces and appliances fill me with pride. I made this.

Brianna handles the financial side—taxes, bills, paychecks. Nic is the artist and marketing wiz who designed the place. But the menu is all mine, and it's the food people talk about most. Well, that and the amazing drinks from our hotter-than-sin bartender.

"Hey, Anna. How's it going?"

Speak of the devil and he shall appear. Asher Ramstad casually leans against a nearby table, snacking on a burger. How the man eats like a teenager and looks like a model, I'll never know. He was our first hire and has become more friend than employee. His eyes fill with concern as they search my face.

Jiminy Cricket, someone tattled about the chicken incident.

"Hey, Asher. Just peachy, sugar." I slap on my best southern belle smile—better start practicing now.

"Mmhmm. Nothing on your mind? No news to share?"

"Well, my big brother is finally getting married. Happy to get a little more estrogen in my family tree. After a lifetime of brothers, I'll have a sister at last."

Asher chews slowly as he studies me. "And we like this sister?"

My eyes prickle again with bittersweet memories, my lips soften. "I love Grace. They've been together for fifteen years, so in a lot of ways she's already like family. She helped me with my hair and makeup and stuff in high school."

"Damn! No wonder you said 'finally'. Why wait so long?"

"Medical residency. Atty says he waited to buy a bigger ring, but the truth is he didn't want her to feel like she had to follow him around for school. He recently moved back home to take over the local practice."

I'm beaming with pride by the time I finish. I love all my brothers, but Atty and I have a special bond. We're also the most alike in how we prioritize family and helping others. Him through medicine, me through food and friendship.

"Very nice. So this shindig will be back in Georgia?" He draws out the vowels.

I laugh at Asher's attempt at a southern drawl. "Darn tootin'."

"Which brother? Don't you have like three?"

"Four actually. It's my older brother, Atty. I don't think either of the twins are even dating anyone. Rhett's still a baby at eighteen."

Asher finishes the last bite of his burger and wipes his mouth on a napkin. "Well, let me know if you need a date. Though I'm warning you now, I plan to go home with one of the bridesmaids and get me some sugar." With a wink and bump of my shoulder, he heads back out to supervise the bar.

Shaking my head at my friend's antics, I smile and feel more myself again. I clap my hands and draw the attention of my kitchen and wait staff. "Listen up. Tonight's special will be a buffalo chicken slider trio with a choice of sauces, served with truffle fries. We're also offering a pan fried Branzino with lemon butter sauce, broccolini, and rice. I got a case of beautiful tomatoes this morning, so Tad, get going on some fresh mozzarella and we'll do a Caprese appetizer. Ryan, what do we have for dessert?"

"Tiramisu, Chef."

"Excellent. Any questions?" I pause and survey the eager faces around me. "Ok, let's have a great dinner service."

A unified shout of "Yes, Chef" answers me, and I get to work.

The sizzle of food hitting a hot pan. The clanks of pans. The tangy smells filling the air. This is my happy place. Here, I create delicious meals for others. I get to be part of someone's first date or graduation celebration. The big moments. Here, I create joy. With a genuine smile on my face, I lose myself to the magic of the kitchen.

CHAPTER FOUR

New Beginnings

I'm worried about Davy. He promised he'd write, but it's been over six months since he shipped out and I haven't heard a word.

Not for my graduation.

Not for my birthday.

Not even at Christmas.

Every time the mail comes my heart leaps, hoping today will be the day I hear from him. Praying for news that he's safe. A thick envelope full of apologies and explanations of some extended mission. Then it drops to my stomach when the mailbox is empty yet again.

We've never gone this long without talking. Even when he was in basic training, I'd gotten a few letters. I've sent him a letter every week with updates from home. Twenty-five envelopes—all un-answered. It's like he's a ghost—and considering he's behind enemy lines, I'm afraid he really might be.

The plate of cookies shakes in my hand as I climb the Hawthornes' front steps. Before I can chicken out, I knock on the big oak door and wait.

Mrs. Hawthorne answers the door with a tired but happy smile. She still works too much, but I understand the need for distraction from the constant worrying. I try to smile in return, but I fear it might look manic.

"Bella, dear, how great to see you! Are those my favorite macadamia nut cookies? Come on in for a visit."

We walk through the sparse living room. Everything looks exactly the same as when they first moved in. A series of school pictures hang along the hallway, showing David growing up. The last picture is his official Marine Corps headshot. My fingers trace his handsome face for a moment before I continue on to the kitchen.

"Well, this is a pleasant surprise. Besides my monthly book club and weekly backgammon games with your father, I don't get to socialize much. Let's use the fancy dishes." With a conspiratorial wink, Mrs. Hawthorne pulls out her china tea cups and dessert plates. She puts the kettle on, and sits across from me at the worn wooden table. "How's school going, dear?"

"Pretty good. First semester is almost done. I'm doing general business studies online at the community college so I can help at home. Not sure what to do with it, though." It's because I'm too distracted worrying about Davy, but I'm not going to say that to his mom.

She grabs a cookie and takes a large bite. Her eyes close in bliss. "You should be doing this! Anyone with a gift in the kitchen like you shouldn't waste it. David's right that your cooking is heaven-sent."

My heart lurches at his name. Trying to act cool, I pick up a cookie and study it. "How's he doing? Have you heard from him lately?"

"Oh, yes! He did very well in his specialized training, and he's settling in on his first deployment. My David never fails to send a letter every month."

Everything goes still as her words reverberate in my brain. My chest burns and my pulse pounds in my temple. She's gotten a letter? Every month?

A high-pitched scream sounds.

Just as I'm sure it's coming from me, Mrs. Hawthorne stands up to grab the kettle. She settles back in her chair across from me and pours us both tea with a proud smile—completely unaware that she's ripped my heart out.

"Are you ok, dear? You look a bit pale." Her tone turns concerned.

"Probably haven't eaten enough today." I stuff the cookie in my mouth and sip my tea to hide my quivering lip.

Don't you dare cry.

I quickly change the topic to ask about this month's book club selection, and Mrs. Hawthorne dives into an animated retelling of the latest thriller they are reading. After a polite amount of time, I say my goodbyes, claiming I should start making dinner for the boys.

That night, as I cry into my pillow, his face haunts me. He pinky promised he would write. Our pinky promises used to be sacred. The clock shows two in the morning by the time my tears have dried out. In their place is hellfire rage, and a new purpose.

I boot up my laptop and research cooking or hospitality programs—anywhere but Georgia. The University of Florida catches my eye—they have management and food science courses and the tuition doesn't look bad. I spend the rest of the night working on my application.

For the next month, I throw myself into my studies, helping with the boys, and secretly applying for scholarships. Atty's living on campus this year, so we only see him on weekends. The twins are rarely around. Much too busy being cool high schoolers now, but they manage to make it home to eat. Rhett's only eight, so I help with homework and school events to stay distracted.

Guilt gnaws at me for not telling my family about my plans. They all have their own crap to deal with. No need to upset everyone if I don't get in. When that big envelope arrives almost two months after I apply, there's no more procrastinating.

I break the news to Dad over his favorite French toast casserole on a crisp April morning.

His face lights up with a proud smile and glimmer in his eyes. "Your cooking is a gift and you should share it with the world. You can do anything you set your mind to, baby girl. If you feel this is the best way to get there, I support you."

We both end up sharing a tearful hug. True to his word, Dad does everything he can to help me find more scholarships and even drives me to campus on that first fall day. Atty and the twins haul boxes into my new dorm while Dad and Grace unpack, and Rhett plays a video game on my bed. It's a family affair.

There are many tears and enough hugs to last until Christmas as they climb into the cars to start the three-hour drive back home. Of course, I'll miss my family, but I need this fresh start. A chance to figure out who Annabel Bennet is.

I dry my face and head back to my triple suite. A petite brunette and stunning girl with black hair sit in the common area as I unlock my door.

The brunette turns to me and gives a little wave. "Oh, hello. You must be one of our new roommates. I'm Brianna and this is Nic."

I take a deep breath. Time for the next phase of my life to begin.

"Hey, I'm Anna."

CHAPTER FIVE

Memory Lane

My eyes burn with unshed tears. I squeeze them tight, then open them wide, trying to concentrate on the task at hand as my vision blurs. Looking up at the ceiling, I will the flow to stop and blindly toss the chunk of onion onto the growing pile.

"Told you, if you light a candle, the fumes from the onion won't make your eyes water." Brianna pushes a lit votive closer to me. The discomfort clears almost instantly.

I take a swig of my wine. "Why do you always have to be right?"

Bree smiles at me over the kitchen island and takes a sip of sweet tea. "It's a blessing and a curse."

"Don't you have a husband to go curse with your help? Where in the heck did Nic go, anyway?"

Her hand darts out to grab a piece of pepper from my prep bowl. I try to slap Bree's hand away, but the petite woman is too fast. Dang pregnancy hormones are making her superhuman. I blame her husband, that feisty leprechaun got me into this mood.

"I don't know. Bathroom?" Bree hops off the stool and comes around the counter to give me a side hug. "You know girls' night is sacred. Wasn't about to abandon you in this shit mood. I left him at home playing some game with the boys. Figured it was safer to keep him away from you and knives." She snags another pepper and runs back to her stool, cheeks puffing out.

How is this woman so small yet so fast?

A shout comes from the direction of my bedroom. "Found it!" Nic enters from the hall with a thin book held over her head. She grabs the stool next to Bree and drops the book with a thud.

I see the words "Hitchcock High" on the cover and immediately try to grab it away from her. "Nicolette Kato-Atherton, why the heck were you diggin' through my things?"

Memories haunted me all night thanks to Atty's call. At two a.m.—you know, when all good decisions are made—I dug out my old yearbook and poured over the pages. Trying to sort between history and fantasy.

"Because you've been annoyingly close lipped and Irish could only give so many details about Mystery Man." She acts gruff and still gives Colin a hard time, but deep down, I know she's a big softie for him. "If you grew up together, he has to be in here." She flips the pages until she finds me.

Bree leans in for a better look. "Aw, look at little Annabel. He's probably in her brother's class though. You went too far."

Dang her logic and problem-solving skills. I go back to chopping vegetables and chicken for kebabs. The blade makes satisfying thuds as I use unnecessary force. I dart glances at my ex-best friends, trusting my knife skills to keep my fingers intact.

"Hold up! Atticus Bennet? No one is allowed to say shit about my fancy-ass name anymore." Nic looks up at me, one perfectly plucked ebony brow arched.

"Momma loved to read. We're all named after whatever she was reading when she went into labor. So Atticus Finch from *To Kill a Mockingbird*."

Bree looks thoughtful. "So *Annabel Lee*, that's a poem, right? Edgar Allen Poe?" At my nod, she claps her hands in excitement. "This is fun. Who's next?"

"There are the twins, Huck and Tom." I drop the cutting board and knife in the sink and grab the soaking skewers.

"Easy. *Adventures of Tom Sawyer*, Huckleberry Finn and Tom Sawyer." Bree's love of reading almost rivals Momma's—of course, she's getting them all correct.

"No shit? Please tell me he's legally named Huckleberry." I nod and her grin widens. "I freaking love your family."

I laugh as I arrange cut vegetables and chicken into kabobs. "Just don't call him that to his face. Last but not least is Rhett, the baby."

Brows furled, Bree appears stumped. A slow smile spreads over Nic's face. "Frankly, my dear, I don't give a damn. Rhett Butler, *Gone with the Wind*!" The two high five. "Ok, back to Mystery Man. Colin said his name was David, right?"

"That one!" Bree points to a picture on the next page. "David Hawthorne. Says here he was varsity football and joined the Marines after graduation."

Nic looks up at me, a calculating gleam in her eyes. "So why'd he come to Friendship Springs?"

I shrug my shoulders as I keep stabbing the chicken and vegetables, picturing David's stupid, handsome face. "Beats me. You'll have to ask the man yourself."

"You didn't ask him when you saw him?" She keeps staring me down.

I refuse to admit I never got an answer to that question. "Didn't come up." I hold her stare, mentally screaming at her to let it go.

Nic can always tell when you're holding something back. She picks apart people like I pick apart recipes. It's so annoying when she uses her powers for evil.

Bree ignores us, still flipping through the yearbook. "Oh, look at this one!" She stops on a full-color picture of a football game.

"That's probably the state championship." David caught the ball and scored an amazing eighty-yard touchdown to win the game. The cheerleaders and fans had swarmed the field to celebrate with him.

"Is that your brother? Who are the girls?" Bree's eyes shine with innocent curiosity.

Guess I'm not getting out of this anytime soon.

With a sigh, I wash the chicken and marinade off my hands, then take a fortifying gulp of wine. Should have gone with something stronger. Thinking twice, I refill my glass and walk around the island to inspect the photo over my small friend's shoulder..

At the center is David, of course. Atty's smiling face shows next to him. He'd been one of the first to run out. Eyes bright, he has one arm around David's shoulders, and another around Grace, looking like the American dream in her cheerleader uniform. On David's other side, stands a curvy brunette in a matching outfit who stares up at him like he's a god.

I point them out as I name them. "My brother Atty is here. That's my future sister-in-law, Grace. David, and that was his girlfriend, Holly. Ugh, I bet she's a bridesmaid. She always hated me, no clue why." My Moscato turns bitter in my mouth at the memories. Regina George had nothing on Holly Morris and her queen bee ways.

Nic snorts to my left, and I jerk my head to her. "What?"

She levels me with a sardonic brow. "I bet she did."

"What's that supposed to mean?" My fist sits on my hip as I brandish my wine glass like a weapon.

"You said that's his girlfriend, right?" She jabs her finger at Holly's face while staring at me. At my nod, she continues. "She's looking at him. Who's he looking at?" Nic uses her finger to trace a line from his eyes to a blond girl cheering in the stands.

Me.

"Damn, is that you, Anna?" Bree turns to look up at me.

"That doesn't mean anything. David and I grew up together. He was basically a fifth brother." Until he wasn't. My eyes search for answers at the bottom of my wineglass.

"Um, according to the hundreds of 'brother's best friend' tropes I've read, it could mean something." Bree's eyes dance with excitement.

"I think I liked you better when you were anti-romance." Bree's eyes round and I feel a twinge of guilt.

It's true though! A year ago, Bree would have backed me up from Nic's meddling. I pull her into a side hug. "I'm sorry, Bree. It's been a weird week. Between surprise reunions and my brother's announcement... I'm just overwhelmed."

"It's ok. We all have off days." Bree excuses herself to pee, leaving me and Nic alone with that stupid yearbook still open. I should have burned that thing years ago.

Nic flips the page and finds a photo from graduation. I'm standing between Atty and David in their caps and gowns. Their arms are around my shoulders, and mine around their waists, all smiles for the camera. "You seem close." She lets her unsaid question hang in the air.

"Yea, well, that was another lifetime." I catch the bottom of the book and close it with one finger. Like it could bite me. "Please, just let it go, Nic. We didn't part well and I don't want to discuss it. I'll be civil tomorrow because Colin invited him. I'll smile and make nice because Atty asked me to. But I don't need a new friend and I'm not interested in reuniting with an old one."

Hands up in surrender, Nic takes a step back. "Ok, if you say so." She's so not letting it go.

With a groan, I throw back the rest of my wine and then tidy up the kebob prep. When Bree returns, I'm stacking tupperware boxes into two canvas totes on the counter.

"What's all this?" Bree cocks her head and rests her hand on her rounded belly. I don't think she even realizes she's doing it. Despite my rotten mood, I smile at the sight. It's great to see Bree so calm and happy. She had a rough couple years there, but between her fabulous new job, her crazy-in-love husband, and a baby on the way, she's thriving.

"I made a few things for the cookout. Figured you could take them to your house tonight and I'll bring the rest tomorrow." I run through my mental checklist, making sure this is everything.

"There's more? Anna, this is too much."

Nic puts a hand on Bree's shoulder. "Pfft. What's the use of having a chef for a best friend if you don't let her feed you?" She still has that calculating look in her eye.

Yup, definitely not letting it go. Maybe I shouldn't have cooked so much.

Some people go for a jog when they're stressed. Others get a quick dopamine high from sex, or chocolate, or cat videos. Hey, I don't judge. Me—I cook. And my family and friends know it.

Bree fights a yawn, saving me from another interrogation. "Better get Preggers home before she falls asleep. I'll be over early to help you set up." I carry the bags of groceries out, hug my friends goodbye, and turn back to the restaurant that is my pride and joy. Debating what to do next, I stand indecisively.

If I go back upstairs, I'm just going to bake something. I don't particularly want to be alone either.

Decision made, I cut through the kitchen to a chorus of greetings from my staff and make my way out to the bar. Grabbing a seat on the end, I wave down Asher for a drink.

"Hey boss, what're we having tonight?" Asher rests his hands on the bar and leans towards me. His biceps bulge and pecs pop under his fitted company polo. He really is gorgeous. He keeps his dirty blond hair shaved on the sides and longer on top, which waves past his chin when it's down. Today he has it pulled back in a little bun, highlighting his piercing blue eyes.

I will myself to feel something. Anything like the electric current I felt when I looked up and saw David standing there. Goodness, was that only a few days ago? Nothing. No spark. Not even a butterfly wiggles in my stomach.

"Shit." I deflate in my chair and rest my chin on my palm, eyeing him again.

Asher rocks back as if hit. "Wow. Don't think I've ever heard you swear before." Without breaking my gaze, he grabs a shot glass and a bottle, neatly pouring the amber liquid by muscle memory. "What's up?"

I wave my free hand at him, wildly gesturing at all of him. "I'm not attracted to you." Grabbing the shot, I throw it back and the cinnamon whiskey burns on the way down.

Strong fingers take the glass from my hand. Asher refills it and throws it back himself. The empty glass clinks on the bar top as he grimaces. "God, that's awful. I'll never understand how you girls drink that stuff. I'm not sure if I should be offended. This have anything to do with the chicken massacre?"

Groaning, I squeeze my eyes shut. "You heard about that?"

"Everyone heard about that. Tony has a big mouth."

With a tortured moan, I push myself up over the bar and grab the bottle of Fireball and a highball glass. "Memories better off buried." I pour the whiskey into the glass.

My cell vibrates in my pocket. I dig it out to find a new email from Grace.

Hey ladies!

Can you believe it!? Thank you all for agreeing to stand up with me. You all mean so much to me. We can't wait to celebrate with all of you - so we decided September is too far away! We're planning a bachelor/bachelorette getaway over the 4th of July! Mark your calendars. Ace booked a giant cabin by the lake for a weekend of fun. Details attached. Can't wait to see you there!

Love,

Grace

I double click the header to see the rest of the recipients, then clutch my whiskey glass. It's a veritable who's who of my least favorite people from high school: Mae Sullivan, Tinsley Ellis, Hope Allen, and—of course—Holly Morris. Ok, maybe that's harsh. Tinsley was never mean to me and I don't know Grace's cousin, Hope, well.

Scanning the message again, my eyes widen. A joint bachelor/bachelorette? As in a weekend stuck in a cabin with the groomsmen. Including the incredibly sexy best man I'd rather avoid. Just peachy.

Being alone suddenly doesn't sound so bad.

Waving at Asher, my whiskey still in hand, I head back through the kitchen to my apartment. The yearbook on the counter taunts me.

Knowing better, I flip back to a photo of the cheerleading team. Holly's stupid face sneers up at me. If Holly was my personal torturer, Mae was her second in command. This is going to be the longest three months of my life.

With a growl, I toss the book into a basket of magazines and head to bed. Tomorrow is going to suck. If I'm going to play nice, I need some sleep.

I can't wait for this wedding to be over.

CHAPTER SIX

Summer Nights

DAVID - AGE 11

This is going to be the best summer ever. Mr. Bennet put an addition on their house and helped us build a clubhouse out of the extra bits. It's right on the property line and he says it's for all of us. It's finally finished! Bella convinced our moms to let us have a camp out tonight.

"There. It's perfect." Bella stands next to me and surveys the inside of the little shack. Christmas lights "borrowed" from the garage cling to the ceiling over a mosquito net. A box fan sits on bricks in one corner to battle the oppressive Georgia heat. Flattened boxes line the ground for some cushion and protection from the dirt. Blankets and pillows snuck from both houses dot the two full air mattresses crammed side by side.

Ace ducks in the door with an extra-long extension cord. "Looks good, Bug."

The twins come in behind him like a tornado. "We want to camp out, too!" Huck, the more outspoken of the two, glares at his big brother. Tom comes in more quietly to stand next to his twin, copying his expression.

The family resemblance is strong as Ace crosses his arms and returns the glare. "We're in middle school now. We don't have to play with babies."

Huck shoves him. Well, tries to anyway, the bigger boy doesn't budge. "We're not babies. We're six!"

"And I'm twelve. So I get double the say." Ace places his palm on Huck's forehead and pushes him arm's length away. Huck's fists miss as he keeps swinging.

"Bella is still in elementary school, same as us." Even at six, no one can beat Tom at logic. Us three older kids eye each other, trying to think of a plan.

"That's ok, Atty," Bella says, her voice all sweetness. "If they think they can handle sleeping out all night. All alone. Nothin' but us out here." She pauses and looks thoughtful. "Well, us and the coyotes."

"Coyotes?" Huck's voice squeaks.

"Mmhmm, and bats." The twins are now eyeing each other nervously. "Momma read this book about a bat that could turn into a man. You know what it ate?" The boys shake their heads, eyes wide. "Blood. The fresher, the better."

"You're making that up." Tom gulps.

"Yea, w-we're not scared." Huck's clenched hands tremble at his sides. A rustle outside the clubhouse makes them jump. "What's that?" they ask in unison.

Bella looks at them, all innocence. "Probably just a rattler."

That girl is downright scary when she wants to be. I swear she can convince anyone to do anything. Best stay on her good side. Especially if I want snacks.

"Let's get out of here!" Huck is running back to the house before he even finishes the sentence.

"Wait for me!" Tom trips on the extension cord as he shoots off after his twin.

Ace laughs and gives Bella a high five. "Good one, Bella."

We collapse onto the mattresses, Bella in the middle. "Why do I have to sleep on the crack?"

"Because you're the smallest." Ace adjusts the pillow behind him and splays out more.

I scoot closer to the wall. "Here, Bells, there's room on this one." Bella smiles at me and squirms near, pulling her pillow and blanket with her. The scent of magnolia reaches my nose as she settles in. Her small body gives off heat where her arm touches mine. A funny feeling rises in my belly. Am I hungry? Guess I should have had more spaghetti for dinner.

We stay up telling stories and making plans for the summer ahead. As the moon brightens through the slats in the walls, we grow tired and quiet. Cicadas sing in the trees, almost drowning out Atticus's snores.

"It's not fair." Bella grips the blanket over her chest as she stares up at the twinkly lights.

I roll on my side to see her better. There's barely enough light to make out the frown on her face. "What isn't?"

"Even the twins get to go to baseball camp this year. Why am I always left behind?" She turns her head and I see sadness in her eyes.

Careful not to wake Ace, I drop my voice to match hers. "Well, your dad does run the baseball camp, Bells. Makes sense for the boys to go with him."

"Daddy says I need to stay home and help Momma. How come I gotta stay home with momma and learn girl things while they get to go off and play?" The bridge of her freckled nose wrinkles.

My chest feels tight. I don't like it when Bella's sad. She's usually the one cheering me up. I roll flat on my back and think of how to respond. "Well,

I'm glad you're going to be around this summer. Who else would I hang out with?"

"You're not going to camp too?" The mattress dips as she sits up to look at me, causing Bella to slip closer.

"Nah, I don't like baseball much." I don't mention that Mom's been working extra shifts again and I don't want to stress her out asking for expensive camps. If I say something to Bella, she'll probably start a bake sale and give me the money.

"Oh, ok then." She settles back down facing me. I tug the blanket back over her shoulder. "Thanks. So are you ready for middle school? It'll be weird not seeing you at lunch."

"Yea, it's only one year, though. Then you'll be back with us. Plus, we'll still walk to school and back together. You'll see, nothing's going to change."

"That's good. Hey, Davy?" Her voice sounds sleepy.

I turn to look at her. "Yea, Hell's Bells?"

"I'm really glad you moved here." She snuggles deeper into her pillow, the mattress bouncing under us.

I smile at her as her eyes drift closed. Long lashes rest on polka-dotted cheeks. "Me, too, Bella. Me, too."

Chapter Seven

Scoping the Competition

David - Now

I can't believe Ronnie talked me into this. Why do my palms tingle? Is my shirt too tight? My eyes dart from the house number and then back to my phone, checking for the fourth time that I'm in the right place. Stalling, really.

Swallowing, I raise my hand and knock before I can change my mind. Shifting the bouquet in my hand, I wait. The door opens to reveal cautious brown eyes.

My mouth goes dry as Bella stands in front of me. Her hair is pulled into a high ponytail. A pink jumpsuit accentuates her long legs, the gold belt highlights her narrow waist. The beautiful girl of my memories has blossomed into a gorgeous woman.

"Hi." I clear my throat and try again. "Hi, uh I brought these." I shove the yellow roses at her. "Sorry, they didn't have magnolias." Shut up! Don't ramble.

She looks at the flowers like they might bite her. When she takes them, she holds them away from herself. "Uh, I'll go put these in the kitchen."

Shoving my hands in my pockets to hide their tremble, I follow her into a neat kitchen. With its gleaming white counters and cabinets, it's a scene straight out of one of the home magazines at the dentist. "You must love cooking here." Bella stiffens, head still stuck in the refrigerator. "Anything I can help with?"

Bella straightens and shoves trays of food at me. None too gently either. "Here, why don't you put those push-ups to use." The way she mutters it, I'm not sure I'm supposed to hear her. My lips quirk as I fight a smile. For a second there, I see a hint of the Bella I remember.

Without a word, I stand with my arms outstretched as she loads them up with stacked trays of meats and vegetables. It all smells amazing, but she was always the best cook I ever met. Bella grabs a couple more covered dishes and speeds out of the kitchen. I follow her through an equally stylish living room towards an open patio door. There are no pictures I can see. At least I don't have to look at more proof she's happier without me.

The sun blinds me as we step outside. Bella walks up to a smiling Colin manning an outdoor kitchen. He wraps his arm around her when she approaches. Acid fills my mouth and I quickly swallow it down. She whispers something to him, and Colin looks over at me, all smiles.

"Good to see you, David. Welcome to our home. Why don't you put those down over here?" He points to a cleared counter space with his spatula.

Bella mutters something at Colin I don't catch and walks off. I follow her with my eyes as she approaches a group of young men. Each as stupidly good looking as Colin.

What is in the water here?

A muscular blond man with a bun lazily rests his hand on her shoulder as he leans in to whisper something. She laughs, transforming her whole face. It's the first time I've seen her smile in ten years. And it's all for him.

My heart aches. I rest my hand on my wallet, taking comfort from my lucky charm.

"So, how long have you been out?" Colin's voice startles me. Real smooth, Marine. His eyes sparkle with mischief.

"Not long." What is this guy's deal?

"What are your plans now? Did you say you were moving here?" He flips a burger, completely at ease, while I'm uncomfortable as hell.

"Yes. Got a place near the town center. A buddy from the Corps and I opened a security business."

He nods, looking impressed. "You should do well with that. Lots of businesses and homes around here would pay for professional security. Actually, I'd love to hire you to do here."

My body stills, sensing a trap. "Here?"

The spatula loosely gestures to the mini mansion behind him. "Yea, we don't have a security system, and with the baby coming…" he trails off. "Well, I'd feel safer knowing my girls are protected."

Baby? Girls?

I clench my jaw to keep my expression neutral, but my heart is shattering. Bella's having a baby? Why doesn't Ace know? He might forget a casual boyfriend, but he'd tell me something that big!

Unaware of the critical hit he's landed, Colin's eyes drift somewhere behind me. His lips twist up into a grin and his eyes practically have hearts in them. It's the same look Ace gets every time he sees Grace. Dammit, he really loves her.

"Here she is. Shouldn't you be sitting, *a ghrá?*" He holds out his arm and I watch in utter confusion as a petite brunette with a very pregnant belly tucks herself against his side. She beams up at him and he leans down to capture her lips in a passionate kiss.

What the fuck? Is this one of those throuple things? What has Bella gotten herself into?

"Oh hush, I'm not the first woman to have a baby, and I won't be the last." She turns to me with a bemused smile, her cheeks flushed. "Are all men as overprotective as my husband?" She lays her hand possessively on his chest and a sapphire ring with a diamond band wink at me. Huh?

The brunette's head tilts, and she squints at me before recognition lights in her blue eyes. "Where are my manners? You must be David. I'd say I've heard so much about you, but our Anna's been annoyingly close lipped."

What's with the "our Anna" shit again?

"David Hawthorne." On auto-pilot, I hold out my hand for her to shake, her grip firm and efficient. I dig deep for my rusty southern charm to hide my utter confusion. "I'm sorry, I met Colin, but we haven't been introduced, Miss..."

Her cheeks redden further. "Oh, isn't he a charmer? I'm Brianna, one of Anna's best friends. Have you met Nic yet?" She gestures towards a striking woman with jet black hair chatting with Bella, man bun guy, and another man with dark hair and fancy looking clothes.

"No, can't say I've had the pleasure." I do my best to smile. Maybe if I'm friendly, she'll let slip some useful intel.

"Oh, you should. The three of us were college roommates, now we own Pop together." A black blur races by, distracting Brianna's train of thought. "Dammit, Riley got out, I better get him. You boys have fun." With another kiss for Colin and a smile for me, she waddles deeper into the yard.

I'm starting to think I misread this whole situation.

"You're lucky, *boyo*. When I first met Brianna, Anna threatened to maim me and Nic offered to bury my body." Colin chuckles as he removes the burgers and uncovers a plate of skewers.

The woman they pointed out as Nic rushes over to Brianna, fancy clothes guy right behind her. Together, they lead the pregnant woman to a nearby chair. The black blur jumps into her lap and I finally see the source of all the drama. It's a small black dog who promptly lays down with his nose tucked against Brianna's swollen belly.

My eyes sweep the rest of the crowd. Anna is still smiling at man bun guy as he talks to her. She rests her hand on his arm and laughs. My hands fist at my sides and my jaw aches as I clench my teeth. I'm not sure I can do this.

Behind me, Colin chuckles, drawing my attention back to him. "You don't have to worry about Asher. They're just friends."

I study his relaxed posture, his easy smile as he flips skewers on the grill. What's his strategy here? "I actually thought you were with Bell—uh, Anna—when I met you."

Another laugh. "Hell, no. She's more like a sister, man." I said the same thing once. "Now, him you might have to worry about." Colin jerks his chin back at Annabel.

Another man has joined the group. He's about Bella's height, good looking in a wholesome good-ole-boy way, tan with dark hair. He eyes Bella with blatant interest and leans into her space. She neither leans away nor towards him.

"Deputy Ramirez has been sniffing around since I got here last year." He steps closer and hands me a plate of grilled skewers. "My money's on you, though. Not just because he threatened to shoot me before."

"It's not like that, I..."

I don't even get the words out. Colin holds up a hand to stop me. "Save it. It's exactly like that. I'm a sucker for second chances, so let me know if you need a wingman." With a clap on my shoulder and a wink, he turns back to manning the grill.

Feeling a little shaky, I concentrate on the mission at hand to calm my swirling thoughts. I place the plate on the nearby table, already covered with dips, sides, and platters of meat.

A shadow appears over the food as a woman stands by my side. "So, you're the mystery Marine."

Here comes round two of the questioning.

"Yes, ma'am. And you would be the other best friend, Nic." I tip my head to her and grab two empty plates from the buffet, handing her one.

"Who scooped me? Was it Irish?" The glare on her face would make my drill sergeant shit himself. She's got nothing on Annabel Bennet in full rage, though.

"Brianna, actually." I load up my plate as I work my way down the spread, Nic close on my heels. By the end of the table, my paper plate is threatening to buckle. Then I spot the pile of praline cookies and pick up three.

"I got my eye on you." Her thin brows lower as she stares me down. My lips twitch into an amused smile, which only makes her eyes widen. "Something funny, Soldier Boy?"

Giving in to the building chuckle, I turn to her fully. "I've always wondered how Bella could stay away from her family for so long. But now I see it. She made a family here. Also, heads up darlin', Marines aren't soldiers. We're just Marines." Her mouth pops open, but no sound comes out. "Now if you'll excuse me, I've been dreaming of these cookies for a decade, and I'm going to go enjoy one. Ma'am." With a last nod of my head, I join Colin at a patio table, where he introduces me to some of his coworkers and friends.

Asher—AKA man bun guy—is goofy, but a straight shooter. He actually reminds me of Ace a little—well, younger Ace anyway. The other guy is Johnson, he looks like a complete pretty boy, but once he starts talking, I realize he's a bit of a nerd. The two of them get into a spirited debate about some sci-fi show that became popular while I was away. Colin throws in comments occasionally, but appears happy to sit back and watch the banter play out.

As the party winds down, I gather dishes and bring them into the kitchen. Asher follows me, arms filled with platters. We chat about various things, his job at Pop, my time in the Marines. My chest aches as I remember so many similar nights with Ace cleaning up after parties with the Bennets. We exchange numbers and I feel like I might have made a friend here.

When everything is clean, we step out of the kitchen to find practically everyone gone. Moans sound from the living room. Sharing a curious look and shrug, we head off to investigate.

Nic lounges on a loveseat, holding a rope for the dog to tug. Brianna reclines on the larger couch, her feet in Colin's lap as he rubs them. Well, that explains the moans. That means the blond ponytail peeking over the armchair in front of me must be Bella's.

I step forward and rest my hands on the chair, and clear my throat. "Thank you for the invite, Colin. Brianna, Nic, nice meeting you. I'll, uh, see ya 'round, Bells."

Nic throws the toy at Bella. "Ow, what the... Nic!" The poor dog is running between the two women, eyes on the rope, tail wagging like crazy.

"See your *friend* out, Anna. Don't want to be rude." Nic's look dares Bella to argue.

With a lot of grumbling, Bella pushes herself out of her seat and passes me with a muttered "Come on." We walk to the front door in silence. She did a damn good job of avoiding me all afternoon.

I pause on the walkway, trying to think of a way to extend this moment together. "Thanks for including me."

She snorts from the top step. "I didn't." Her arms cross over her chest and she cocks a hip. "Why are you here?"

From my lower ground, I have to look up to meet her eyes. "Colin invited me." The dark brown swirls with fury and hurt. Her body radiates with tension as she glares me down.

Call me a bastard, but there's a perverse satisfaction knowing I still affect her. If she was truly indifferent to me and our history, she would have no problem slapping on the southern charm and small talk.

She tosses her blond head back with a groan, her fingers curl like she's imagining wringing my neck. My lips twitch as they fight to smile. Getting under Bella's skin has always been fun. Though, it's usually Ace making her angry and me smoothing the tension.

"You know what I meant. Why are you here? In Friendship Springs?"

I search her face, debating how to play this. How much to reveal this early in the game. "Probably the same as you. It's an up-and-coming location for new businesses with decent taxes and cost of living."

Her eye twitches briefly as she dissects me, judging my words. "And that's the only reason?"

Careful, boy. Remember that promise to never lie? "What other reason could I have that would convince my business partner to move here, too?" I rock back on my heels and spread my arms wide, hoping to convey innocence.

She studies my face for a few more tense beats. "It's a small town. You should be friends with Colin—goodness knows he could use some more guy friends. But I'm not looking for a friend. I like my life here. I'm *happy* here." Her eyes glimmer in the street lamps as she swallows. "So, welcome to Friendship Springs, neighbor. I'll be polite, recommend some local spots. Even let you borrow a cup of suga'. But I have no intention of taking a trip down memory lane with you."

I gulp as I fight the emotions rocking me. Spine straight, her eyes burn into my very soul. Pain and rage radiate from her like a physical blast. My fingers itch to smooth the hair off her face and soothe her. My arms long to pull her against me, beg for her forgiveness and another chance.

After all, her pain is my fault, and old habits are hard to break. Even after a decade apart.

"I understand, Bells." No longer able to resist the temptation, I step towards her, tuck a strand behind her ear and leave a ghost of a kiss on her cheek. "For what it's worth, I missed you," I whisper, before heading to my truck. She's still frozen in place as I drive away.

CHAPTER EIGHT

Boy Next Door

ANNABEL - AGE 18

My body is humming. I'm at prom with David Hawthorne. Star running back of the varsity football team, David Hawthorne. Clubhouse-camping boy next door, David Hawthorne.

He looks handsome in his suit. Basic training has changed him, his shoulders are firmer under my hands as we dance. We're surrounded by dozens of my classmates, but I couldn't name a single one.

I feel like Cinderella in my golden dress, dancing the night away with the charming prince. Something has shifted tonight, and I don't want it to go back to normal.

Davy's fingers find the exposed skin between the laces of my dress. They slowly stroke the base of my spine as we sway to the music. Electricity sparks outwards from the contact, and I shift closer. His lips brush my temple and biceps tense under my hands. The pressure on my back urges me even closer until his thigh rests between mine, our bodies flush together.

An ache builds in my core with each bump of David's leg. His comforting smell surrounds me and my heart skips a beat. My eyes drift closed as Davy's fingers continue to stroke my bare skin.

This is the most intimate experience of my life, and he hasn't even kissed me.

The lights of the gym turn on, shattering the spell. David smiles at me and tucks a curl behind my ear. "Ready to go?"

I release a deep breath and look around the emptying room. "I guess."

With David's hand still at the small of my back, he leads me out. The silence is thick in the truck until David opens my door in front of my house.

I let him help me from the same cab I've jumped down from a dozen times before. "Thanks for tonight."

"You don't have to thank me, Bells. Pretty sure I had a better time tonight than at my own prom."

I smile at him through my lashes as I fuss with my clutch, not wanting the night to end. "You were wonderful. Doing all the traditional prom stuff for me. Even photos."

His lips twist into a sexy grin. "Well, I pinky promised to always be there, didn't I?"

"Yea, you did." A warmth spreads in my chest, and I catch my lip between my teeth. Davy's eyes darken as he stares down at me.

"I'm not all that tired," I say. My eyes dip to his mouth as they part on an intake of breath.

"Oh yea?" His voice rumbles like a purr, and I press my thighs together to relieve an ache.

Lifting my eyes back to his, I lean in as if pulled by a magnet. Davy's hands cup my elbows as I rest my palms on his chest. He whispers his pet name for me a moment before his lips ghost over mine in the barest of touches.

He starts to pull back, but I rise on my toes to chase him. I want more. With a pained groan, his hands clutch me closer and his tongue probes the seam of my lips. Eagerly, I open for him.

Holy crap. I'm kissing David Hawthorne.

I've been kissed. A little. But they all pale compared to this kiss.

Davy pulls away and rests his forehead against mine. We're both panting for breath.

"Come on." I grab his hand, and we dart across the dark lawn to the clubhouse.

A flip of the switch sets the old Christmas lights aglow overhead as the air mattresses hum to inflate. With a boldness I didn't know I possessed, I walk up to David until we're chest to chest and kiss him. Gently at first, then deeper.

Without breaking contact, I peel his jacket off his shoulders, then get to work on the buttons of his shirt. His breath hisses as my hands finally touch his smooth skin. Together, we sink to the mattresses still entwined.

David's hand leaves my waist and strokes down my hip and thigh until he finds the dress slit. I arch my neck and moan as his rough fingers trail up my leg.

He stiffens above me. "Christ, Bella. We gotta slow down."

"I don't want to slow down. This feels right. I want my first time to be with someone I trust. Don't stop."

David's weight lightens as he pushes up to search my face.

"Please, David. You're shipping out soon. If we stop now and something happens to you, I'll regret missing out on this night for the rest of my life."

His cheek bulges as he clenches his teeth. "You sure?"

I cup his tight jaw. "Never been surer."

His nostrils flare a second before his lips capture mine. This kiss is different. Full of hunger, but infinite patience. Possession. Protection.

My head falls back as his hands continue their exploration of my thigh. Hot kisses trail down my exposed throat and chest. Blunt fingers find my covered center already wet. Davy groans against my neck as he teases my clit through my cotton panties. I spread my thighs wider, desperate for something, but not quite sure what.

Needing no further invitation, David guides my underwear down my legs, then strips off his dress shirt. He takes a condom out of his wallet before tossing it aside.

Nerves build as his hand finds the sensitive bud again. I lose myself to the sensations as his lips capture mine. One thick finger tests my entrance and I tense. With soothing sounds and nipping kisses, David waits for me to relax before easing into my tight passage. He strokes and teases as a pressure builds. Slowly, he eases a second finger, and then a third. Something snaps inside me and my body locks down around him as wave after wave of pleasure course through me.

David nips at my bare shoulder. "Beautiful." He unzips his pants and his hard erection springs free. I gulp at the size. He rolls on the condom and positions himself at my entrance. His eyes are filled with lust as he looks at me, but he holds back. "Are you absolutely sure?"

"Absolutely." I grab his tight butt and pull him closer.

The thick head of his dick stretches me as he pushes in. The sensation is strange but not unpleasant. David's arms shake as he hovers over me. "This might hurt a little. Try to relax."

With a hard thrust and a flash of pain, he's fully seated inside me. He holds still as I adjust to the intrusion, dropping sweet kisses along my face and whispering loving nonsense. "Shh, baby. Just relax. It'll get better. I promise."

I smile at the words we've whispered dozens of times over the years and shift experimentally beneath him. The discomfort is easing and as I shift my hips, that pressure builds again. I run my hands up Davy's bare back and pull him back to my waiting lips.

He slowly moves, and I tentatively meet him stroke for stroke. My legs shake around his hips and David reaches between us to pinch my clit, sending me over the edge into another shattering orgasm. My eyes fly open and I call his name as I meet his gaze.

My core clenches around David. I feel him swell impossibly larger before he cries out my name. As we both come back down, we share a tender kiss.

David carefully pulls out and deals with the condom. He settles back on the mattress and tugs me onto his chest, wrapping us in a spare blanket. My fingers trace invisible shapes on his skin as he cuddles me close.

"I set an alarm for early—I have to return the tux and you need to sneak back in. For now, let me hold you."

We whisper together in the night. Talking of everything and nothing. When I drift off to the scent of cloves, it's the best sleep I've had in a long time. I just might be falling for David Hawthorne.

CHAPTER NINE

Chef's Special Sandwich

ANNABEL - NOW

My feet slap the pavement in a comforting rhythm and shake off the last tangles of dreams and memories better off forgotten. There's nothing quite like the silent morning streets of downtown Friendship Springs to reset your emotions.

Feeling refreshed after my three-mile circuit, I return to the back door of Pop, greeted by the scent of freshly-baked bread. My new pastry chef is kneading dough on a floured surface.

I've been filling in on top of being head chef since we opened. Goodness knows I have enough of Momma's old recipes upstairs and years of stress baking skills to keep us in the black. I've been trying to convince Bree and Nic to expand for a couple of years now. Part of that is showing I can delegate and step back a little to spread myself further, so last month I hired Ryan.

"Morning, Chef. Good run?" As his eyes sweep over my body, I'm self-conscious of my running shorts and tank. Ryan's attractive enough, I suppose, with his gray eyes and athletic frame. Kneading bread is great for the arms, though evidently not as good as combat. Not that I'm comparing him to David.

The appreciation in his eyes leaves me uncomfortable. I may encourage a more relaxed kitchen and enjoy camaraderie with my staff, but I would never sleep with an employee. I cross my arms over my chest, hugging myself. "Uh, yeah. I was about to head up, but it smelled so good in here I couldn't help but peek in."

A flirty grin spreads on his lips. "First batch is cooling over there," he nods towards the six-foot racks near me with his chin, "why don't you have one for breakfast?"

"Oh, thanks. I'll, uh, grab it to go."

Feeling awkward, I take a hot roll and speed up to my apartment to shower and change for work. By the time I return, my lunch staff has already arrived. Immediately, I relax to the familiar sounds of plates clattering and oil sizzling. With a smile on my face, I lose myself to the chatter and bustle of a well-run kitchen.

I'm checking dishes for quality control at the pass when one of our servers, Vicky, flies through the kitchen doors blushing heavily.

"I think I'm in love." She fans herself with her order pad. When she sees me smirking at her with one eyebrow raised, she flushes even redder.

"Oh yea?" I chuckle at the girl's discomfort. At twenty-one, she's one of our younger servers, waiting tables to pay for college. Sweet, but a bit of a hopeless romantic. Not like I can talk—I wasn't that different at her age.

"I simply adore a man with a southern drawl." The fanning starts again. "And a soldier with tattoos? Sign me up."

I stiffen at the description. No, it couldn't be. Only yesterday I told him I didn't want to be friends. "What did he order?" I ask through clenched teeth.

Vicky stills, clearly noticing the shift in my mood. "Um, he said to ask for the chef's special sandwich."

"That son of a... Meeka, take the window." My lips curl into an evil smile as an idea hits me. Vicky gasps and falls back a step as I slap two pieces of yesterday's white bread onto a plate. Vaguely aware that all eyes are on me, I dart back and forth from the pantry and walk-in refrigerator until I have what I want. "Raj, do we have any of those salt and vinegar chips left?"

"Yes, Chef." He brings over a container covered in cling wrap. "Might be a little stale, though." I wave him off as I grab a jar of peanut butter and slather it on the bread. Pickle slices and a handful of the chips join the spread before I smash the other half on with a satisfying smoosh.

Plate in hand, I'm already at the kitchen doors when I hear Vicky wail behind me. "What did I do wrong, Meeka? I only said he was cute."

"I think he's already taken, Vicks."

Ha! If I wasn't so set on kicking that man where the sun don't shine, I'd swing back and make it clear how *not* taken he is.

My eyes adjust to the dimmer light of the dining room as I scan for his hulking presence. I find him in a small booth and stalk towards him. Asher calls out to me from behind the bar, but I hold up my hand to stop him and continue across the room.

The thunk of the plate dropping to the table is loud in the quiet room. The jerk even has the gall to look amused as I stare him down.

"Thanks, Bells. Looks good." David calmly maintains my glare as he lifts the sandwich to his mouth for a large bite. A bit of green juice dribbles out the other side as his teeth close with a satisfying *CRUNCH*. His bearded jaw twitches as he swallows, but his eyes stay locked on mine. "New recipe?" He reaches for a sip of water.

"Yea, what'cha think?" My voice drips with saccharine southern sweetness. I dare him to say something.

"Well, pickles aren't my favorite." My smile curves until my cheeks hurt. Of course I remembered that little fact.

He takes another bite. *Crunch.*

"But the mixture of textures is interesting. You've always been one to think outside the box, Hell's Bells." *Crunch. Crunch.*

Damn infuriating man. My smile dims. *Crunch.*

He's always been like a placid lake that runs deep. Whenever Atty and I would get into it, Davy was always the calming presence, keeping us out of trouble. *Crunch, crunch.* I should have known it'd take more to get under his skin.

He pushes the empty plate away slightly, a smile on his stupidly handsome face. "Thanks again, Bells. Any chance for dessert?"

Teeth clenched, I grab the plate. "I'll send Vicky back out with a menu." I turn on my heel and head back to the kitchen doors. Asher watches me walk by with a curious expression. I only grunt at him. The kitchen doors are still swinging slightly, like someone just ran back in.

Tameka and Vicky stare at me with wide eyes as I toss the plate in the sink on my way back to the pass. "He wants dessert—go get him a menu." Grabbing the next ticket from the line, I shout over my shoulder. "I need two crab cakes and a Cesar salad." A chorus of "Yes, Chef" washes over me like a healing balm as Vicky scurries back out of the kitchen.

The rest of lunch and dinner speed by. I quickly forget about David and lose myself to the hum of the kitchen again. After nearly twelve hours on my feet, I collapse into bed, half asleep before my head even hits the pillow, and enjoy a dreamless sleep.

The next day, I throw myself into my normal routine. Everything is great until another ticket comes in for "Chef's special sandwich." This time, I send the plate with a server, but peek through the kitchen doors as he takes a bite into the tuna and mustard on a Hawaiian roll.

Every day, David comes in for lunch and I create something I know he'll hate. Every day, David eats it with a smile and a request for a dessert menu. What is his game?

By Friday, I'm out of ideas. I'm a foodie at heart, so these combos aren't exactly second nature to me. As I'm eyeing the various spreads and fillings, Tony approaches and hands me a small cup full of a red, gelatinous spread.

"What's this?" I eye the mixture dubiously.

"Ghost pepper jelly."

My eyes widen as I look at his wide smile. "No!"

"Yup... maybe with peanut butter? Or chicken salad? With pecans and grapes?"

Chuckling, I reach for the bowl, but he snatches it away from my fingers. "I want to deliver the plate."

"Deal!" Only I have something more devious in mind than chicken salad.

Grabbing the bowl back, I get to work. I gather fresh sandwich bread and a few different cheeses. After buttering the bread and placing it on the griddle, I arrange the cheese on one half and a thin spread of the jelly on the other. When it's all toasted and gooey, I press it together and move it to a waiting dish. At the last minute, I throw a handful of perfectly good fries on the plate, too.

Tony eyes it dubiously. "What?" I ask. "I'm not completely heartless. Plus, if he sues us, I can't pay anybody." Nodding in agreement, Tony takes the plate and heads out to the dining room. Tameka and I rush to the kitchen door to watch.

David looks up at Tony curiously as he approaches. He eyes the sandwich and asks a question before taking a bite. Satisfaction burns through me as his eyes bug out and he grabs his water, downing it in three gulps. His eyes flash in my direction and I duck back, hoping he didn't spot me. With a deep breath, he squares his shoulder and takes another bite. Then another. He mops his forehead with his napkin and pants in obvious discomfort.

Tony comes back to the kitchen with a smirk on his face. "Guy's got it bad, Chef." Tameka shushes him as she throws a towel in his face. I ignore the banter, my sole focus on the man powering through a deathly spicy sandwich.

Asher plops a glass of milk and a pill bottle on the table in front of David and sits in the booth opposite. The two talk for a bit, sandwich gone. David gulps the liquid like a man dying of thirst. Asher stands, pats him on the shoulder before heading back to the bar, shaking his head.

My stomach twists. I almost feel bad. *Almost.* This probably isn't what Atty meant by being nice. With a sigh, I send a basket of rolls and fresh cinnamon butter along with a brownie sundae out to his table, then get back to work.

Hours later, I'm still conflicted as I scrub the kitchen. It's after two in the morning. The sound of the bass no longer thumps through the wall, a clear sign it's past closing time. Asher pushes through the kitchen doors with the bank bag in his hands.

"Remind me to never get on your bad side, Anners. You about done torturing the guy?"

"Yea." My heart twists with fresh guilt. "It's no fun when he doesn't react, anyway." I pick at the already spotless counters.

"Ready to talk about it?" He leans a hip against the counter I'm scrubbing. The kitchen is empty besides us.

"I don't know what you're talking about." I inspect an invisible speck of grime as I avoid his gaze.

"Cut the bullshit. If you don't want to talk about it, I won't pry. But don't disrespect my intelligence. For over five years, I've watched you be the quintessential southern belle—all charm and manners. Some guy from your past shows up and you turn into Dennis the Menace. Which is strange enough, but he just takes it with a smile and comes back for more?"

With a sigh, I throw the rag down and brace my hands against the surface. "We grew up together. Completely inseparable. As close as two kids could be." I turn to Asher. "Got as close as two teenagers can get too." He cocks an eyebrow and I nod my head before looking down at the counter. "Then he up and left. Shipped out and never looked back. Leaving me to pick up the pieces and move on."

I chance a glance up at Asher, unsure what emotion I'll find. He's watching me intently. Listening without any judgment on his face. "I did move on. I left my family and built a life here. And he shows up after a decade? Why now, when I'm happy?"

"People make mistakes, Anna. Especially if you were only kids. He showed up. He's putting in the effort." With a grunt, I turn and lean against the counter next to him. Asher bumps his shoulder into mine. "I'm not saying sweep it all under the rug. Just hear the guy out. Maybe you'll get some closure out of it." I nod as I stare at my feet, knowing he's right. "Ghost peppers?"

My lips quirk up. "It was Tony's idea."

Asher shudders. "I'm pretty sure that's a war crime."

I laugh and relax for what feels like the first time in ages. "Thanks, Ash. You heading out?"

"Yea, you heading up?"

"Not quite yet. I want to try out a new idea for Atty and Grace's wedding cake. It'd be easier in the big ovens."

His gorgeous blue eyes squint in concern. "You want me to stay?"

"Naw. You probably have a hot date. I'll be fine." I wave him off and start pulling out ingredients. This crazy idea for a maple bacon cake with brown sugar frosting has been stuck in my head all day, and I want to try it out. The urge to bake has nothing to do with my conflicted feelings over Davy's reappearance in my life.

"Ok. I'll drop the bank bag in the office. Don't forget to lock up!"

I immediately start frying bacon in a pan with some brown sugar. Once it's caramelized and crispy, I transfer it to a paper towel to cool. The drippings get strained and added to the chocolate cake batter. Like a machine, I mix batter and prepare cake pans.

Once everything is in the ovens, I pull out the stand mixer and whip up butter for frosting. The whir of the motor is a comforting sound in the silent kitchen.

Some caramel would really tie this whole thing together.

Grabbing more butter and sugar, I set a heavy pan on the burner and light the gas with a click and a whoosh. As my butter melts, I check my frosting. Pale yellow and perfectly fluffy. Excellent. I steal a taste of the sugary concoction on my finger, closing my eyes against the heavenly flavor.

My ears are still ringing in the sudden silence as I turn off the mixer. Wiping my hands on a nearby towel, I throw it over my shoulder. There will be plenty more taste tests to come. My lips spread in a smile. What is the point of being a chef if not to lick the spoon?

A sound behind me freezes my smile in place. I start to turn, but pain blossoms across my back and knocks me off balance. The towel falls off my shoulder onto the pan of caramel as I try to catch my footing. Large hands grab me from behind—one locks around my arms, the other over my mouth. Wildly, I lash out. My nails dig into a thick wrist and I struggle against a firm grip.

Eyes wide, I glance around for a weapon. Where are all the darn knives?

The handle of the pan catches my attention. Moving quickly, I bite down on the hand covering my mouth as hard as I can. I dive for the caramel and swing blindly. A roar of fury sounds as the hot metal makes contact with flesh.

Without looking back, I rush for the office, already reaching into my pocket. Numb fingers grapple with my phone and I thank Atty for making me practice the emergency SOS feature on my cell. Hands grab my ankles and I pitch forward, throwing my free hand out to break my fall. The impact with the cement floor jars through my entire body. I curl into myself as a shoe connects with my ribs.

Through the rushing in my ears, a shrill alarm registers.

The door slams as my attacker runs out the back. I lay on the floor panting, tears burning my eyes. As I sniffle, an acrid smell overwhelms my senses. I crack my eyes open and realize its smoke burning my eyes, not tears. Bright orange flames dance above the stove as the cheap towel burns.

Whimpering, I shuffle towards the blaze. I drop a dirty cake pan over the flames to cut the oxygen, then quickly shut off the burner. The fire is out, but black smoke is still heavy in the air.

Sirens grow louder as they approach, the only sound in the sleepy town. The back door flies open and I hear my name. I turn as muscular arms pull me against a firm chest.

CHAPTER TEN

Jungle Juice

Some guy is leaning over me at this party. He's talking, but I can't hear a thing. The music blasts out all the other sounds in the room. I take another sip from the red cup in my hands. What was this again? Oh yea... Jungle Cruise... no... Jungle Juice!

The room sways. I stumble a bit in the heels I stole from Momma's closet and nervously tug at the hem of my minidress—a gift from Atty's girlfriend. My body jerks the other way. Is the floor moving? Is this a boat?

The guy is back. Why are my shoulders so heavy? His hot breath is on my neck. Ugh. Shrugging away, I point to my ear. "I can't hear you." The music is so loud, I have to yell.

He grabs me and leans in close enough to practically lick my ear. "Hey, beautiful, let's go somewhere more quiet, heh?"

I try to say no, but he leads me like a doll, anyway. A door opens to a study or something. The red couch is soft as I sit down. The guy leans into me, his hot breath makes my skin crawl.

"I'll go get you another drink. Don't move, sweetheart." His weight leaves my side and his footsteps retreat.

I don't want to be here. I shouldn't have come out alone. Momma would be so mad.

As I lean into the cushion, something hard jabs my rib. Cellphone! I fish my phone out of my bra where I'd stashed it earlier. Squinting at the numbers as they dance in front of my eyes, I hit my number one speed dial.

Ring... ring...

A deep voice answers. "Hey Bells, what's up? Everything ok?"

"I don't think so." My tongue feels like lead in my mouth. And so dry.

"Annabel, where the hell are you?" Did his voice get deeper? Why does it make me happy? "Annabel, answer me."

I jerk as my mind comes back to the phone. "Some party. Billy Becket's place. I don't feel so good. And this guy..." I stop to swallow. Seriously, why is my tongue so heavy? And itchy?

"What. Guy?" Each word drips with fury.

My thighs squirm. Dude, what? Arguing voices through the phone break my train of thought. "I don't know who he is. He took me to a room and left me here. Something about more Jungle Juice." Is that statue moving? Why is the room spinning?

"Hell's Bells, you're wasted." A loud slam through the phone draws my attention back to the call. An engine roars and tires squeal. "I'm coming to get you, Bella. I'm ten minutes out. Just stay on the phone with me. Ok? Can you do that for me?"

My entire attention focuses on his voice. "Yea. Davy?" My voice catches on a sob. The room dips and spins around me. My stomach gives an uncomfortable lurch. "I don't like this."

He draws a breath and groans. "Me, either, baby. I'm on my way to get you. Stay with me, though. Can you walk? Is the guy there?" His words end in a growl.

I shudder. "He's not back. I might be able to walk if I take my shoes off."

"Leave the shoes and try to head towards the front door. I'll meet you outside. I'm driving as fast as I can." Tires squeal and a horn blares in my ear.

"But they're Momma's favorite pair!" My tone sparkles with southern spice.

"I'll get the damn shoes, baby. After you're safe." Davy sounds like he's almost begging. That's a first. "Just come meet me. Almost there, just keep talking."

I weigh a trillion pounds. One foot in front of the other feels impossible. The walls keep moving. The sea of swaying bodies trails on for miles. The boom of the speakers vibrates through my body. I'm almost to the door when it slams open.

A furious Mediterranean god stands before me. His eyes smolder as he scans the crowd. I step forward to draw his eye. My vision tunnels in on those warm hazel eyes. I watch as they scan me from head to toe and back. How his lips form a curse.

A heavy arm snakes around me and grabs the side of my breast. But Davy is still in front of me. So who the hell is touching me?

In slow motion, my head turns and I see the mystery George of the Jungle Juice. I lean away from him, but my ankle buckles. As the room pitches, my shoulder connects with a broad chest and I look up to see my avenging angel.

Deft hands pull me upright, Davy wraps his letterman jacket around me and keeps me in his muscular arms. His chest rumbles under my ear. "I will be back for you." The words make me shiver even though I don't think they're for me.

A gentle arm surrounds my shoulders and leads me to a rusty pickup by the curb. My head drops to Davy's shoulder. He scoops me up like a princess and somehow gets me into the cab.

"Stay here, baby. I gotta take care of something real quick." He reaches across to buckle me in and caresses a hair off my face.

I turn towards him but can barely keep my eyes open. "My shoes, right?"

Davy snorts. "Yea, Bella, your shoes."

There's a slight tingle at my forehead, then the slam of a door jolts me. My eyes try to adjust to the interior of the truck. My eardrums seem to bounce with the beat of a drum. Or maybe that's my temple?

Sweet Jesus, why do people drink?

It could be seconds, or it could be hours, but Davy eventually returns. The light comes on, stirring me further in my seat.

"Here are your shoes, baby." He tenderly places them on the floor, then rests his hand on my knee. The knuckles are raw and bruised. Gently, I lay my smaller hand over the wounds.

"Annabel, are you ok? Did anyone," he gulps, "touch you?" His fingers grip my leg and his thigh tenses next to mine. I shake my head and purse my lips as I fight back tears. "What in the hell were you doing there, Bella? Alone? Wearing that?" His hand vaguely gestures to all of me.

"It shouldn't matter what I wear, David!" I pinch his hand.

"That's not what I meant, and you know it. Why, Bella? This isn't you." His voice sounds almost sad.

I take a shaky breath and end with a gasp. "It's all too much. I feel so much all the time. Momma. Rhett. How utterly alone I am." I turn to him with blurry eyes.

He flips his hand so our fingers can lace. "You have your big, wonderful family."

"Rhett has Dad. The twins have each other. Atty has Grace. Who do I have, Davy? You know why I drank? I wanted to forget. Just for a moment, I wanted to pretend it's all ok."

A burst of curses erupts as Davy unbuckles my seatbelt. Strong arms pull me across the truck bench to rest on his chest. My nose burrows into his neck. A deep inhale of his comforting scent.

"You're not alone, baby. You'll always have me." Davy's voice rumbles under my ear.

"You have Holly and Atty. I'm just your friend's kid sister. You'll leave me too." I sniffle.

Davy ducks his head to meet my eyes, but I look down as he cups my face and strokes my cheek with his thumb. My lip quivers.

"Hey, now. I remember a pinky promise to be your friend over Atty's. And pinky promises are sacred." I sneak a glance at his handsome face. His eyes are serious, but his mouth twists into a little grin. "Hell's Bells, have I ever let you down?"

Half a decade flashes through my foggy mind. "No, you haven't."

"And I ain't gonna start now. If you need me, I'll be there. I'll always put your happiness first, Bella."

I turn my tear-lined face up to him and hold up a single finger. "Pinky promise."

"Pinky promise." He returns the shake, then releases me slowly. "Now let's get you home. You're lucky Ma is pulling a double at the hospital. You can sober up at my house and sneak back home in the morning."

I fall asleep on the way, tucked into Davy's side with my head on his shoulder. When I wake before the sun the next morning, I'm on Davy's bed with the mother of all headaches. Over my dress, I wear a Hitchcock

High Football sweatshirt. A weight on my hand catches my attention as I stir. Behind me, Davy is asleep on his bed, still fully dressed, and his fingers clasp mine. Careful not to wake him, I detangle myself, swipe the waiting bottle of water and aspirin off the nightstand, and sneak home, hoping no one notices I'm still wearing his sweatshirt.

CHAPTER ELEVEN

I'll Always Be There

DAVID - NOW

The bed creaks as I readjust for the dozenth time. Its three a.m., but I can't sleep. Something nags at the back of my head. An annoying tickle I just can't quiet.

I used to get like this on deployment. Some damn inconvenient sixth sense before a mission would go wrong. Ronnie says it's anxiety and PTSD, but my gut knows. Danger is out there.

With a sigh, I swing my legs out of bed, taking a moment to run my hands through my hair. So weird to feel it stick out past my fingers. Yet another thing to acclimate to in civilian life. I concentrate on the churning feeling in my stomach, chase it down to try to determine the source. Convinced it's not just the sandwich repeating on me.

In the distance, a siren screams. It's close enough to have me up and moving. With jerky motions, I pull on a pair of shorts and a black tee. Next up is yesterday's socks off the floor and sneakers on without even untying them. Barely slowing, I grab my keys and head out my front door. My feet take me where my gut already knows the sirens are headed.

The rubber soles slap the pavement as I race down the empty street. No harm taking a jog past Pop, check for lights in the apartment above. That's it. I won't stop, just make sure Bella's fine. Then maybe this vice around my heart will loosen and I can sleep.

As I turn the last corner, my worst fears are confirmed. Flashes of red and blue brighten the night in the parking lot outside Pop. Heart pounding, I'm already yelling her name before I reach the police barrier.

"Bella!"

An officer holds me back. He keeps talking about protocol, but I don't give a shit about his protocol. Not when my girl needs me.

My frantic eyes finally see her. She looks so small. Her shoulders hunch as she clings to a gray utility blanket. Another official stands with her, his hand on her shoulder while he talks to her.

A second set of hands hold me back as I struggle to get to her. "Bella! Annabel!"

Her head jerks up and I see the trail of tears on her dirty face. Recognition and something else I can't quite place flash in her eyes. She drops the fabric and runs towards me.

"Davy." Her voice catches as she says my name. It's all I need to spur myself on. I twirl and duck away from the officers before vaulting over the barrier.

I meet her halfway. My hands clasp at her arms desperately as I pull her to me, crushing her against my chest. A moment later, I push her back away and cup her face so I can search her eyes.

My mouth runs dry. "Are you ok? Are you hurt anywhere?" I check her for signs of injury. Her eyes are wild and fresh tears spill over as her fingers tangle in my shirt. At her slight headshake, I wrap her in my arms again and bury my face in her hair. She smells of magnolia, smoke, and fear.

I clench my eyes to stop my own threatening moisture as I drop kisses to the crown of her head while I whisper comforting words. Her shoulders shake with sobs as I hold her close. I almost lost her.

Again.

A throat clears, shattering the moment. I lift my head, still holding Bella protectively against me. Of course, it's Officer Dickwad. The guy is clearly into Bells and staring daggers at me as I hold her.

Bella lifts her face from my chest, but stays inside the circle of my embrace, fingers locked on my shirt. Victory flashes through me. Despite everything, she still trusts me when the shit hits the fan.

"Anna, I still have a few questions for you. Did you see your attacker? Was anyone else in the building?"

Attacker? I stiffen, my arm tightening around her as she whimpers slightly.

"No. I was alone. I was working on a new recipe in the kitchen and didn't realize someone was there until I felt the hit." She curls tighter into herself and fresh panic courses through me.

It takes a lot to scare my Bella.

"Any camera feeds we can check?" Officer Ramirez eyes her over his notebook.

Bella shakes her head. No cameras? A growl escapes my chest. I'll sure as hell fix that tomorrow.

Ramirez keeps glaring at me over Bella's head. If looks could kill... well I'd probably only have a flesh wound... but the guy hates me. Feeling's mutual, buddy.

"You should find someplace else to stay tonight, Anna. Can I give you a ride somewhere? Brianna's maybe? Or Nic's?"

My fingers flex on her hip. "She'll stay with me." Pressure on my chest increases as Bella relaxes further into me.

"I don't think..." Not letting the man finish, I hold up my hand and give him my best superior officer look before gently pushing Bella back and smoothing the hair out of her face. I catch the eye of a female EMT hovering nearby and jerk my chin to call her over.

"Bells, baby, why don't you go get checked out upstairs and pack a bag? You can stay with me tonight and we'll figure the rest out tomorrow." With a last kiss to her forehead, I carefully untangle her fingers as the EMT guides her away. I watch them walk away, ensuring they get to the back of the building safely.

"Who the fuck do you think you are?" Spit flies from Ramirez's mouth as he steps closer to me.

I stand to my full height, a solid four inches over the deputy. My chest puffs out and my sleeves constrict my biceps as I clench my hands by my sides. "I'm the guy who's been there for every skinned knee and crisis since she was eight years old. I'm the guy who held her hand on the worst day of her life. And I'm the guy who's going to install security cameras in that goddamn kitchen tomorrow and make sure she's never in danger again."

For a moment, doubt flickers in his eyes. In an instant, they harden and his lips twist with hate. "Then where the hell have you been lately? I've known her for years and never heard of you."

My jaw ticks as I stare him down. He shrinks back slightly as my rage grows. "In the Marines, serving my god-damned country. Any other questions?"

My stomach churns. I'm drowning in guilt and taking it out on this chump. He's right. Where the hell have I been? Why do I deserve to be here now? The first contract, sure, that's forgivable. But I signed up for a second all on my own.

The back door opens and Bella emerges with a small duffle. I step back and get a grip on myself. She doesn't need my emotional baggage right now.

When she's close enough, I grab the bag from her, tossing the strap over my shoulder. My other hand anchors at the base of her spine while she leans into me. Just like that, my confidence returns. She fucking chose me. "Got what you needed, Bells?"

Eyes wide and glassy, she nods. The cops hold the crowd back as I lead her down the street. The two blocks to my house pass in silence. I keep an eye on her as I unlock the front door and usher her inside. Turning the lights on as I go, I put her duffle on my bed. Seeing her standing there, lost, breaks something in me.

Gently, I press on her shoulders until she sits on the edge of the mattress. Kneeling, I slip off her shoes and socks one at a time. Moving quickly, I turn the taps for the bath and grab a fluffy towel from the closet. When I return to her, she's sitting in exactly the same spot.

Squatting down in front of her, I rub her arms until she meets my eyes. "Come on, you should take a bath and then get some sleep. Why don't you pull out your pajamas?"

She blinks up at me for a moment, then starts as if waking from a dream. "I should call... someone. The kitchen staff needs to know..." Her brows crease, and she digs into her bag for her phone.

My larger hands still hold her shaking ones. "Shh, I'll take care of it, baby. All you need to do is grab your pajamas and take a bath." Eyes still glassy, she nods slowly, grabs some clothes and then walks woodenly into the bathroom.

My breath rushes out as I pull my cell from my back pocket. Scrolling through my contacts, I shoot off text messages to Colin and Asher informing them of the situation and that Bella is safe with me. Next, I send a note off to Ronnie, asking him to stop at Pop first thing and start a security survey for alarms and cameras.

Bella re-emerges as I'm bumping the last of my morning appointments. Her fingers twist the bottom of her tank top and she shifts from foot to foot as she eyes me through her lashes.

I pull the sheets back and step out of her way. "Come on, Bells, get some sleep. Everything else can wait a few hours."

She looks around as she crawls under the covers, like she's seeing her surroundings for the first time. Bella hesitates. "Is this your room? I don't want to put you out."

"I haven't bought a guest bed, yet. It's fine. I'll sleep on the couch." The indecision is clear in her eyes. I gulp. "Hell's Bells, just let me help." At the old nickname, her eyes soften and she settles on a pillow. I pull the comforter up to her chin and chance one last kiss to her forehead.

I'm at the door, shutting off the lights, when she calls out, "Wait." I turn back. Her eyes glitter with determination as she raises the corner of the covers. "Stay. I... I don't want to be alone."

For a heated moment, I search her face. I see vulnerability, but also resolve. Silently, I approach, still holding her gaze. I toe off my shoes and socks and settle onto my back, careful not to touch her.

We lay in silence. The sheets rustle and the bed dips as she scoots closer. Icy fingers lift my arm and she molds herself against my side. Her head lies on my shoulder, her fists clutching my shirt again as her body trembles.

I turn my face into her hair. "Shh, I got you, baby." I stroke her back and her shudders eventually slow. I tuck my chin down to glance at her face. The stress lines around her eyes have smoothed and her long sooty lashes rest on her freckled cheeks. "You'll always have me, baby. Promise."

Her nose wrinkles, and she rubs her cheek against my chest. "This doesn't mean I forgive you. I'm still mad."

Her voice is heavy with sleep. I'm not even sure she knows what she's saying. Despite her words, the way she clings to me fills me with lightness for the first time in years. With her in my arms, the darkness feels less bleak. I drift off, and for once, there're no dreams to haunt me.

Restless, I stir in bed. The scent of magnolia is overpowering, and I press my face into my pillow, chasing it. As I wake fully, last night comes flooding back.

Bella.

My eyes snap open and I find myself alone. The mattress next to me is still warm, so I didn't dream it. Pans clatter and the smell of coffee drifts through the cracked bedroom door.

She didn't leave.

I rush through my morning routine before heading to find her. My breath catches and I freeze at the sight of Bella in my kitchen. Her blond hair is in a messy knot on top of her head. Her long, tan legs are on full display below her tiny sleep shorts. I smile as I realize she stole one of my sweatshirts.

She looks damn good here. My heart flips painfully. Like she belongs.

Coming up behind her, I carefully place a hand on her shoulder as I reach over her head to grab two mugs. "Smells good, Bells." I pour two steaming cups of coffee, adding extra milk and sugar into the one I set by her elbow. She murmurs her thanks as she transfers the eggs and bacon onto waiting plates.

I sit at the counter and pull my plate towards me. The first bite melts in my mouth. God, I've missed her cooking. It's the same eggs I've been eating all week, so why does it taste so much better when she does it?

Her lips are pinched and eyes narrowed on her plate as she picks up a crispy piece of bacon. Uh, oh. I know that look. Bella's gearing up for a fight. I gulp down my coffee and wait for the fireworks to start.

She squares her shoulders and looks at me. Here we go. "Thank you for last night. For being there, for letting me stay, and calling Asher." She swallows as she maintains eye contact. This is hard for her, I can see it in her eyes.

"I'll always be there. I pinky promised, didn't I?" My voice is gravelly, contradicting my flippant words.

Bella slams her fork against the counter with a loud bang. "But you weren't. If pinky promises are so sacred, then why did you break them all?" Her eyes flash with fire and steel.

"Annabel..." Her name is half plea, half prayer on my lips.

"Don't 'Annabel' me. You were my friend first. So why did you shut me out?" Her voice quivers with emotion. The tip of her nose reddens as she stares me down. "Atty asked me to make peace, and I've tried to let it go. But I can't. If our relationship meant anything to you, how did you just walk away? Why is Atty so worried about you?"

I swallow the lump in my throat. "I was a dumb kid and thought I was protecting you." She scoffs and turns from me. Rushing around the counter, I grip her waist and turn her to look at me, but she twists her head away.

I pinch her chin lightly to lift her eyes up to mine. "Things got real dark over there, Bells. *I* got real dark. I couldn't be your Davy and survive those horrors. You had your own shit with your mom, and the boys, and school. I refused to bring you down with me." The rage in her eyes flickers for a moment. Hope blossoms in me. "I know I have a lot to make up for. I'm here to do the work, just let me try. Let me be your friend and prove your Davy's still in here somewhere."

She stares at me and a thousand emotions cross her face. Disbelief. Hope. Fear.

Bella sucks on her teeth and appears to come to a decision. "Alright, I'll try to keep an open mind until after the wedding. For Atty." I practically melt with relief. "But I'm warning you, David Hawthorne. You get one chance. If you blow it, I'll never talk to you again after the wedding."

I squeeze her arms. "That's fair. Let's finish eating. I'm meeting Ronnie over at Pop in an hour to install some security equipment. You're welcome to stay here if you want." She shrugs and turns back to her breakfast.

The rest of the meal is silent. After, I give her a quick tour of the living room, setting her up with the remote to the tv. Before I leave, I surprise her with a tight hug, mostly to convince myself she's here and ok. My heart swells as she returns the squeeze half-heartedly. Promising to return soon, I reluctantly leave her.

Chapter Twelve

Snooping

He came for me. The words keep repeating in my head. David came for me. At three o'clock in the freaking morning, he showed up like my personal hero. Like he always did.

Until he didn't.

For a half hour, I sit on his couch and scroll through options on Netflix. I put on a superhero movie but quickly lose interest. Looking around the room, I realize he's left me alone with all his stuff. My teeth gnaw on my lip as I debate. This is the perfect opportunity to snoop. Figure out who this version of David is and why he's really here.

As I inspect the nearly empty bookshelves, my phone vibrates in my pocket. I pull it out to find a group video call from Bree and Nic. Preparing myself for the interrogation, I swipe Accept.

Both my besties look concerned, so I slap on a smile. Nic has her earbuds in and sweat on her face—she's probably on her exercise bike. Bree's forehead wrinkles as she stares at the screen, a teacup balanced on her swollen belly.

"Hey y'all. Guess you heard about the fuss?"

"Are you ok?" Bree asks. "Colin said you were attacked? Asher said there's smoke damage? What happened?"

"Jeez, Bree, one question at a time." Nic slurps from a water bottle.

"I'm ok, shaken up a bit, mostly. Madder than a wet hen." My eyes continue to scan the shelves. A well-worn book on the end catches my eye.

"Why were you still in the kitchen at three a.m.?"

I smile at Bree's tone. The baby's not even here yet and she sounds like a mom. "I was working on a new recipe. Maple bacon chocolate cake with brown sugar frosting and caramel. You know those ovens are way better than mine upstairs."

Bree moans through the phone. "Did the cake survive? Now I want that! Damn cravings."

"Are you fucking serious right now? You're worried about a damn cake?" Although Nic's breathless, her tone is acerbic.

Still laughing at their antics, I pull the book from the shelf. It's an anthology of Edgar Allen Poe's poetry.

My brows pinch as I flip the well-worn pages, my friends still bickering in the background. The book naturally spread to a particular poem, as if the spine has been conditioned to hold this spot from countless readings. The edges are smeared and various stains cover the margins. I look up at the title and my heart flips in my chest.

Annabel Lee.

"What the fuck are you wearing? Wait..." Nic leans closer to the phone, her shiny forehead taking up the entire camera. "That's not your apartment!"

I look down at the giant Marine crest on David's sweatshirt and curse. Well, G-rated cursing, unlike my besties, Mrs. Trucker and Miss Sailor, over here. After ten years of friendship, I've mostly gotten used to their language. Momma would wash my mouth out with soap if I talked like these two, and some childhood lessons are hard to forget.

The air felt chilly after a night tucked next to David's warmth. I saw the sweatshirt on his dresser and grabbed it before sneaking out of his room to make breakfast. With his clove and cinnamon smell embedded in the fabric, it was too comforting to take off. Wish my besties didn't catch me red-handed, though. They'll never let it go, now.

"The police didn't think I should stay at the apartment last night. Billy was quite adamant. Didn't want to wake either of you up."

Nic's eyes narrow in her patented I smell bullcrap expression. "Mmhmm—except Billy is no Marine. Who's the only Marine we know, Bree?"

"Would that be the same man who texted my husband and Asher at three-thirty about the break in?" Bree is trying and failing to look innocent.

"Bitch! You had dirt and didn't share?"

At least they're distracted from me again. I slip the book back onto the shelf and wander into the kitchen for a glass of water before propping myself up in David's ridiculously comfortable bed. That's the only logical explanation for the best sleep I've had in years, despite all the chaos.

Bree pulls me back to the conversation. "So why did you call David if you wouldn't call us?"

"I didn't, actually. Uh, he just kind of showed up?" It sounds more like a question than an answer.

"Showed up... in the middle of the night? Are you hate fucking or something?" Trust Nic to be the blunt one.

"No! I don't know what he was doing nearby. He was suddenly there yelling my name and fighting through cops to get to me." I feel my cheeks heat and my stomach flip at the memory. "It was like something out of a Bonnie Tyler song."

The call falls silent. I make sure we're still connected. Bree practically has cartoon hearts in her eyes and Nic is staring slack-jawed. "What?"

Nic shakes her head and opens and closes her mouth a few times. "Need more details."

"I don't know. It's a little fuzzy. Billy was asking me questions. Then I hear my name and look up and there's Davy. Two cops held him back, but he simply vaulted the barrier to get to me. Then when Billy said I shouldn't stay at the apartment, Davy took me to his house and drew me a bath."

Bree sniffles. "That's so romantic." She grabs a tissue and blows her nose like a dang fog horn. "Damn hormones."

Nic leans back on her bike and mops her face with a towel. "And where is your streetwise Hercules now?"

"At Pop, installing a security system." Bree still looks like she's about to swoon—better change the subject. "So Bree, whatcha still doing at home? Shouldn't you be at the office by now? Or do executives not work?"

Last year, Bree got her dream job after uncovering a massive scandal at her company. Well, Bree and her now-husband Colin. Girl has a corner office at a major research and development firm, a devoted husband and a kid on the way, yet somehow still finds time to balance the books at Pop. She's unreal.

"Working from home. I decided pants were too hard today." We laugh. Bree tilts the phone down to show her impressively pregnant belly better. "You're both tall, you don't get it. I'm fun-sized and I'm growing a baby with Celtic warrior genes."

"Celtic warrior?" I ask.

"Maybe I've read too many historical romances lately. Damn hormones."

"Listen, I'm fixin' to get dressed. Should probably call Asher for a damage report, too." I sigh. We've been saving up to expand Pop, but depending on the repair bill, that might get pushed back. Again.

"You sure you're ok? We can take care of the damage if it's too much." Bree's face clouds with concern.

I smile at my friends. They really are the best. "Thanks, sugar, but I want to stay busy."

"If you need a place to crash for a while, you can use my apartment. I've got photo shoots in New York City over the next couple of months. Then I'm flying to England for some family shit straight from JFK."

Besides being one-third owner, interior designer, and the marketing genius behind Pop, Nic is a successful photographer. She does both magazine and catalog work, but the photos she takes for herself are breath-taking. We've been after her to submit to a gallery for years.

"Everything ok? When was the last time you went back?"

"Yea, overdue summons from Grandmama Dearest. Need to put in an appearance for the sake of the family name or some bullshit. I'll bring back the good chocolate."

We say our goodbyes and hang up. Clothes in hand, I head to the bathroom to freshen up. Halfway to the door, I realize I forgot my deodorant and whirl back to get it. My toes connect with a moving box, knocking it over. Dropping my clothes to grab my aching foot, I hop up and down.

Fudge that hurts.

When the stinging finally fades, I tentatively put weight on my foot and wiggle my toes. I can already tell there's going to be one heck of a bruise, but no serious damage. As I lean down to straighten the box, a piece of paper with my name on it catches my eye.

What is this?

Opening the box further reveals a leather notebook with scraps of paper peeking out. I open the book to the page where I saw my name and find a clipping of an article from when Pop opened half a decade ago.

My knees feel weak as I slide down the side of the bed to sit on the floor. The pages hold a decade's worth of pictures and clippings. My high school graduation photo. An article about the county fair blue prize my pie won that summer. A photo from move-in day at the University of Florida. Track meets in college. Every major review or article of Pop is here. Even the one about speed dating last year.

It's all here. Every major life event in the last decade is here.

I close the notebook as tears blur my vision. How did he do this? His words from earlier replay in my mind. *I thought I was protecting you.* He really didn't stop caring. He couldn't be here in person, but he still found a way to fulfill his pinky promise.

The notebook digs into my chest as I hug it, giving in to the threatening sobs. I cry for the brave boy who went off to war. For the brokenhearted girl he left behind. For the man who came back only to be scorned. But mostly, I cry for the lost time. The wasted anger.

When the tears finally dry, I feel lighter. The burden of my pain lifted a bit. Carefully, I put the notebook and box back where I found it. Better rush through the rest of my morning routine, I have things to do before Davy gets back.

I'm dressed and waiting impatiently in the kitchen over a heating pan. The thud of a truck door sounds in the driveway, spurring me into action. I place the prepared sandwiches into the heated pan to melt the cheese and brown the bread. By the time the front door opens, I'm practically jumping out of my skin.

"Bells?" His deep voice causes my heart to flip in my chest.

"In the kitchen." With a breath to calm my nerves, I transfer the gooey sandwich to a waiting plate by a glass of Coke. "Hope you're hungry. I made lunch."

Davy's eyes are wary as he enters the kitchen and lowers himself to the stool by the dish. Suspiciously, he sniffs at the sandwich.

A laugh bubbles out of me. Davy's eyes jerk back to me at the sound. "I guess I deserve that. It's the real thing. No ghost pepper sauce." I bite my lip, suddenly nervous.

The neatly trimmed beard accentuates his grin, and I feel it all the way to my core. "Hell's Bells, ghost pepper? The heart burn was probably the reason I was up at three am."

My cheeks heat. "I'm sorry, Davy. For the sandwiches and for my general attitude since you showed up. We didn't part well, but you were my best friend for most of my life before that. I owed you a chance to explain." I can't quite meet his eyes as I stand across the counter from him.

A warm hand covers my nervous fingers, surprising me into looking up. A thousand emotions dance in his hazel eyes. Regret. Hope. And an disarming vulnerability. "You have nothing to apologize for, Bells. You had every right to be pissed, but I hope you let me make it up to you now."

I smile shyly. Physically, at thirty, Davy hardly resembles the nineteen-year-old boy who was the center of my world. Once I let go of the hurt and anger, I can see he's still the same caring friend I remember. It might be nice to have my friend back. That is, if I can shove any lingering romantic feelings aside. "I'd like that. To get to know each other again."

He smiles, and a shot of electricity hits me in the gut. Reminding myself we're better off as friends is going to be hard.

After one more squeeze of my hand, he brings the sandwich to his mouth. His eyes close as he takes a bite. The worry lines on his face soften and he smiles in satisfaction. "Bells, you still make the best grilled cheese I've ever had."

I chuckle as he eats like it's his last meal. Nibbling on my own sandwich, I give into my curiosity. Who is David Hawthorne now? "So... physical security? How'd the football star-turned-Marine get into that?"

Sandwich gone, Davy takes a sip of cola and leans back. "Not sure I'd say football star. I specialized in electronic surveillance in the Marines." He shrugs. "This seemed like a logical transition to life outside the Corps. A way to help people with the skills I learned and make a living."

"Electronic surveillance, what exactly does that mean? Cameras and stuff?"

He tilts his head from side to side, hedging. "More or less. Could be video, audio, GPS tracking, some data mining. We sell DIY kits in our store but also offer full-service installs. Like what we did at Pop today."

I shudder at the reminder of last night. Swearing, David pushes out of his chair and comes around to rub my arms. "I'm sorry, Bells. How are you holding up? Can I do anything?"

"You've already done so much. We should probably head over there at some point. You can show me how to use the new, fancy alarm and I can pack up some stuff. Nic's traveling for the next couple months and offered me her apartment."

His eyes dim like he's disappointed before he quickly masks it. "Are you sure you want to go over there today? There's no rush. I walked Asher and Colin through the controls and there's a manual. The only thing I didn't tell them was the PIN to your separate apartment system." He lets go of my arm to pull a white card out of his back pocket and hand it to me.

The business card has his name and contact information. On the back, Davy scrawled a code in his bold handwriting. "Zero. One. Two. Nine. That's..." I look up at him with wide eyes.

"Your Momma's birthday." He gives me a sad smile and then reaches up to tuck a strand of hair behind my ear. I feel the rush of warmth I'm starting to get all too used to. "Why don't you stay today? I'll make some popcorn, we can watch a movie. Catch up some more. I'll take you to Pop tomorrow and help you pack whatever you need for Nic's."

I run my tongue over my teeth as I weigh my options. My heart wants to stay and reunite with my childhood best friend. Hide away from the attack for a while longer. My brain is telling me this is a very bad idea. I fell for him once, I'm not sure I'd survive it again. There are a million ways this could blow up in my face, but when I open my mouth, I say, "Sure."

CHAPTER THIRTEEN

She's Gone

ANNABEL - AGE 16

I think this is it. The doctors said there wasn't much time left and we should say our goodbyes. How do you say goodbye to your mother? How do you keep going, knowing she won't be there to share your life?

We've all gathered around Momma's bed. When the chemo stopped working, she decided to spend the rest of her time at home with her family. Rhett is lying next to her, holding her hand. At the foot of the bed, Huck and Tom flank her feet. Dad sits in a chair by her side, holding her other hand and telling her we'll be ok. I sit behind Rhett with my hand on his back, while Ace stands by Dad, comforting him.

This has been our role for the last two years. Look out for our younger brothers. Keep the family together.

As I look down at Momma, I hardly recognize her. Her once sunny hair is pale and limp. Cheeks once rosy are white, and her lips are slightly blue. She doesn't open her eyes. I wouldn't even be sure she was still breathing but for the sickening rattle in her chest every so often.

We sit. And we wait.

My eyes feel gritty from all the tears that have fallen and dried on my face. I can't remember the last time I've showered or eaten something. And honestly, I don't care. The only sounds in the room are the ticking clock, the occasional sniffle, and that rattle that will haunt me for the rest of my life.

The hours stretch on. Then… it happens. I watch Momma's final breath leave her body in an agonizing wheeze. She's at peace at last.

And our hell begins.

Rhett starts calling for her, squeezing her hand. I pull him to me and he clings, sharp nails digging into my shoulders as hot tears bathe my neck. As my father collapses forward, still clutching Momma's hand, and Ace moves forward to hold him, I carry Rhett out of the room and down the hall.

As I rock Rhett on his bed, I fight back my own tears. My eyes and throat burn with the effort, but my baby brother needs me to be strong. First, Tom pads into the room, looking pale and lost. He crawls onto the mattress to my left, leaning his head on my shoulder. Moments later, Huck follows, mirroring his twin perfectly on my right. We say nothing, simply sit together for comfort.

I don't know how long we sit there. Long enough for the ambulance to come—no siren. I hide Rhett's face as the EMTs take her away and silent tears course down my face. The house feels colder and too still. The sun fades, bathing the room in an orange glow as the twins shuffle back to their room. I transition a sleeping Rhett into bed and tuck him in, like I've done most of his life.

The hall is quiet. Both Dad's and Atty's doors are closed.

I tiptoe down the stairs to the kitchen. This is the room I associate most with Momma. She taught me to cook here. She listened to me complain about school and fed me cookies when I was sad here. Sometimes I wonder if she knew even then what the future held. Is that why she was so adamant I learn to cook?

The numbness I've felt all day gives way to a soul-crushing grief in a moment. Suddenly, being in this kitchen without her is too much. It doesn't matter that she's been too sick to leave her room in months. I don't want to be here without her. Covering my mouth as my breath catches on an ugly sob and my eyes blur, I run out the back door as quickly as I can.

My legs pump as I tear across the backyard. My muscles protest, but the pain in my thighs is a welcome distraction from the pain in my chest. I have no destination in mind, anywhere except my house will do.

When my muscles finally give out, my knees sink into the dirt by the creek. I dig my fingers into the damp earth. My back arches as I fight the emotions I'm not ready to handle. Despair. Relief. Anger. I scream at the heavens, raging at a God my mother praised until the end.

What is the point of this? How is this part of some bigger plan? Why did she have to leave me? Why didn't she go to the doctor sooner? If she wasn't so busy taking care of five children, would she still be here?

Arms wrap around me as I hunch over, my tears turning the dirt to mud. A warm chest presses against my back, and a head rests on my shoulder. "Shh, Bells. You'll get through this. I'm here, whatever you need." My fingers dig into Davy's arm as I continue to sob. Red half-moon marks bloom on his skin, but he says nothing.

"She's gone, Davy… she's…" A fresh wave of grief takes me. My stomach clenches and twists so hard I think I'm going to be sick. When I'm out of tears, I feel numb.

That's not quite true. I feel empty. Like a vacuum has opened up and taken everything. Like I'll never be ok again.

"Come on, you're freezing. Let's get you cleaned up and warm." Davy stands and pulls me up with him. He has to support my weight with his arm around my waist. I trip multiple times, my body as unresponsive as my emotions.

The week is a blur of arrangements and well-meaning but unwanted visitors. The refrigerator is overflowing with grief casseroles. They are disgusting and no one feels like eating, anyway. With no reason to cook, I scrub the house until my hands bleed. I make sure everyone has black outfits for the funeral.

Every minute Davy's not at school or football practice, he's with us. He keeps pushing protein shakes on me, anything else I can't keep down. I don't know what I would do without him. Every time Rhett cries for Momma, I break a little more. Davy steps in at those moments, distracting Rhett so I can catch my breath.

The service is beautiful. White lilies, magnolias, and roses overwhelm the church. We Bennets stand together in the front pew. Dad and Rhett, then Atty, me, Huck, and Tom in a row. We stand tall and silent, all our tears finally spent. It drizzles at the cemetery, like even the angels are weeping for our loss.

As I watch my mother lowered to her final resting place, a pressure builds from deep within. I want to run. I want to throw myself on her casket and beg the heavens to give her back. Just as I think I can't take it anymore, a warm palm and calloused fingers touch my hand. The scent of cinnamon and clove surround and comfort me. I lean back on my heels, finding Davy right behind me, lending me the strength I desperately need.

My fingers squeeze his mercilessly, but he doesn't complain about the pain. At this moment, he is my lifeline. Silently, he gives me the strength I need to push through. I'm still empty, but with Davy's support, I feel a little less broken. Like maybe there is a possibility of us surviving this nightmare.

CHAPTER FOURTEEN

Running & Questions

DAVID - NOW

The sun is rising as I open my eyes. A night uninterrupted by nightmares. It's a miracle. Most likely thanks to the angel in my arms. I smile as I look down at a still sleeping Bella tucked against me. She started the night staunchly on her own side of the bed, but sought me out in her sleep. Now she's wrapped around me like a damn python.

What a way to go, though.

I enjoy having her in my house. Not only for the amazing cooking—though, that alone would be enough. With her here, my nerves are less frayed. Having her here is soothing. Calming. Like aloe on a sunburn.

Sitting on the couch yesterday was so easy. Bella's walls are cracking. She's letting me back in.

As a friend.

I'm not complaining. I'm happy she's talking to me at all and showing me hints of my Bella. The girl I fell head over heels for half a lifetime ago and never looked back. I'm a patient man. I'll wait as long as it takes, and I'll happily accept whatever she gives me.

I just want to be in her life.

She stirs in my arms and blinks her eyes awake. I note the exact moment she realizes where she is and her brows pinch in confusion. Might as well face the awkwardness straight on.

"Mornin'." My voice grumbles from lack of use.

"Mornin'." The flush of her cheeks sends blood to my cock. Please don't move your leg, or you'll get a big surprise.

As if hearing my thoughts, Bella carefully untangles herself from around my body. I instantly miss her closeness. Sitting up in bed, I bend my knees to camouflage my growing erection.

"I should get going..." Bella is avoiding eye contact, which is never a good sign.

Desperate for this cease-fire to continue, I blurt out the first thing that comes to mind. "Want to go for a run first? Then I'll take you back and help you pack."

"Since when do you run?" Her nose wrinkles in confusion and it's absolutely adorable.

I shrug. "Basic training? I've kept at it, though. It's good for stress."

"Yea, ok. Glad I packed some workout clothes. Do you want to use the bathroom first?"

"You go ahead, I'll pop down the hall."

When the master bath door closes behind Bella, I grab some exercise clothes and rush to the other bathroom. Bracing my hands on the sink, I look down at the tent in my gray sweatpants. I palm my erection, hoping for relief, but it only fans the flames. I check the lock over my shoulder before giving in and stroking my aching cock. The quick release leaves me far from satisfied, but at least I don't have to worry about my running shorts not fitting.

Once we're both ready to hit the pavement, I lead her on my favorite route. After a five-minute warm up, I pick up the pace. Her long legs easily keep up with me. As she runs, Bella's face relaxes, the tension eases from her shoulders. When we get back to my place after the six-mile run, we're both winded. I toss Bella a towel and a bottle of water as we enter my kitchen.

"Thanks. It's been too long since I've gone for a long run." She tosses the towel around her neck and guzzles the water.

"I go every morning. You're welcome to join me, the company would be nice."

She eyes me cautiously, her teeth dig into her bottom lip. "Yea, sure."

I step closer. My fingers itch to free her lip from her teeth. "What's wrong?"

"Do you think it's safe to stay in my apartment?" Her eyes wary, she fidgets with the edge of the towel.

My heart aches to see her scared. If I ever get my hands on that son of a bitch, I'll kill him. "With the security system and cameras, I think you'll be safe enough." She nods, but her teeth dig deeper into her lip. Warring with myself, I give in to the urge to comfort her and cup her arms with my palms. "Hey. If I didn't think it was a good idea, I'd say so."

"Nic's apartment is so far away. I like my place…"

I grin at her. "Well, you can't beat the commute to work."

Her lips curve in the ghost of a smile. "I guess I'm just a little scared." Bella hunches into herself.

It kills me to see her feeling so small. "That's completely normal, Bells." A thought occurs to me. "Give me your cell."

Her eyes jerk up to mine. "What?"

"Your cell." I hold out my palm for her device. Eyebrows pinched, she pulls it out of her pocket and hands it to me.

"First, you need a PIN or thumbprint on this thing." My thumbs fly over the device as I search for the settings and apps I'm looking for. Once I'm happy, I hand it back to her with a grin.

Her eyes dart from the phone to me. "What did you do?"

"I installed our panic alarm app for you. It will send a silent alert to me and my partner, and enable GPS tracking so help can get to you. I also programmed my number in there. If you want to talk or hear a noise or just don't want to be alone, call me."

Her eyes round as she processes my words. "Thanks, Davy."

I smooth her sweaty hair behind her ear and drop a quick kiss to her forehead. My chest swells with warmth. It almost feels like when we were kids. "Seriously, any time, Bells. Now let me jump in the shower and we'll get you back to your place in time for work." I leave her standing in the kitchen, clutching her phone against her chest.

An hour later, I'm walking through the front door of Smith and Hawthorne Security with a spring in my step. Ronnie waves to me from his chair as he talks on the phone. I sit at my desk and check emails while I wait for him to finish up.

Bells looked nervous outside Pop, but having the kitchen full of people seemed to help distance her from the attack. Asher and Colin did a great job of removing any signs of the fire.

"Hey, man. How's your girl doing?" Ronnie's face pinches with genuine concern.

"I think she'll be ok. Thanks for dropping everything for those installs yesterday. I appreciate it."

He tilts his chair back and grabs a Skittle out of the bowl on his desk. The man is a sugar addict. "Anything for family. You know that. She got any idea who would have a motive?"

I shake my head. "Were you able to pull any footage from nearby cameras? ATMs or traffic cams?"

"There weren't any with a view of the back door. Clearly Friendship Springs is too trusting and our business plan is solid." Ronnie grew up in a busy city and doesn't understand small town Americana.

"Well, if the fucker comes back, we'll get it on camera. I also set her up with the panic button app."

"Good call." His gaze turns thoughtful and Ronnie chews on his cheek for a minute. "Something about this doesn't feel right."

My stomach drops. "What do you mean?"

Ronnie leans forward, hands clasped between his knees. "The bank bag was still sitting out when I got there. In plain view. If this was a simple B and E, why did the asshole not grab the money?"

My pulse ratchets up as Ronnie's comment sparks a thousand thoughts. "If it wasn't about a quick grab, why else would someone break in?" I hold Ronnie's gaze.

"I don't know, man. But I don't like it."

Neither do I.

CHAPTER FIFTEEN

Earning It

I close my eyes and let the sounds and smells of the busy kitchen distract me from my swirling thoughts. In the light of day and full of my staff, the room is thankfully absent of signs from that night. Probably helps that I'm running the pass instead of cooking tonight. "Where are my scallops? Ryan, how are the lava cakes coming?"

"Right here, Chef." Ryan appears on my left with a tray of plated desserts for the fortieth birthday party in the back section. As I reach across him to garnish the mini-desserts with powdered sugar and raspberries, I accidentally bump his arm. He winces and bobbles the load.

"You ok?"

"Yea, overdid it at the gym, is all. Here you go, Chef. I'll get the next tray." He is still holding his arm as he walks away.

With two large parties in the house tonight, the kitchen is buzzing. The hours fly by as I expedite and check orders.

I keep waiting for a ticket requesting the chef's special sandwich. It's well past lunch and dinner's almost over, but still no ticket. I shake my head at myself. Davy spent the last two days dealing with my crap, he's probably stuck at the office playing catch-up.

"Ugh, he's hot and all, but I'd rather have the tips."

I look over at Sara, one of our newer servers, as she approaches the pass. "What's that? Customer giving you trouble, Sara?"

She blows her bangs out of her face and gives me a pained look. "This guy has been sitting in my section for over an hour. He's done eating but won't leave. He's super fit and those tattoos are dreamy, but a girl's gotta pay rent. You know?"

My breath catches at her description. "Dark hair? Beard?" Butterflies explode in my belly.

Sara tilts her head. "Yea, actually."

"Tony, take the pass." Without waiting for a response, I push through the double doors to the dining room. Asher calls a greeting as I near the bar, but I'm too busy scanning the crowd to respond. Then I see him. Davy's sitting at a table in another snug polo, with glasses perched on his nose as he types away on a laptop. His brows pinch in concentration and my fingers itch to smooth them.

When I reach his table, Davy looks up at me. His features soften and his lips form a sexy grin. "Hey, you. How's work going?"

I can't stop the smile that spreads across my face. "Well, it'd be going better if someone wasn't harassing my waitstaff." Davy snaps to attention, his eyes scanning the dining room for signs of trouble. "I mean you. Sara can't make tips if she can't turn over the table." His sheepish expression makes me chuckle. "Come on, you can work in my office or up in my apartment. Have you had dessert yet?" I grab his beer and step back, waiting for him to follow me.

"No, not yet. I had pork belly for dinner, it was delicious. You've created something incredible here, Bells." He grabs his stuff and tosses a fifty-dollar bill on the table before following me back to the kitchen. We pass a shocked-looking Sara and Tony as I bring Davy to the tiny office at the back of the room.

"Thanks, Bells. What time are you getting off?" He settles in behind my desk, dwarfing the chair as he re-opens his laptop.

"I usually close. You hanging out for a bit?"

"If that's alright. Figured I'd stay while I type up some proposals."

If he's the same Davy I remember, he's most likely staying to keep an eye on me. Be nearby in case I need him. A warmth spreads in my gut at the proof he still cares. "You're welcome to work from back here anytime. Want to help me with something after closing?"

His eyes sparkle with curiosity, but he's grinning when he says, "Sounds great. I'll wait here."

The rest of the dinner service is uneventful. When I wander back into the office, Davy is looking at a picture of me, Bree, and Nic on my desk. "That was the day we opened." I smile at the memory.

"You look happy. I'm glad you found your people, Bells." He puts the frame down almost reverently before turning back to me. "So, what did you need help with? Something wrong with the security system?"

I rock back on my heels. "Nope. I never got to try that new recipe the other night. Thought you could be a taste tester."

His white teeth flash in that sexy grin. "That, I can do."

"Come on, think I'll bake upstairs this time."

He follows me as I set the downstairs alarm and head up the stairs to my apartment. After placing his laptop on the couch, he pulls up a bar stool at the kitchen counter.

I grab an apron off my pantry hook and toss it at him, hitting him square in the chest. "Nah-ah, mister. You gotta earn it."

His lips curve as he stands. Lordy does that beard suit him. "Yes, chef. What do I do first?"

I'm already half in the refrigerator pulling out ingredients as he swaggers up in my apron. "Get the sugar, flour, and cocoa from the pantry." I pull out my frying pan and get it heating. Still need to test this recipe. Think I'll make cupcakes this time, though.

"So," Davy starts as he places the canisters on the counter by me, "the bachelor/bachelorette party is in a couple of weeks. Do you want to drive up together? Save on gas."

I'd forgotten about the trip in all the chaos. Funny, I'm dreading it a bit less now that I've decided to be friendly with Davy. Atty was right, it is time to bury the hatchet. Not that I'll ever tell him. "Yea, that sounds great. Now start measuring the dry stuff."

We get to work. He's actually a decent helper. I repeat the steps from that night, glad he's here to drown out the lingering memories of the attack. As we work, we chat. Catching up on the last decade. Any remaining reservations I have about trusting this man fades. It's hard to keep my walls up when it's only the two of us. We slip back into being Davy and Bells—like the last ten years apart never happened.

"How'd you meet Brianna and Nic?" Davy purses his lips in concentration as he pours caramel into the cupcakes I've already cored.

"They were my suite-mates when I transferred to UF. We hit it off immediately." I follow behind him, piping perfect swirls of brown sugar buttercream on the filled cupcakes.

"When'd you start going by Anna instead of Bella?" His eyes dart to mine briefly, then he goes back to staring at the desserts like they might explode in his face.

"About the same time. After everything that happened in Hitchcock, I just wanted a fresh start." Davy winces before his features smooth again.

"When did you get the tattoos?" I nod my head at the Marine crest on his forearm and the trail of flowers peeking out of his short sleeve.

I'd gotten to see a little more of the quarter sleeve during our run. I'm pretty sure they're magnolia blooms. They're all black and gray and beautifully done. My fingers itch to lift his shirt and look closer.

"At twenty, Ronnie and I got the crests on our first leave. I got the first flower soon after and then kept adding. Do you have any?"

I dip a fork in caramel and flick it back and forth over some wax paper. "Me? Heck, no. I'm not a fan of needles. They are beautiful though. Ok." I place the caramel nests and some candied bacon onto two cupcakes. Picking them up, I hand one to Davy. "You earned your taste."

His white teeth sink into the soft chocolate cake. Davy's eyes close as he moans. I watch as his tongue darts out to lick the frosting from his lips and my core clenches. My thighs press together to relieve the tension.

Settle down, Annabel. Been there. Done that. Got the t-shirt. No need for a repeat disaster. Nic is always proclaiming the benefits of a healthy sex life. Maybe I should get one.

"Hell's Bells, this is sinful." Not unlike my thoughts. "Is this for Pop or the wedding? Because I want more of it."

I gulp as he takes another giant bite, flexing the muscles in his neck. Weddings are a good place to pick up someone. Right? Too bad the rest of the groomsmen are related to me.

"I'm actually not sure if Grace wants me to bake her cake. Guess I'm a crappy maid of honor."

"Naw. You've had a couple hard weeks. You'll get all the details when we head up." Davy grins at me, then shoves the rest of the cupcake into his mouth, making me chuckle. "Dang, it's late. You ok here tonight? Or were you heading to Nic's?" His eyes crinkle with concern.

"I'm good. Gotta test out my new fancy alarm." I smile up at him with confidence I don't quite feel.

"I'm only two blocks away if you need anything. Seriously, anything at all, call." After a brief pause, he pulls me into a hug and drops a kiss to my crown. It's so quick I don't have time to squeeze him back.

I see him out and arm the system before setting the kitchen to rights. After checking the doors and windows twice, I crawl under the covers, trying to ignore how cold the bed feels alone. How every creak or hiss of the dishwasher makes me jumpy.

Tossing and turning, I chew on my cheek. "Screw it," I mutter as I grab my cell and scroll through my contacts. He answers on the second ring.

"Bella, what's wrong? You ok, baby?" I close my eyes at the concern in his voice. My heart flips at the endearment, the tightness around my chest loosening a bit.

"Just checking," I squeak.

Rustling comes through the phone, like Davy's settling back in bed. "I told you I'd answer, Bells."

"Yeah, but you didn't pinky promise." I trace the pattern on my comforter, wishing I could see his face.

Davy's chuckle rumbles in my ear and makes my toes curl. "You and your pinky promises."

I smile until my cheeks hurt. "Pinky promises are sacred." It was always our thing.

"Well, then I pinky promise. Why aren't you sleeping, Bells?"

"I'm fixin' to, but I can't." He chuckles again. The sound reverberates through me and my muscle relax. "Whatcha doin'?"

"Trying to sleep. You're safe, Bells. If anything trips the alarm, I'll get an alert on my phone. I'll be there before anything can happen, I promise."

I swallow, "I'll let you sleep. Oh, and Davy?"

"Yea, Bells?" His voice is low and raspy.

"Want to meet up for a run in the morning?" I bite my lip as I wait for his reply.

"I'll meet you outside Pop at eight. G'night Bells."

Smiling, I roll towards the nightstand. "Goodnight, Davy. See y'all in the morning."

CHAPTER SIXTEEN

Road Trip

DAVID - NOW

I check my phone for the hundredth time in an hour. Bella should be here any minute for our drive to Hitchcock. I've updated the outgoing message on the phones and emails, sent out statuses to all open clients, and even dusted. Where is she? The bells ring on the front door as it opens.

"There you are. Oh..." Instead of the blond currently occupying every waking thought, I find her friend's husband. "Hi, Colin. What's up?"

His lips curve into a mischievous grin. "Take it you were expecting someone else?" I swear the man is half leprechaun for all the mischief he stirs. "You wouldn't happen to be waiting for a certain chef, would you?"

I grunt at him as I lean back in my seat. "Yea. We're both heading back home for the holiday weekend, so we're driving together. It's her brother's bachelor party." Narrowing my eyes at the lack of surprise on his face, I continue. "But you already knew that, so what can I do for you?"

He strides in and pulls out Ronnie's chair before dropping into it as my phone vibrates.

Bella:

Hey, can you pick me up at Pop? I may have overdone it with the snacks…

Typical Bella, making too much food. One mystery solved, I chuckle and shake my head.

Me:

Yea. Just need to get rid of an annoying customer that walked in.

K. I'll wait at my place. The coolers and luggage are by the door.

"Coolers. Plural?" I mutter to myself.

Hell's Bells, is it all going to fit in my pickup?

Har har. Just make the sale already and get here.

I shove my phone back in my pocket and turn towards Colin. Dark smudges shadow his eyes and he slouches in the chair. "You good, man?"

"Yea." He rubs his hand down his face. "Bree's right miserable. Doctor put her on bed rest until the baby comes. Once the baby gets here, everything will settle down."

I let out a bark of laughter. "You know you get *less* sleep after the baby's born, right?"

"Oh yeah, and what do you know?" He scrubs a hand over his tired face.

"We were in middle school when Bella's youngest brother was born. Bella and I babysat a lot. I remember how hard those days were."

Colin sits back in his chair, green eyes wide. "No shit? Didn't realize it was such a big age difference. They don't come down much."

"Rhett graduated high school last month, so I'm not surprised. Don't think you stopped in to gossip about Bella's family, though."

"You're right. Any news on the break in?"

Eyeing Colin carefully, I consider my words. "Shouldn't you be asking the authorities?"

"Cut the bullshit. I know you're investigating."

"How do you figure that?"

He stares me down, any signs of the former lightness gone as a hard gleam fills his gaze. "Because if it was Brianna, I wouldn't let it go until I caught the bastard."

My fingers scratch the scruff of my beard as I hold his glare. "He covered his tracks. There was no video footage or clues. We're hoping it was an isolated incident."

Colin's eyes narrow. "Hoping. Which means you don't think it was."

Slowly, I shake my head. "The bank bag was sitting right there. The way Bella cooks, she zones everything else out. He could have gotten it and slipped out without her noticing. My gut says she's the target, not Pop or an easy buck."

"Bollocks." Colin runs his hand through his brown hair, leaving it standing on end. "I'll sleep better when you finish installing the alarm system at my house. If anything happened to Bree..." His eyes pinch as he looks at me.

"I hear ya. The rest of the equipment should be here in a few weeks. Until then, the girls have the panic app installed on their cell phones and you have the basic alarm set up."

He nods absently and stands, gripping my shoulder in a brotherly squeeze. "Yea. You go get your girl, I'll head home to mine. She sent me out for ice cream, lemonade, and last quarter's books from Pop. Says if she's stuck in bed, she might as well get a head start on the taxes. The woman doesn't understand the meaning of rest."

He pretends to be annoyed, but I can see the love shining in his eyes. The guy's got it bad for his wife.

When I get to Pop fifteen minutes later, I find Bella staring at two large coolers and a full-size suitcase, plus a couple of those reusable shopping bags that are overflowing with food and drinks. "Hell's Bells. You realize it's only four days, right?"

"Well, I don't know what I'll have to work with at this cabin. The invite wasn't exactly full of details. I had to pack a little of everything to be safe."

The first cooler is heavy as hell when I pick it up. I don't miss the way her eyes drop to my muscles as they flex under the strain. Or the way she licks her lips. It takes multiple trips and some creative arranging, but I get it all in the bed of my pickup. I'm catching my breath with my hands on my knees when Bella appears next to me.

"Thanks. The totes are for the road trip, though." She pulls the bags out and crams them in the cab by her feet.

"Bells, how much do you expect to eat on a three-hour drive?" I shoot her a grin as I climb in. "Ready? Here, you get copilot duty." I unlock my phone, set up maps, and hand it to her after connecting it to the console.

The miles fly by as we joke around and tease each other over music selections. Gotta hand it to the girl, the snacks are worth it. Shouldn't have expected anything less, though. I take a sip from the growler of sweet tea we're sharing.

Sneaking a glance at her, I find her eating a soft pretzel she's dipping into a tupperware of cheese sauce. Realizing she's caught, she blushes and covers her face as she chuckles with a mouth full of food. "Want some?"

Keeping my eyes on the road, I lean towards her and open my mouth. "Ahhh." I chance a peek at her. She looks unamused. "Come on, can't dip and drive!"

Snorting, she dips the pretzel into the cheese and feeds me a bite, totally missing my mouth. "Your aim is off, Bells." She giggles. I freeze as her thumb wipes the gooey cheese off the corner of my lip. Then, quick as a viper, I close my mouth around her finger, sucking the sauce off with my tongue. I don't miss the way she gasps and blushes. "What else you got in your bag of tricks?"

Bella gives her head a little shake, then digs through the bags at her feet. "Fruit kebabs, some trail mix, sausage balls, and homemade chips."

My lips quirk up. "Sausage balls?"

"Yea, like meatballs, but a little spicier and filled with cheese." She opens a container and bites half of something round before holding it in front of my mouth. Blindly, I take the bite, catching her fingertips lightly before she can retreat. It's spicy with hints of cheddar and biscuit. "They're better warmed up."

"Those are bangin'. You'll have to heat them up when we get there. You excited? When was the last time you were home?"

Her nose wrinkles as she closes the Tupperware and returns it to the bag. "Easter? I missed Christmas because of Bree's wedding." She gnaws on her thumb as she looks out the windshield. "It'll be nice to see Dad and the boys. Not so sure about being stuck in a cabin with the bridesmaids, though."

I study her briefly as I check my blind spot and change lanes. "I thought you and Grace were close?"

She waves off my comment. "Wasn't talking about Grace. Haven't spoken to the rest of them since high school. It'll be fine. I'll hang out with my brothers, leave the girls to their own thing."

A lump of guilt forms in my throat. I'm not an idiot, I know Holly and Bella never got along, and I'm to blame. "It won't be that bad, Bells. We're not in high school anymore." My eyes dart between the road and her face, trying to read her expression. As I open my mouth to reassure her again, an engine growls and a loud pop sounds just to my left.

Every muscle tenses, and my vision narrows to points. The sounds of people screaming, running for cover, as alarms wail echo in my head. A pressure on my thigh grows, drawing my attention back to the present.

"Davy? David, are you ok?" It's Bella's hand gripping my thigh, and my fingers grasp hers like a lifeline. I take a deep breath and mentally list three things I can see, hear, and feel to ground myself fully in my body. "Is that from the darkness you mentioned?"

I check my blind spots and change lanes to stall as I gather my thoughts. "Yea. It's better than when I first got out, thanks to therapy. Mostly just nightmares now, but sometimes something shocks me back there. Wasn't like I was on the front lines, but saw too many devastated towns full of scared families just trying to survive. Everyone deserves to feel safe in their own home."

She nods thoughtfully. "The security company makes sense. Does it affect you often? The darkness?"

The concern in her voice is a healing balm to my stiff muscles. "There's good days and bad. Mostly good since I've moved to Friendship Springs." I squeeze her hand, keeping it in mine as we travel the final stretch in silence.

The sky is golden by the time we pull up to our destination, and warm lights glow from large windows dotting the front. To the side of the structure, a small lake reflects the setting sun. The cabin itself is a sprawling two story home surrounded by pine trees. A few trucks, a Jeep, and a sedan litter the driveway. We're probably the last to arrive, so I lay on the horn to alert the cavalry.

Laughter floats through the air as the door opens, and a smiling man emerges. "About time you made it!" Ace ambles down the porch and approaches the truck. As I pull him into a one-armed squeeze, Bella comes around the hood.

"What about me?" She cocks a hip and plants a fist on it, pretending to be mad.

Ace's eyes widen, and his face splits into a grin. He scoops Bella up in a bear hug that lifts her clear off the ground. "Bella Bug!" He lowers her to her feet, brows pinching as he darts a look between us. "Wait. You guys drove together?"

Bella and I share a look before answering in unison. "Yea."

With one arm still slung around Bella, Ace turns back to me. "And no one died?" I laugh and Bella socks him in the ribs. Ace immediately rubs the spot. Big baby.

"Tom, Huck," Ace yells back to the house. "Come say hi to your sister and help carry shit."

"Good idea. She packed two coolers." I shake my head as I drop the tailgate to reach for the first one.

"Rhett's not here?" Bella asks. Ace shakes his head no.

Two more men exit the house and jump off the porch steps. They push into each other as they approach. God, how long has it been since I've seen the twins? At twenty-five, they look nothing like the gawky teenagers I remember.

Tom gets to Bella first, wrapping her up in a quick squeeze with a peck on the cheek. His curly blond hair is shorter and slicked back and the smile on his face accentuates his cleft chin and firm jaw. His muscles stretch his gray tee as he lifts a cooler and heads back to the cabin. "Damn, she stress cooking again?"

"Baby bro decided to stay with Dad since he can't drink yet. Guess he didn't want to be DD when we go clubbing tomorrow. What's up, sissy?" Huck grabs Bella around the waist and spins her in a circle, making her screech.

For identical twins, they're complete opposites. Huck wears his curly hair long and messy, with a black beanie pulled over the mop. A black barbell winks in the fading light as he quirks a brow at the remaining cooler. "Jesus, sissy, you know it's only four days, right?"

I chuckle but cough to cover it when Bella stomps over. "Like any of you are going to cook this weekend? Uh-huh. Didn't think so. Now git." Bella playfully swats at Huck's butt. As he grabs the cooler, I'm surprised to realize he's packed on almost as much muscle as me.

"That doesn't explain the clothes, Bug." Atticus grunts as he swings the suitcase out of my truck and heads back up. I grab my duffle before snagging the totes from Bella. The grateful smile she gives me makes my chest warm, and as she climbs the porch steps before me, her ass in those tight jeans makes my dick twitch.

This is going to be a long weekend.

A delicate hand with scarlet nails grabs my arm, stopping me at the door. "Well, if it isn't David Hawthorne. Looking good, doll. We should catch up."

My jaw clenches as I take in the woman touching me. Long brown hair, red lips, red crop top, denim shorts. I feel nothing as I look at her. "Holly." I jerk my arm out of her grasp and continue to the kitchen with the food.

One look at my Bells and I know she saw the greeting. She's busying herself unpacking and preheating the oven. If I didn't know her so well, I'd think she was completely calm, but the loud clacks as she lays containers out on the counter tell me otherwise.

I put my bags down and walk up behind her as she sorts everything. She tries to step away, so I plant my hands on her hips to keep her still, before dropping my voice so the others don't hear. "You good?"

"Peachy." She pops the "p".

"Bells, I swear I haven't spoken to her since I graduated high school. There will be no…'catching up'."

Her lips thin as she looks at me over her shoulder for a tense minute. She drops her eyes back to the counter and murmurs so low I almost miss it, "It shouldn't matter to me."

I open my mouth to argue with her, but a blur of red speeds around the corner, screaming.

"Bella!" Reluctantly, I release my hold on Bella and step back slightly as Grace grabs her in an embrace. The two are laughing and chatting, so I continue to put the food away. Soon, the little redheaded spitfire sets her sights on me. "David! Give me a hug."

"Heya, Gracie." My shoulders relax as I engulf her much smaller frame.

Grace looks over her shoulder, but Bella's disappeared already. "How's it going?"

"Better before Holly cornered me at the door and Bella shut down."

She winces. "Sorry about that. Holly's ex-husband got engaged, and she's not handling it well."

"Yea, well, if Bella kills me on the way home because of it, you'll absolutely be sorry."

CHAPTER SEVENTEEN

Pulling Punches

I tug on the hem of my white t-shirt for probably the hundredth time. Why did I come out tonight again? So far sophomore year is as annoying as the last.

My eyes drift over the room from the beanbag I've claimed in the corner. A dozen teens pepper the semi-finished basement, most of them coupled up. The guys are almost all on the team, sporting jeans and matching Hitchcock High football shirts. The girls are in barely there shorts or skirts and tank tops. Everyone sprawls on available surfaces, chatting and drinking from red cups. Across the room, Grace sits in Atty's lap, laughing as he grins up at her.

Oh, yeah, that's why I'm here. When Atty mentioned the party to Momma, she insisted I should go, too. Something about being young while I'm still young enough to enjoy it. Daddy backed her up, said he'd be home to help with the boys.

Davy sits at Atty's side, with Holly plastered to his arm. All four of them have ignored me since I've gotten here.

Hazel eyes meet mine and wink.

Ok, well, not all of them, Davy checks on me every so often. I force a small smile and look away, continuing my scan of the room. Maybe some punch will help. How long do these things usually go for?

As I fill a cup from the bowl, one of Grace's friends comes up to me. "Hey, Baby Bennet. Isn't it past your bedtime?" I'm barely four months younger than Mae, so wouldn't it be her bedtime too?

I bite back the smart retort on the tip of my tongue and settle for a sigh. Momma always says you catch more flies with honey than vinegar. "Hi, Mae. Want some punch?"

I turn towards her, smile plastered in place, and hold the cup out slightly. She reaches as if to take it, but taps the bottom edge at the last second. Red liquid pours down my light shirt and pants. "Oops, clumsy me. Better take care of that."

My eyes blink, trying to process the horror movie playing out in front of me. Unsure how best to navigate this situation.

Cool fingers grasp my hand and tug me up the basement stairs. "Come on, honey, let's get a new outfit." Grace barely comes up to my shoulder, but she pulls me up to her room with the strength of a linebacker. Before I can protest, I'm pushed into Grace's bathroom and told to strip.

What the heck am I going to do now?

"Put this on." A wad of yellow fabric hits me as Grace chucks it through a slit in the doorframe.

I pull the dress over my head and reveal a stranger in the mirror. The soft cotton sundress is a little snug on my frame, accentuating curves I didn't realize I had and barely brushing my mid-thigh. The straps are thick ribbons that tie into bows on both shoulders.

When I open the door, I find Grace sitting on her bed, waiting for me with a smile. "Damn, that looks way better on you." She hops up and stands next to me, staring at our reflections. "Honey, if I had legs like yours, I wouldn't hide them! Why do you always wear jeans?"

I shrug. "It's easier when I'm running after Rhett. Protects me from tics... and plastic swords."

Grace tsks, then stretches on her tippy toes to pull out my scrunchie. My hair falls in a blond cloud around my shoulders, complimenting the yellow of the dress and making my skin look golden. "That's better." Her lips spread into a grin. "I'm glad you came tonight. We should hang out more often, without the boys."

My cheeks warm, and I return her smile. "I'd like that. I honestly don't have any girlfriends."

She grips my arms in a little side hug. "Come on, Jedi was asking about you. We can't waste this outfit."

The dash back to the basement is as swift as the race up. True to her word, Grace brings me over to a boy sitting in a group by the stairs. He has red hair and a kind smile that spreads as we approach. She introduces us, pushes me towards him, and runs off with a wink.

"So, Bella, are you a cheerleader with Grace? I've seen you around practice."

"Oh," my cheeks heat again, and I force a laugh. How could anyone mistake me for a cheerleader? "No, Grace is dating my brother. I'm usually there waiting with him for David." I nod my chin at Davy and Atty.

Jedi looks over, his eyes widening. "So you and Hawthorne...?"

An indelicate snort escapes at the idea, drawing his eyes back to me. "Heck no, he lives next door. The three of us have always walked home together."

The tension in his shoulders relaxes, and he leans closer to me, his lips curling again. "That so?" His eyes darken as they sweep over me from head to foot. "You're obviously an athlete, though. What sport do you play?"

I laugh again, sounding much more natural. "I run a bit. Thinking about trying out for the track team this week."

"I'd cheer you on." His eyes drop to my bare legs. "Are you coming to the game next weekend? There's a bonfire after. I'd love to take you." Jedi's warm hand cups my arm. It's a strange, not entirely unpleasant, but still kind of weird feeling.

"David!" Holly's shrill voice cuts through the party. I glance up to meet cold hazel eyes for a moment before she pulls his attention back to her.

My stomach clenches and I turn, wide eyed, back to Jedi. "Maybe. I'll have to check if I'm babysitting Friday night." His grin spreads until a dimple forms in his cheek. He's sort of cute. Ok, this isn't so bad.

"Bella. You forgot your phone again. Dad needs to talk to you." I jerk my head, surprised to see Atty standing next to me, holding out his cellphone.

I excuse myself and climb a few steps to muffle some of the noise. "Daddy?"

"Hey, baby girl." He sighs, sounding tired, "sorry to interrupt your party, but I can't find Rhett's stuffy. I swear I've shown him every one, but he says they're all wrong. Says he can't sleep without it." The sounds of sniffling grow louder in the background as Rhett's exhausted voice whines for Mr. Roar.

"It's ok. He probably wants his T-Rex, that's been his favorite lately. Last I saw it was when we made a pillow fort on the couch after dinner." I hang on while my father bangs down the stairs to the living room.

"Got it! You're an angel. Having fun?"

I smile, thinking about Jedi. "Yea, I am."

"I'm glad, sweetie. Enjoy your night. Love you."

Hanging up, I head back down the steps, stopping short at the sound of Holly's voice. "Baby Bennet, Jedi? Really?"

"What are you talking about, Holly? Bella's nice. And hot."

"It's pathetic. Grace only invited her because Annabel doesn't have friends of her own. That's why she's always tagging along after Ace. So sad."

My eyes burn as I clutch the phone to my chest. Is that true? Am I pathetic? Even if Grace is being genuine, do I even belong here?

No. No, I don't.

I run up the stairs and out through the front door, only stopping when I reach the sidewalk, lungs heaving. Looking up at the stars above, I ground myself in their constancy as a single tear breaks free.

"Bella, what happened?" I didn't hear him approach. It only proves how jumbled my mind is right now.

"Daddy can't find Rhett's toy and he's crying. I gotta head home. Here." I turn, shoving the phone into Davy's large hand, keeping my head down so my hair hides my face.

"I'll drive you back, it's late." He takes half a step forward. If he comes any closer, he'll know I'm lying. He won't let it go until I tell him everything, and it'll be a huge scene with Holly.

Now, that would be pathetic.

"No," I yell as I step back. "It's barely three blocks. Go back to your friends."

"They're your friends too." I loudly say nothing. He breathes out in a huff. "Just promise you'll text when you get home, so I know you made it."

"Yea, I promise."

He taps my canvas-covered toe with his. "Pinky promise?"

My lips quirk into a smile, despite my best efforts. "Yea, pinky promise. Tell Grace I'm sorry and I'll return the dress after I wash it."

I jog to my house without looking back. The only light on is Momma and Daddy's room, so I take a chance and sneak around back to the kitchen door. I grab my forgotten phone off the charger and tiptoe back out and to the clubhouse. The screen flashes with two text messages.

Davy:

> Did you make it?

Grace:

> Bummer you had to go :(keep the dress, it looks better on you. Shopping on Sunday? Only us?

I shoot off a quick message to Davy first. If I don't, he'll just show up and ruin everything. The old air mattress squeaks under my weight. I lean back, the rough walls biting into my bare shoulders.

Do I want to go shopping with Grace? I think I do.

It was nice having her help me with the dress, and I liked the way I feel in it. Momma's been too tired to do things like shopping for a while now. Usually it's me and Atty running to the store and making sure the boys have clothes for school. I run my tongue over the teeth as I consider my options.

Just the two of us sounds wonderful.

I send her a text saying just that, then lay my head back and close my eyes as the tears fall. From now on, I'll stay in my own little bubble. Time with Atty and Davy is fine at home, but no more Baby Bennet tagging along. Monday, I'll sign up for the track team and hopefully make some friends.

Worst case, I'll have a new lunch table to escape Holly and Mae.

CHAPTER EIGHTEEN

Making Music

The cold water does nothing to cool my temper. I snap a towel off the rack and bury my face in the soft material. Fighting the urge to scream.

She'd touched him. Like she had a right to.

Then I remember, she does have a right to. More than me, anyway. She'd once been his—publicly—unlike me. Nope, I'd just been the extra Bennet. The one that had to tag along with Atty.

So here I am. In the tiny powder room of this giant rental, having a mini meltdown over ancient history. I dry off and sneak back, happy to find the coast clear. All the food is away except for the sausage balls and fruit skewers.

Well, there goes my excuse to hide in the kitchen.

Looking around at all the groups of folks, I'm not sure where to go. The main room of the cabin is a wide open space dominated by a gigantic stone fireplace. Worn leather couches form a U on an equally worn rug. A monstrous plank dining table lines one side of the room. It could easily sit twenty on its long benches. Behind it, a staircase leads to presumably more bedrooms upstairs.

Huck splays on a couch, relaxed and confident with a beer between his fingers. He's added to his tattoo collection since the last time I saw him. Mae and Tinsley sit with him talking. Tinsley now wears her hair shorter. It suits her. The dark pixie cut highlights her bright blue eyes and pale skin like a fairy-tale princess.

A shrill laugh pulls my attention to Mae. She, on the other hand, hasn't changed a bit. As she leans over to put her hand on Huck's arm, I'm afraid her generous breasts will pop out of the low-cut tank she's wearing. Grimacing, I turn away. It's so weird to witness girls I went to school with drool over my little brother.

No sign of Tom or Grace's cousin Hope. She's about Rhett's age, so maybe she skipped the party as well. That's too bad. I probably could have stuck to her all weekend. No memories there.

Grace and Atty sit at the long table. Despite my discomfort being here, I can't help smiling as I watch them. Her petite frame fits snugly under his long arm. They truly are perfect together. I don't think they realize they do it, but if they're in the same room, you can bet they're wrapped up in each other. It could be the years of long distance, but I hope they never lose it.

Davy sits next to Atty at the head of the table in a heavy conversation. Seeing his dark head tipped towards my brother's fair one makes my smile spread further. Happier childhood memories spring to mind, all of us sitting around the kitchen counter doing homework after school while Momma made dinner.

Then there's Holly. Although she's talking with Grace as they both lean over a magazine, she's as close to Davy as possible. Who the hell wears a crop top and mini shorts in the woods? Hasn't she heard of ticks? Rocky Mountain spotted fever is no joke!

She stands up slightly to better see the picture, practically draping her breasts on Davy's arm. Sweet Jesus, I can see her butt cheeks. Stomach twisting, I turn away and busy myself getting the sausage balls in the hot oven.

"Hey Bella Bug! What are you making? I'm hungry," Atty yells from the table.

I raise my hand and wave at him without turning around. Don't need another view of Holly's desperation. "Yea, yea. You always are. I'll throw together some small plates."

This is good. Cooking, I can do, saves me from having to be social. Surprisingly well stocked for a rental, the kitchen boasts a double wall oven, eight-burner gas range, microwave, and coffeemaker. I can work with this. It takes up a quarter of the main area, with a long peninsula counter to define the space. Raiding the fridge, I gather my ingredients and get to chopping, mixing, and preparing.

"Hey y'all, fire's going out back." Tom bursts through the French doors by the kitchen, just as I'm adding garlic to a pan. I startle, using a little too much force and splatter hot oil on my wrist with a hiss and clang of a utensil hitting the floor.

A loud clatter reaches my ears a minute before warm hands grasp my arm and pull me to the sink. Glancing up from the running water, I find Davy's brows drawn together into a sharp V. His large, tan hands cradle my red wrist like it's about to break.

"Davy, I'm fine. More startled than hurt."

His eyes burn with concern and something a little wild as he looks into mine. Not sure why he's so concerned over a little oil splatter. Is this connected to the darkness? Watching him lock up on the road had been frightening.

Atty walks up behind Davy and claps a friendly hand on his shoulder. David's hands turn to steel and I see his entire body tense up at the contact. How do I help him?

"Yea man," Atty says, oblivious to the tension, "she's had way worse. Good thing you missed the time she nearly cut her fingertip off."

"Or the candy apple incident," Tom shudders as he steals a slice off my abandoned cutting board. "That blister was nas-tay."

My tongue runs across my teeth as I hold Davy's gaze. Touch seemed to ground him in the car. I lay my uninjured hand on his. "Everything's ok, Davy."

Slowly, the clouds clear from his eyes. He releases a shuddering breath and nods his head slightly.

"Come on, let's move this party outside!" Atty lets out a woop then grabs Grace around the waist on his way to the doors. They all head out, but Davy stays still.

"Aren't you coming, David?" Holly calls from the door.

"Go on," Tom pushes off the counter to stand on my other side, "I'll stay and help Bella." I smile at Davy and he slowly looses his fingers, taking a slow step back. "Take the balls with you, man." Tom holds the tray of sausage balls out.

Davy takes the tray. His lips quirk slightly as he grabs one off the plate and pops it in his mouth before heading out the door with one last look back at me. What horrors he must have seen.

"Ok, Chef. What'cha need?"

I glance at the now burnt oil smoking on the stove. "Well, we gotta restart the shrimp. Can you rinse out that pan while I chop more garlic?" Tom rolls up his sleeves, then the pop of water hitting a hot pan reaches my ears. "So, you dating anyone?"

Laughing, Tom tosses a towel at me after drying the pan. "Heck no. You know Huck stole all the social genes in the womb." I chuckle because it's true. "I got all the brains, though." We share a smile.

I point to the oil for him to add it to the pan and toss some shrimp in shredded coconut. "You happy?"

"Yea. I work way too much, but I love what I do. Business strategy is like a giant game of chess, and you know how I excel at games. Huck drags me out once a week so I don't turn into a mushroom in the apartment. Plus, I've been spending more time with Rhett, helping him get ready for college." Tom is watching the oil shimmer in the pan as he slowly tilts it to coat evenly. Huh, guess he's learned a couple of things.

"He doing ok?"

A grin spreads across his face as he looks at me over his shoulder. "That kid has a crazy head for numbers. He's a pain in the ass, though, that's for sure. It's gotta be karma for me and Huck raising hell. Don't know how you kept the three of us in line without killing us."

"Come on now, you make it sound like I raised you." I laugh dryly.

Tom's eyes are piercing as he stares me down. I fidget under his sharp gaze, and am surprised when he changes the subject suddenly. "So how're things at Pop?"

"Good. Really good, actually. The restaurant is always busy these days."

"But?" Tom leans his hip against the counter and crosses his arms as he continues studying me.

I sigh as I concentrate on scraping the fresh garlic into the hot pan. "We're about as far as we can go. I want to expand, add an event space, maybe do some weddings."

"What's stopping you?"

"Money. Don't get me wrong, we're in the black every month, but can't save up enough profits to reinvest in a project that big yet."

"Why don't you put more capital into the business?"

Stalling for time, I carefully toss the shrimp into the pan and wait for them to brown. "I couldn't ask Bree and Nic to invest more. They already did so much to help me the first time."

He hands me a pair of tongs, then lines a plate with paper napkins for me. "Yeah, but they have other jobs besides Pop, right?" I nod. "You could bring in a fourth partner. Why not put in more of your money and be the majority owner? It's your dream after all, why shouldn't it be mostly yours?."

Huh. Never thought of it that way. I carefully flip the shrimp. "Where would I get the money, though?"

"You could take out a business loan."

That I had actually thought of before. "I don't have any collateral—I literally live at the restaurant and still drive the same beater from college." Fully cooked, I transfer the shrimp to the waiting plate and shut off the burner.

"How much do you have in savings? Let me invest some for you and I'll get you what you need."

"You can do that?"

He uncrosses his arms and lays a gentle palm on my shoulder. "Yea. I've been trading for years. You've always been there for us, Bells. Let me do this for you."

"Wow, thanks, Tom." I slip my arms around his waist for a quick hug.

His arms close around me tight, and he drops a kiss to my crown. "I follow the Pop account online. It's impressive what you've done. I'm damn proud of you, sis." After one last squeeze, he steps back. "I'll bring these two trays out. You coming?"

"Be there in a sec. Let me just dress it up a bit." I wave him off as I sniff back sudden tears. When I'm far away, it's easy to forget how much

I miss my brothers. Tom has blossomed into a great man. I need to be better about calling him more. Once my emotions are under control and the shrimp is magazine ready, I head outside.

Everyone is sitting out by a large, circular fire pit with built-in benches. I hand the plate to Atty as I pass by, who happily grabs some food before passing it along. My eyes sweep the circle, looking for a place to go. I freeze as they land on David positioned between Tom and Holly.

She's leaning towards him and talking animatedly, but he's staring at me. He tilts his chin and scoots closer to Tom, leaving barely enough space for me.

I shouldn't.

Would I actually rather sit next to Holly all night than watch her flirt with Davy?

God help me, but I really think I would.

Decision made, I cross the circle and squeeze into the gap before Holly thinks to fill it. My thigh is digging into Davy's, but neither of us move. "Hey, Holly. How have you been?"

Holly's smile is so brittle it might shatter. "Annabel, hi. I was actually catching up with David. So if you don't mind moving, darlin'."

David's voice vibrates through my chest. Dangit, I'm basically sitting in his lap. "Sorry, Holly. I need to talk shop with Tom. You understand." David turns his back completely as he draws Tom into a discussion about cyber security.

"So, what are you up to these days?" Blast you, David, for leaving me with the psychotic cheerleader of my nightmares.

"Real estate." Holly flicks her brown hair over her shoulder. "Number one agent in the county three years in a row."

"That's great, Holly. Congrats." I can see her being good at that. She always was good with people. Well, *other* people. And she can spin almost anything.

"And you're, what? A cook now or something?"

I open my mouth to agree when David cuts me off. "Actually, Bells owns her own restaurant. Best in the city, four years running."

As Holly's features pinch in anger, I picture my hands choking the daylights out of David Hawthorne. "Well, bless your heart. Excuse me, darlin', my drink needs refreshing." Without waiting for a reply, Holly stomps off towards the coolers to grab another hard seltzer. Instead of returning to us, I see her squeeze in on the other side of the circle next to Tinsley.

I scoot over into the vacant spot so I'm not sitting on top of him anymore. "Gee, thanks."

David leans in, his breath fans on my cheek. "What'd I do now?"

"Like Holly didn't already hate me enough. You had to throw gasoline on that particular fire."

His eyes drop to my mouth and back up to my eyes. "I didn't like her calling you just a cook."

I roll my eyes. "But I am a cook."

"No, Bells." He tucks a strand of hair behind my ear. "You're so much more." My lips part on a gasp and my eyes wander to his full lips.

"Listen up, everybody." Atty's loud voice startles me and I jump away from David as he chuckles lightly beside me. "Grace and I want to thank y'all for being here. Both this weekend and the fifteen years that led us here. All y'all are our family, and we love you. So let's pretend we're not responsible adults, get drunk, and have a party!"

Everyone cheers. Groups form and break up as people mingle. I stay in my spot, content to watch.

Huck approaches with two plastic cups, his guitar strapped to his back. He hands me both before unslinging the instrument and plopping down next to me, reclaiming his drink. "Big bro said to get drunk, Sissy. Bottoms up." We tap cups and I chuckle. "How are you doing in the big city?"

"Good. You should come visit—maybe get some sun." I bump his shoulder and point to his pale skin.

"Yea, maybe." We sip our drinks in silence for a beat before he continues. "It's good to see you here. We all miss you." I open my mouth to reply, but he cuts me off with his hand on my knee. "Don't get me wrong. I totally get why you left." His eyes shadow and his jaw clenches. "Too many damn memories in that house."

I blink back tears as I wrap my arm around my younger brother. "I'm sorry my leaving made it harder for you."

He squeezes me back, and I'm shocked at how strong he's gotten. "You needed a fresh start, but I still missed you."

"I missed you too."

Huck takes a big sniff and blinks quickly. "Enough with the heavy shit. How about some music?" He settles his guitar on his knee and starts expertly strumming out some of the classic rock and country tunes we grew up listening to.

Tom comes over and sits on Huck's other side. They sing together when he gets to "The Devil Went Down to Georgia." A rare treat to hear them in harmony like that.

Thick fabric lands across my shoulders. I look up to see David as he sits back next to me. He tucks the blanket around me and settles his arm along the back of the bench behind me. I sneak a look over at Atty to see if he's watching, but he's too busy whispering to Grace as she sits in his lap across the way to notice. It doesn't have to mean anything, it's nice for things to feel like they used to. Before everything changed. Deciding to give in to the moment, I settle back into David's warm chest and enjoy the music with my family.

CHAPTER NINETEEN

Bow & Tie

"**S**niper! Two-hundred feet ahead. Get him!" I turn and target, but the gunner gets me first. "Dude, I hope you're better at the real thing." Huck throws a pillow at me as the video game resets.

I recently graduated from basic training and am enjoying ten days of leave at home before shipping out for my specialized coursework. Mom is working a double to make up for the time she missed flying out for graduation, so I'm hanging out at the Bennets' today, catching up.

"Whatever, man. I'm going to go get a drink." I head towards the kitchen, calling back. "You want anything?" He waves me off, already concentrating on finding his next target.

The smell of toasted pecans and caramel draws me in. I walk up behind her as she pulls a tray out of the oven. "Hell's Bells, what smells so good in here?" I snake an arm around her waist and tickle her side, then grunt as her elbow drives into my stomach. I dance away as I steal a praline cookie off the cooling rack. "Gotta be faster than that, Bells. I'm a stealthy Marine now." When the tickles and teasing get no reaction, I study her more closely.

The apron over her pajama pants and t-shirt sports splatters of flour. A quick survey reveals baked goods covering every surface of the kitchen. Cookies. Brownies. Breads. Is that a whole roasted chicken? "Uh, Bells, what's with the stress baking?"

"Prom."

I jerk at the sound of Grace's voice. She's leaning against the archway to the living room, expression unreadable but eyes assessing. I gulp.

"Prom? What about it?" My eyes dart back and forth from Bella to Grace, unsure who will answer.

Grace pushes off the wall, her red ponytail swaying, and heads towards a basket of muffins. She lifts one, unwraps it, and takes a bite while giving me an annoyed look. "Bella's date backed out, so she refuses to go."

My stomach twists and the skin on my neck itches. "What date? I'll kick his ass."

"Just some guy at school. He got back together with his girlfriend." Bella doesn't even look up from her next batch of cookies.

"Well, when is it? I'm sure you can figure something out." I lay my hand on her shoulder, trying to draw her attention.

She ignores me and keeps mixing. "Tonight." My eyes widen as I turn to Grace for help.

Her blue eyes sparkle. "I told Bella she should still go. She already has the tickets and the perfect dress. You only get one senior prom."

"I'd feel dumb going alone." Bella's shoulder rises under my hand and she ducks her head.

Seeing her like this reminds me of the darkness of her grief, and how we almost lost her. "I'll go."

"You will?" The girls shout in unison.

I'd do anything for Bella, even wear a monkey suit. "Why not? Grace, get her ready. I gotta see a man about a tux. What time does it start?"

A Cheshire Cat smile spreads across Grace's face. "Seven."

Bella is staring at me in shock, so I rub her arms and push her gently towards Grace and check my watch. She's still watching me over her shoulder as Grace herds her up the back stairs.

I grab my keys and rush to the next town, my tires squealing as I swerve into a spot. The truck door barely shuts as I skid to a halt in front of Bow and Tie—the only formal shop within fifty miles of Hitchcock. The owner, Mr. Kazazntzakis, is flipping the sign to "Closed" as I knock on the door.

"Young man, we are closed." He points to the sign he's just turned on the door.

I lay my palm flat on the glass. "Please! It's a matter of life and death!"

His bushy eyebrows lower over his eyes in a stern look. "Seriously, son?"

"Uh, well... Look, I'm trying to help a grieving girl get to prom. So close enough, right? Her life, her mom's death?" His expression softens and I'm filled with hope. "Please, sir. She's already lost so much, I can't let her lose this, too." I grip the handle, willing him to unlock the door and let me in.

"Oh, all right." He holds the door for me as I slip in. "This would be for the Bennet girl, I'm assuming."

"Yes, sir."

"My Martha helped her pick out a dress with that Allen girl. Would be a shame to waste it." He ushers me to the men's side and prods me onto a small platform. The man is a wizard at his craft and I'm measured and pushed into a changing room with a black garment bag in under five minutes.

I admire myself in the mirror. This tux fits better than the one I rented last year! As I approach the counter to pay, a flash of gold by the register catches my eye. Delicate petals of hammered gold surround a simple rhinestone and pearl center. Gold leaves shimmer in the light as I pick up the hairpin. It'll look beautiful in Bella's blond hair. "This too, please. Can't forget flowers."

I smile at the man and fish my wallet out of my crumpled jeans. Mr. Kazazntzakis waves me off and hands me a pair of dress shoes.

"Those Bennet kids deserve a break. Just get the tux back first thing tomorrow. I need to press it for the Sullivan wedding." He winks at me and pushes me out the door, my clothes thrown in the garment bag and shoes dangling from my fingers. Checking my watch again, we only have about an hour.

Butterflies dance in my stomach as I pull my old truck into the driveway. I walk up the same cracked steps I've run up a thousand times . For probably the first time in a decade, I ring the Bennets' doorbell instead of walking in. I want to get it right. Bella deserves a happy memory and I refuse to half-ass this thing just because I'm a fill-in.

Mr. Bennet answers the door and smiles at me. "She's almost ready, son." His warm hand lands on my shoulder. I hadn't noticed before, but I now have a few inches over Mr. Bennet. "Thanks for doing this. I didn't want her to miss it."

I turn to tell him it's not a big deal, but all words disappear. There, at the top of the stairs, stands the most beautiful woman I've ever seen. She's pulled her blond hair into a bun at the back of her head. Loose curls flutter by her cheeks as she descends. Gold fabric shines along her torso and hips, flaring out behind her. A flash of tanned thigh peaks out with every step of her gold strappy heels.

She's an angel.

Her entire attention is on each tread, so I am left to look my fill. Bronze shimmers at her eyes and cheekbones. Her dark brown eyes look bottomless, with their bold black eyeliner and lashes. White teeth dig into reddish-brown lips.

Bella looks up at me and I'm a goner. She smiles hesitantly and shrugs her shoulders. After a decade growing up together, I can read this girl—no, woman—like an open book. She's nervous and a little uncomfortable. My face hurts and I realize I've broken into a giant grin.

She's still my same Bella, just shined up a bit.

"Hell's Bells, you look beautiful." I step forward and raise my hand to help her down the last few steps. As she stands next to me, I can make out a slight flush to her cheeks. "I got you something." Pulling the hair clip out of my suit coat, I hold it up for her to see.

Bella smiles sweetly. "Magnolia. I love it."

"May I?" She nods and turns her head to give me better access. As I lean in, her fresh magnolia smell hits me and my heart beats faster. My fingers graze the side of her throat as I secure the pin behind her ear. I can feel her pulse matching mine. Our eyes meet over her shoulder and I feel myself tip closer, caught in the moment.

A throat clears, bringing me back to reality. Mr. Bennet is still smiling by the door, his eyes bright with emotion. Upstairs, Grace stares at me with a raised eyebrow. "Boys," she calls, "Bella's leaving if you want to see her."

Clumping footsteps bounce down the hall as Mr. Bennet goes to get a camera. Four boys stomp down the stairs with varying degrees of enthusiasm.

"Wow, Bella, you look like a real princess!" At seven, Rhett is big into heroic knights, pretty princesses, and dangerous dragons. Bella stoops to give him a kiss on the cheek, then wipes off the smudge with her thumb.

The twins are more reserved. "You clean up good, sis." Tom gives her a high five as he passes Bella to stand behind Rhett. "Yea, watch out for hands!" Huck jumps over the railing to escape a slap to the back of the head from Atticus.

Ace is silent as he approaches Bella. His eyes glimmer and he purses his lips to fight some emotion. He pulls her into his arms for a bear hug and whispers into her ear. She nods and squeezes him back.

"Atticus Finch Bennet! I swear, if you ruined her makeup." Grace rushes down the stairs for a last inspection and a sisterly smile.

Mr. Bennet snaps a few pictures, then engulfs us both in a squeeze. Pulling back, he cups Bella's jaw in one hand and looks into her eyes for a moment. "I love you, baby girl. Have fun. Be safe."

The whole Bennet bunch follows us onto the front porch. But I only have eyes for Bella as we walk away. My body hums. Electricity shoots across my skin everywhere we touch. It's not the first time I've felt this way around her. But it's the first time I'm not fighting it. And the first time I think she might feel it too.

CHAPTER TWENTY

Pockets

The sounds of screams and explosions still echo in my head as I jerk up in bed. It takes me a few pounding heartbeats to remember where I am. As my breathing slows, I look around the mostly dark room. Can't be much later than 0600.

Might as well go for a run. After that episode in the car, I've been feeling extra jumpy. No way I'm getting more sleep.

I slip through the silent house—everyone else is still asleep after a night of drinking. As my sneakers fly over the country roads, my mind wanders to a certain blond with chocolate eyes.

Things have been going so well in Friendship Springs. I thought I was making actual progress. Do I like that it took some traumatic, violent shit for Bella to let her walls down? Hell no. Am I proud to admit that some fucked-up part of me is grateful for the growing closeness regardless of how it happened? Also, hell no.

Then Holly had to go and open her big mouth. I don't know why I ever dated her. Ok, not exactly true. I was fifteen, and she was friends with my friend's girlfriend. It wasn't rocket science.

Look, when your graduating class has less than fifty people in it, you don't have a lot of options.

Maybe not all hope is lost. Bella did lean against me out at the firepit. It honestly felt perfect. Sitting out with the Bennet brothers, Bella snuggled up to my side. Good music. It was the best parts of my childhood all rolled up into one night. I'll do just about anything for more nights like that. If only I can stay the hell away from Holly.

As I slow to a jog in the cabin's driveway, the sun is fully up, but the house is quiet. I'm still too worked up to go in, so I walk around to the back porch to cool off. I'm shocked to see Grace sitting in a rocker with a blanket and steaming mug of coffee. As I slowly climb the stairs, she tosses me a bottle of water and nods to the rocker next to hers.

"Don't worry, no one else is up yet. Looks like everyone took Atticus's speech about being irresponsible a little too far. We won't be seeing them until at least noon."

I chuckle as I settle into the chair and happily chug half the bottle of water.

"So..." Grace eyes me over her mug, "how goes Operation Get the Girl? The real answer. With details, please."

Staring at the lake, I sigh and think of how to respond. "She wouldn't even talk to me at first. And I told you I thought she was with that Colin guy. She tried to poison me for a week, then some shit went down..."

Grace holds a hand up and shakes it at me until I stop talking. "Hold up. I said details. Poison?"

I chuckle at the reminder. "I went into Pop for lunch every day for a week asking for the 'chef's special sandwich,' because..."

"Yea, your weird obsession with her grilled cheese, I remember. Focus, David, what about poison?"

"She kept making the most disgusting sandwiches I've ever had. The first one had pickles and salt and vinegar chips, Gracie. The last one was ghost pepper jam on a grilled cheese."

Grace winces and laughs awkwardly. "Damn. Well, our girl is creative. And vindictive apparently. So you just kept showing up and asking for more torture?" I shrug. "That is kind of romantic, in a hella crazy way. So what shit went down?"

Stalling, I take another swig of water, unsure how much to share. Bella has always been strong enough to stand on her own. Hell, she spent a lot of her childhood caring for her brothers. Now that they're fully grown, though, they see her differently. Ace especially can get overbearing with her. If she doesn't want them to know what happened, I can sort of see why.

"Not my place to tell. Leave it at this—I helped her out with some equipment. When I got back, she made me a special grilled cheese." I smile at the memory. It sounds stupid, but that damn sandwich means more than just bread, cheese, and a mystery ingredient. It's us. Our story.

"You and that damn grilled cheese. Are you ever going to tell me what's so special about it?" She gasps and leans forward in her chair, coffee momentarily forgotten. "Is it a euphemism? Eww! Is grilled cheese code for a sexual act?"

Chuckling, I shake my head. "No. It's a literal sandwich she made me when I was nine. We've been in a good place for a couple of weeks now. She runs with me most mornings and we hang out when she's not working or with her girlfriends. Oh God, *please* let her make the wedding cake. The practice cupcakes were the best damn thing I've ever had."

With a bemused smile, Grace sits back and sips her mug. "You, sir, are positively smitten."

"You've known this for almost fifteen years, Gracie."

She scoffs and waves me off. "Yea, but I haven't gotten to see it in action for at least ten. This is fun to watch."

"Yea, if Holly doesn't burn it to hell first." I chug the rest of my water.

She grimaces. "Well, she's going to be too hungover to do much damage today. She's been a real peach lately."

I wipe the sweat from my face with my shirt, grateful to change the topic. "How are things with you? The wedding?"

Grace smiles, the very picture of a blushing bride. "I'm so happy to have Ace home. He's been busy settling in at the practice, but I'm so damn proud of him. He's going to help so many people in Hitchcock, David. It's the healing he needs."

The back door opens and Bella steps out in leggings and a loose sweater that hangs off her shoulder. Two mugs of coffee in her hands. I stand to give her my rocker as she passes me a mug. She tucks her purple painted toes under her, and I lean my hip against the railing opposite the girls.

Grace—damn her—watches the scene with mischief sparkling in her eyes. "So, Bella. I forgot to mention it yesterday, but would you mind heading into town with David today? Y'all need to get a fitting in while you're here."

Bells looks between the two of us for a minute, her brows pinched in confusion. "Are you sure? This weekend is about you. I'll just stop by before we head back home."

"But with the holiday, he won't be open. It's really got to be today. Plus, everyone got so drunk last night you won't miss anything. We'll have plenty of fun tonight. Huck got us into some fancy club."

Bella's eyes dart back to me, like she is begging me to say something. I dare not contradict Grace. The woman is on a mission and who am I to interrupt? I widen my eyes and shrug, hoping it looks innocent.

Then Grace goes for the kill shot. "When you get back, Bella, I'd love your opinion on wedding cakes."

An hour later we're pulling into Bow and Tie and it hasn't changed a bit in the past decade. I open the front door for Bells and rest my hand on the small of her back as we approach the counter. A young girl, maybe seventeen or eighteen, is sitting, scrolling on her phone and blowing a bubble. As the bell over the door chimes, she looks up at us and slaps on a professional smile.

"Welcome to Bow and Tie. How can I help y'all?"

Bella steps closer. "Hey there. We're in the Bennet Allen wedding. The bride was hoping we could get a fitting in while we're in town."

"Both of you?" The girl glances between us as I follow Bells to put my hand on her waist again with a nod. "Ok, I'll take you, miss, to the ladies' section. Sir, if you could step over to the men's area, someone will be right with you." She turns to the curtain behind the counter and yells louder, "Grandpa, customers."

I watch the two girls move over to the dresses, heads already together chatting, as I walk to my designated spot.

"Well, if it isn't the prom Romeo himself. Need another suit to sweep the girl off her feet?" Mr. Kazazntzakis appears in the mirror beside me with a measuring tape around his shoulders. He's a little more slumped, and a lot grayer, but the same intelligent gleam sparkles in his eyes.

I jerk my eyes to the other side of the room, where Bells and the shopgirl stand, but it doesn't look like they heard.

"Ah, so you're still trying to get the girl after all these years?" He tsks as he positions me and uses his tape measure across my back. "Maybe if you spent less time at the gym, you'd have more luck."

"I had the girl, I just fucked up." He slaps the back of my head with his notebook. I duck and rub my aching skull. "What was that for?"

"For letting her go. Why would you do a stupid thing like that, boy?"

"I thought I was holding her back. She needed to chase her dreams instead of waiting for a broken Marine to come home."

"Well, there's your problem. You can't go thinking for a woman. You need to talk to them. Give them the facts. Then wait for them to tell you what to do. That's how I kept my Martha for almost fifty years, God rest her soul."

My stomach sinks. "Oh, Mr. Kazazntzaki, I'm so sorry for your loss."

He pats my shoulder before taking another measurement. "Thank you, son. She beat cancer once, but it got her the second time. She's at peace now, and I believe I'll see her again. Until then, my granddaughter is helping me mind the shop." He nods towards the girls.

"Fuck cancer."

"Well, I could do without the cursing, but I agree with the sentiment." He rolls up his tape as his eyes turn glassy. "Ok, I think the suit I pulled for you should work. Go try it on and I'll double check."

When I return, Bells is nowhere in sight. She's probably changing, too. Feeling a little like James Bond, I tug my sleeves down and look at my reflection in the tri-fold mirror. Mr. Kazazntzaki joins me a minute later and starts tugging and assessing the fit.

"What do you think?" I turn at Bella's quiet voice, and my breath rushes out. I'm staring, I know it, but I can't help it. This whole thing is reminding me of prom. From the vulnerability in her eyes, I think Bella's feeling it too.

Grace is one genius meddler.

The dress is some cloudy concoction—looks sheer at a glance. Purple at the straps and deep V of the bodice, then fades to a pale pink in flowy material around her feet. She's a vision. My dick twitches and I pray I can hide this growing semi.

"Oh my, might have to go up a size in the pants," Mr. Kazazntzaki mutters as he tugs at the pant leg to get it to lay straight.

Shoot me now. "Hell's Bells, you look amazing. What do *you* think?"

"Nice recovery, son." Really could use less from the peanut gallery tailor.

Bella gives a little twirl. "I like it. And look!" She puts her hands on her hips and they disappear into the fabric. "It has pockets!" I chuckle at her enthusiasm. "Ok, I'm going to change. Want to grab stuff to make lunch before heading back? If they're as hungover as Grace thinks, we might not have enough food."

I seriously doubt that, since we brought two giant coolers, but I'll keep that to myself. "Sure, Bells. Sounds good."

She scans my clothes one more time, her eyes heating slightly before she blushes. "You look good in that suit, Davy." With one more small smile, she heads back to the dressing room. My heart clenches and I rub my chest absently as I watch her walk away.

"Well," says Mr. Kazazntzaki, "there may be hope for you yet, son."

CHAPTER TWENTY-ONE

Hell Hath no Fury

ANNABEL - NOW

The bass pumps so loudly it feels like a second heartbeat. The crush of bodies creates a haze for the flashing lights. I smooth the shiny material of my black minidress across my thighs for the hundredth time.

This is so not my thing.

It's for Atty and Grace. That's what I keep reminding myself, anyway.

Huck managed to reserve the VIP section for the night. It's nice in here. The roped-off area is less crowded than the main floor. Groupings of leather couches and chairs give a prime view of the rest of the club while allowing for socializing. Servers in skimpy outfits circulate, dropping off trays of shots on the low coffee tables.

On the dance floor below, Atty and Grace move with the crush of bodies. Completely oblivious to everyone else as they sway together to the music with matching goofy grins. My chest aches. I'm so happy for them, but jealous too.

I feel him approach before his warm hand lands on my shoulder. "Here you go." I look up from the leather armchair I've claimed for the night to see Davy's hazel eyes staring down at me. He looks so good in a navy button-down shirt, sleeves rolled up to expose muscular forearms. It's so not fair when I'm trying to keep things friendly.

David holds a martini glass in his other hand, which he expertly lowers to me. Curious, I take a sip. Hints of apple and cinnamon whiskey dance on my tongue. It's delicious. I smile up at him. "Thanks. Tastes good."

"I see some things never change," Holly scoffs from the chair opposite. No idea how I found myself with the bridesmaids instead of my brothers. An image of Huck and Tom dancing with random girls—and I use the term "dancing" loosely—comes to mind. Yup, that's right. That's how I ended up sitting with my nemesis.

Davy's smile dims, but he doesn't look up from me. "Holly. Ladies. Don't go getting in trouble, now." With one last squeeze of my shoulder and a wink, he strides across to the other seating area where the groomsmen have gathered. His jeans cling to his muscular legs as he moves. I sip my drink as I watch.

"I still can't believe Grace met the love of her life at fifteen. That would be like me marrying..." Tinsley's nose wrinkles adorably as she thinks, "Bobby Mitchell!" She laughs. "What about you, Bella? Who was your high school boyfriend? I can't remember."

Tinsley's expression is open and friendly, but Holly might as well have lasers shooting out of her eyes. She grabs a shot off the table and downs it as she glares at me.

"Actually, I didn't date in high school." I fidget in my seat as Holly gives a sarcastic bark of laughter and takes another shot. "Atty warned away any guy that looked at me twice."

Holly snorts and throws back a third shot as Tinsley frowns at her. "I can't sit through this." Pushing up to her ice pick heels, Holly stumbles off towards the bar for another drink.

It's like being right back in high school. Why can't we all be adults? I blink back tears as I stare into the amber liquid. "I shouldn't have come," I whisper.

Tinsley leans forward and pats her hand on my knee. "It's not you." I level her with a weighted glance, and she winces slightly. "Not really. Holly's just... Holly. She's jealous, but she's not actually still stuck on David. I think seeing you together reopened old wounds that never fully healed. Doesn't help that she recently went through a nasty divorce."

My stomach flips. "Why would she be jealous? She's the one he dated, not me."

Tinsley's eyes narrow. Her brows pinch as she studies my face. "You really don't know, do you?"

The apple martini sinks like a dead weight in my gut. "Don't know what?"

She hesitates, like she's debating how to say something. "It wasn't Ace that warned the guys away. It was David." Tinsley looks around before leaning closer to me. "He was with Holly when you called from Becket's party. She told him if he left, they were done. He didn't even hesitate."

Well, that explains why Holly's never liked me. My hands shake as I lower the glass to the coffee table. I feel lost. First the scrapbook, now this. Did I ever know David at all? I look into Tinsley's kind eyes as every childhood memory replays in my mind. Details I never thought much of before now hold new meaning. "I didn't know, Tinsley, I swear."

Her lips curve into a comforting smile. "That's what I always figured. Don't get me wrong—I get why Holly was jealous. There's always been this connection between you two, but it wasn't sexual." She takes a sip from her Cosmo. Her lips twitch as she glances over at David, sitting with Tom and a few of his high school friends. "Well, until now." Tinsley stands and gives my shoulder one more squeeze. "I'm going to go make sure Holly doesn't end up puking."

Mae runs up breathless, cheeks flushed and eyes bright. "Come on, Annabel, let's dance!"

Why the heck not? I could use the distraction and to burn off some nervous energy. I toss back the rest of my martini and let Mae pull me onto the floor. Grace sees us and smiles over Atty's shoulder with a little wave, then goes right back to their love bubble.

The beat pulses through my body, pushing away lingering thoughts of Tinsley's confession, and I quickly lose myself to the music. Mae and I laugh as we dance to song after song before she heads back for another drink. A glance over at our VIP area and I find warm hazel eyes watching me. My awkward smile and wave has a slow grin spreading on David's face. As the beat slows and another song starts, he stands and prowls towards me.

My heart races. I wipe my sweaty palms on my dress as I watch him eat up the space between us. A heavy arm circles my waist as hot breath fans my cheek and I stiffen. My heart pounds for a completely different reason as memories surface. Other parties where boys touched too much. The attack in my kitchen. My face grows cold and my pulse pounding in my temples replaces the speakers.

David is still walking towards me. I can see him, the confusion on his face transforming into fury. If I stand still, he'll save me like he always does. That thought is enough to spark a fire in me. My fear transforms into rage.

Tonight, there are no damsels here.

I grab the wrist at my waist, digging my nails in as I pry the offending hand away. Turning with the arm I'm twisting, I push the guy's chest with all my might. Of course, he barely moves, but at least he's not touching me. My lip twists as I glare up at the man in front of me. He's average height, but broad-chested. If it wasn't for the sneer on his face, he might be handsome.

Hands grip my hips and pull me behind a strong back. I clutch David's shirt as I shift to his side so I can still see the jerk who grabbed me. David has a solid five inches on the guy and has somehow made himself seem even larger as his chest puffs and jaw locks.

"Hey man," the jerk shrugs and crosses his arms, "it's not my fault your girl was asking for it. Don't let her wander off in a skimpy dress if you're not willing to share."

David growls—literally growls—at the guy and leans forward.

I jump in front of him and put my hands on his chest to stop him from getting into a fight. "Davy, come on, it's not worth it. Let's go back to the group."

His torso might as well be marble under my fingers. The muscle in his throat spasms, but he doesn't look away from the idiot behind me.

I cup his bearded cheeks with my hands and force him to look at me. The hard lines of his eyes soften slightly as he looks at me and his hand shifts to my waist, keeping me near. "Come on, Davy. I'm fine. Just forget about him." Slowly, the tension leaves his shoulders. His jaw relaxes. The hand on my hip pulls me closer into him and we turn to rejoin our party.

"Yea, Davy. Run along. I don't see a purse, so did she leave your balls at home?" The jerk gestures to the Marine insignia tattoo on Davy's arm. "Since when are Marines such pussies?"

My ears buzz with a high-pitched tone and my vision tinges red. Davy's eyes widen on my face as I turn and launch myself at the asshole with my nails out. "He's a bigger man than you'll ever be, you micro-dick fuckwad."

Centimeters before my nails make contact, Davy hauls me back to his chest. My heels kick the air as he holds me off the ground. I flail helplessly and my elbow contacts with something soft. "Ow. Hell's Bells, calm down." I ignore Davy's warning and keep swinging until the world tilts and my only view is a very muscular denim clad-butt.

I arch up and glare at the back of his head instead as he carries me out of the club, still yelling. The crisp air helps a bit. He puts me down on the sidewalk and uses his body to shield me as I tug my dress down to an acceptable hem length.

Stewing, I pace in front of Davy while he has the audacity to smile as he pulls out his cell. "What the heck is so funny? And who are you texting?" I stop my path to glare at him with my hands on my hips.

"I'm not sure what's funnier, Bells. You jumping to the rescue in a bar fight. Or the fact you said 'micro-dick fuckwad'." He chuckles as he keeps typing on his phone. Annoyed, I cross my arms and glare more. I'm full-on pouting at this point and I don't care.

Davy looks up at me and laughs harder before pulling me into his chest for a hug and kiss on the top of my head. "You cold?" He rubs his warm hands up my arms and, although I'll never admit it to him, I'm grateful for his warmth.

The front doors swing open and Tom comes out, looking around until he spots us. "What the hell did you do now, Bella?" He holds my purse out on one finger like it might bite him.

I try to step closer to my brother, but Davy keeps me close. "Aren't you such a peach? I defended myself from a handsy SOB. I was doing just fine, but David hauled me out."

Davy's chest rumbles against my shoulder. I swear if that man laughs at me one more time. "She's leaving out the part where she tried to claw his face off after calling him a micro-dick fuckwad. So, I'm taking her back before she finishes the deed."

Tom's eyes widen. "Well shit, Bella never swears."

"Oh, so the swearing is shocking, but the violence isn't?"

The guys share a look over my head and shrug in unison. "Yup." I elbow Davy in the stomach and get the satisfaction of a grunt. "Think you proved our point, Bells. Here." He hands his truck keys to Tom. "You're in charge. Make sure they don't get too drunk, yeah?"

Tom tosses the keyring in his hand and eyes the two of us. "How are you getting back?"

"Got a rideshare coming any second. Didn't want y'all to be down a car."

"Ok, have fun, you two. Don't kill each other before the wedding." With a wink, he turns back to the club doors.

David's firm grip keeps me from going after my kid brother. "I hate you both, for the record!"

"Love you too, sis." Without a backward glance, Tom disappears into the building and a black sedan pulls up by the curb, calling David's name.

The ride back to the cabin is silent. When the car stops, I slam out of the door. I stomp into the rental and straight back to the kitchen. Not even a glass of sweet tea can calm my temper. I whirl to face the door as footsteps echo down the hall. Ready for a fight.

CHAPTER TWENTY-TWO

Welcome to Hitchcock High

DAVID - AGE 15

The crisp fall air nips at my cheeks. Good thing I threw on my football sweatshirt. Scanning the outside picnic tables, I finally spot her. She hugs her knees against her chest with one arm and pushes her meatloaf around the cafeteria tray with her fork. The way she glares at the slop has my lips quirking into a smile. Our Bella's become quite the food snob.

My long legs eat up the school courtyard. This summer, I shot up to six feet. I've also bulked up a bit, likely thanks to Bella's awesome cooking. Coach put me on the starting line this year.

Tugging on her ponytail, I straddle the bench next to her. "Hell's Bells, what's with the long face? Already over high school on your first day?" Bella smiles, but I can tell it's fake. She continues to stab at her plate and shrugs at me. I steal a slimy carrot. "What are you doing out here? You could have sat with me and Ace."

She gives me a little side-eye, no comment on the food theft. "I don't think those girls like me very much."

"Who?" Is someone giving her trouble? My eyebrows furl. "Grace and Holly? Naw, they just don't know you yet." She snorts at that.

I take the fork out of her grip and place it on the hardly-touched plate. My stomach twists. This isn't like her at all. "Come on, Annabel. What's really the matter?"

"Do you think Momma's ok?" She stares at a hole in the knee of her jeans.

Hadn't expected that question. "I haven't noticed anything. What's got you worried?"

"She hasn't been the same since Rhett was born. More tired, I guess? I thought it was just having to take care of a little one at first, but have you seen how skinny she is?" Her brown eyes seek mine, bottomless and wide.

"Can't say I have, Bells." I try to picture Mrs. Bennet. She still smiles when I come over and asks me about what thriller I'm reading, just like always. Sure, her blond hair has gotten lighter, the creases on her face deeper, but all our parents are looking older. "Rhett is a bit of a hellion, Bella. He makes me tired." That kid chases me around the yard until I cry uncle.

Bella nods slightly, clearly unconvinced. "Last night I woke up because someone was throwing up in the bathroom. Thought it might be one of the twins at first. Then I heard Momma and Daddy talking, but couldn't make out what they were saying." Her lip quivers and her eyes glimmer. "I'm scared, Davy."

Turning on the bench so we sit side by side, I pull her in for a brotherly hug. "Whatever happens, Bells, we'll get through it. Together."

Her blond head rests on my shoulder as she sniffles. "Promise?" Her right pinky slowly lifts in my peripheral vision.

I grip her finger with mine, and my voice cracks as I finish our ritual. "Pinky promise."

A lump forms in my throat as I swallow. Bella's always been fearless. Seeing her this worried is freaking me the hell out. I want to tell her everything's going to be ok, but I don't know for sure. And one of our dozens of pinky promises over the years was to never lie.

"Come on, you've murdered the meatloaf enough. I got a granola bar you can eat inside." I grab her tray and she reluctantly follows me back into the cafeteria. Dumping her untouched lunch, we head to the table with Ace and some of the other sophomores.

"David, sit here." Holly smiles up at me as she pats the bench next to her. Ace is into Grace, so I usually have to entertain her best friend. She's not that bad. I take a seat and wink at Bella as she settles across from her brother and Grace.

"What the hell is up with you?" Ace looks up from his flirting to study his sister.

Bella sticks out her tongue at him. "Bite me, Atticus."

I chuckle and toss her the promised granola bar. "She's just hangry." Holly tugs on my sleeve and starts talking about cheer practice and getting ready for the first football game.

"So, Annabel, how's your first day going?" Grace's tone and smile are friendly.

"It's Bella, actually." She ducks her head and unwraps the bar. "It's alright, I guess. Mr. Epstein is a jerk, but Ms. Farris seems ok."

A masculine groan catches my ear. "Oh, Epstein is the worst. I could help you study if you want, I still have my notes from last year."

My head jerks up from Holly. Dereck Serrano's smile is wolfish as he looks down at Bells. The hell? I kick him under the table, only getting a raised eyebrow from him.

"I have my notes, too. I'll give them to Ace for you." Thank god for Grace! Holly's insistent fingers pull my attention back to her. I swear she glares at Bella for a moment, but her expression turns sunny when I look again.

The bell rings, and we get up to leave. Dereck is still standing entirely too close to Bella. I shoot a glance at Ace, trying to get him to warn Dereck off his kid sister. Completely oblivious, Ace is busy drooling over Grace and making plans for after school. Holly rambles on next to me, but I'm only half-listening.

Hours later, I'm still steaming as I run out onto the football field for practice. As we break from huddle, Dereck tries to get my attention.

"Hey, Hawthorne. What's up with that Bella chick?" He jerks his head. Bella is sitting in the stands with Ace, reading a book. "She single?"

My vision turns red. I plow into Dereck and his stupid smiling face, and he lands flat on his back. I glare down at his shocked face through my helmet. "Stay away from Annabel. You hear me?" He nods, eyes wide.

"Hawthorne, what the hell, son? You're a running back, not a linebacker. Get your head on straight."

"Sorry, coach." I glare at Dereck one more time. Looking up, I see a few more teammates glancing at Bella. I try to see her as they do and realize she had a growth spurt this summer, too. Her legs look extra long in those jeans. Her sweater clings a bit at her chest and hips.

Ace is completely missing the attention she's getting, too busy staring at Grace in her cheerleader skirt. Guess I'll be the one relaying the message to the football team—and every other guy at Hitchcock High, for that matter.

Bella Bennet is off limits.

CHAPTER TWENTY-THREE

Midnight Snack

DAVID - NOW

I watch Bella storm into the house. She is madder than a wet panther—and so damn sexy. I thank the driver and follow her at a slower pace, hoping she'll calm down enough that I can keep my balls intact.

When that guy grabbed her, I was furious. She's still recovering from a violent attack and doesn't need that shit right now. When she ripped his hands off her and turned on him, I was so proud. When she defended me, I was fucking turned on.

No one's fought for me like that before. Sure, my Corps brothers had my back on a mission, but this felt different. A warmth spreads through my chest even now at the memory. When the insult was against her, Bella had urged me to walk away. When he insulted me, she'd gone practically feral. It's exactly how I react every time I see her in trouble.

Maybe she still feels the same way.

Following the trail of lights, I find her in the kitchen sipping a glass of sweet tea. Feeling bold, I stand behind her and rest my hands on the island, caging her in. The magnolia smell of her hair taunts me and pulls me in.

My Bella. My avenging angel.

"Why'd you do it?" Her voice sounds clipped, but calmer than I expected.

My brows pinch in confusion. I was expecting screaming, not whatever this is. "I'm sorry, were you enjoying the party otherwise? Figured after everything you'd want to get home. Was that wrong?"

"I don't mean tonight."

"What do you mean, Bella?"

The glass clinks against the counter before she whirls to face me. She doesn't fight the circle of my arms, merely stands in them glaring up at me. Tears threaten to fall from chocolate eyes full of fire. Her breaths come in hard pants, her breasts brush my chest with each one. Our mouths are close, I'd only need to bend a little...

"I always thought Atty was the overprotective one in high school. But it was you?"

Shit. How did she find out after all these years? "Bells..."

She's not done yet, though. "All that time? Why?"

I press my forehead against hers, exhaling heavily. God, give me the words. "At first, I didn't know why. I thought it was brotherly protectiveness, didn't realize I was fucking jealous."

Her hands clutch my shirt as she arches her neck back to look me in the eye. "When did it change? Prom?"

Swallowing the lump in my throat, I shake my head. "I finally realized it the night I picked you up from that stupid party. Maybe some part of me always knew, but I couldn't deny it anymore after that night."

Her eyes dart between mine. "Why didn't you come back after your first tour?"

I grip the edge of the counter until my knuckles turn white. "I promised myself I'd put your happiness first. Your restaurant had just opened, and you looked so damn happy. I thought you would be better off without me and the reminders of home." I squeeze my eyes against the memories. The feeling of not being enough.

"That was years ago. Why didn't you move on? Find someone else?"

Opening my eyes, I meet her vulnerable gaze. "There's never been anyone else, Bells. I've always only seen you."

Her lips part as she draws a breath. Her eyes soften and practically glow with emotion. She pushes up on her toes and her mouth captures mine in a searing kiss. Ten years I've dreamed of the taste of her lips.

It feels like coming home.

My hands slide to her hips. Gently at first, then I clutch her, afraid she might disappear. My lips slant to deepen the kiss. Her slight moan and seeking hands against my chest is all the encouragement I need. My hands glide over her ass to hook behind her thighs, lifting her onto the counter for better access.

Bella arches her neck back as I skim my lips along her jaw to her thundering pulse. Blond hair cascades over my arm like a waterfall. My fingers tangle in the silky waves, tugging gently to better expose her neck.

My cock throbs against my zipper and weeps for her, but I'm in no rush. This is the closest to heaven I've been, and I plan to enjoy every minute. My lips and teeth explore the creamy skin on her shoulder and my hand slides the straps out of my way. I trail open-mouth kisses down her chest until I reach her breast. Already perfectly puckered, I draw her nipple into my mouth and circle the sensitive tip with my tongue.

"More." Bella tugs at my scalp, encouraging my path. My lips smirk against her between kisses. I could get used to the longer hair if she runs her fingers through it like that.

As I move to give equal attention to her other breast, my hands explore her thighs and the hem of her dress. I stroke her center through the silk of her panties and groan when I find it already wet. Bella spreads her legs wider for me with a needy whimper that shoots straight to my aching cock.

My finger teases the edge of the fabric before slipping beneath. We both moan as my fingertip finds her wet folds. I tease her slit, coating my finger before circling her clit. My movements are achingly slow. I'm not sure if I'm trying to torture us both or simply extend this moment as long as I can.

"Davy, please." Hearing her breathless voice, I look up to find her chocolate eyes nearly black with desire. It's my undoing. I can't deny my girl anything.

Keeping my eyes on hers, I lower myself to my knees between her thighs. My fingers slide her underwear off her hips and down her gorgeous legs before tucking them into my back pocket. She squirms, so I tug her closer to the edge and pin her in place. I lick her slit, her sweet taste exploding on my tongue. Bella's head falls back as her hands grip the counter behind her for support. I eat her like a man starving.

One thick finger slides into her weeping core as I flick her clit with my tongue. She's so fucking wet and tight. Her greedy pussy is already gripping my finger. As her muscles relax, I work a second in, slowly pumping.

When I feel her thighs quiver by my shoulders, I know she's close. Curving my fingers up, I tap that ball of nerves sharply and she explodes on my mouth. I draw out her orgasm, pumping my fingers until the pulsing stops.

Standing up, I capture her mouth in a searing kiss that is all tongue and teeth. Her hands fist in my shirt, holding tight. She wraps her legs around my waist as I stand between her thighs. As I scoop her off the counter, I snag her purse with my finger and carry her to her room. Kicking the door shut behind us, I lower her to the bed.

Dress bunched at her hips and still in those strappy heels, she looks like a sex goddess. Bella sits up at the edge of the mattress, shimmying the fabric the rest of the way over her head, leaving her naked to my eyes. She reaches for my shirt and watches me through her lashes as she undoes the buttons. As I shuck it off my arms, Bella gets to work on my belt and jeans. She pushes the stiff fabric down with jerky motions.

When my cock is free, Bella grips the hard length in her hand. Her thumb gathers the pre-cum weeping at the tip and rubs it up and down my shaft. With a smirk, she eyes me as she dips her head to lick me like a damn lollipop. My jaw clenches, but a groan escapes as the wet heat of her lips engulf my cock.

Desperate to touch her, my fingers spear her hair as she bobs her head. A tingle starts at my spine and I know I'm in danger of exploding in her pretty mouth. After the wait, I want to feel her pussy around my cock as I come. Lifting her by the armpits, I move her higher on the bed. Kicking my pants off completely, I crawl up her naked body until we are face to face again.

As I capture her lips in a drugging kiss, my cock bumps against her opening. It slips easily through her folds and we both moan at the contact. I freeze at the realization there's nothing between us.

"Shit." I lower my forehead to hers and catch my breath. "No condom. I wasn't expecting... this..."

Her palms cup my cheeks, forcing me to meet her gaze. "I'm on the shot and recently got a screening. I'm good."

I've never gone bare before, and the thought has my balls clenching up. I search her eyes. "Are you sure?"

Her smile is full of affection. "We've wasted so much time already. I trust you."

A warmth spreads through my chest at her sincere words. I lower my head for another kiss as I notch myself at her entrance. Slowly, I push forward, her tight pussy strangling my cock. I give her time to adjust before pushing the rest of the way in.

"Are you ok?" I drop kisses to her jaw.

"Yes," she turns her head to allow me more access to her throat, "don't stop. You feel so good." Her legs latch onto me and she lifts her hips, seeking friction.

I pump into her. Slowly at first, then quickly building as a desperation to reach the peak consumes me. Her moans and clutching hands spur me on. Adjusting my hand to grip her ass, I lift her hips higher to better hit her G-spot.

"Oh, god, Davy. Yes. Right there!" Two more pumps and she screams my name as she comes on my cock. Before the waves of pleasure end, I grip her ankles and hold them over my shoulders. I nibble the tender skin of her ankle as I snap my hips, pounding into her sopping wet pussy.

"Come on, baby. Come for me one more time." I can feel her pussy tightening impossibly more. Leaning forward, I increase the friction against her clit with each stroke. Moments later, the pulses of her orgasm set off my own. Releasing her, I kiss her deeply as my cock swells and empties itself into her perfect pussy.

Careful not to crush her, I reluctantly pull out, dropping a kiss to her hip bone before grabbing a tissue to clean her up. She lies in the bed, flushed and looking completely satisfied. With a twinkle in her eye, Bella holds her hand up and I happily join her.

She settles herself into my side, her head on my shoulder and a leg thrown across mine. "That was better than I remember."

I chuckle at her comment and brush her hair off her face so I can kiss her forehead. "Every time with you is incredible. I've missed us, Hell's Bells."

"Me too. I spent years wondering if I'd made it all up."

I squeeze her. Regret and guilt are thick in my throat. "I'm sorry, Bells. I'll never make you doubt me again."

She turns so she can see me. "Promise?" A vulnerability shows in her eyes as she holds up her pinky.

My lips curve at our old routine. I hook my pinky around hers. "Promise."

CHAPTER TWENTY-FOUR

Rude Awakening

ANNABEL - NOW

As I stir, I snuggle closer to the warm pillow, happy to avoid reality for a few more minutes. I had the most amazing dream and another day with the bridesmaidzilla will seriously ruin my mood. Davy was in it. We'd reunited and had some of the best sex of my life.

Frowning, I wiggle to get more comfortable. This pillow sure is firm. I push at the cushion, trying to soften it. A chuckle vibrates against my cheek. What the...

I blink my eyes open and tilt my head to find Davy's hazel eyes studying me with a sexy grin on his face. Shifting my gaze, I take a moment to appreciate his toned chest, defined abs, and a very naked, very hard cock.

Guess it wasn't a dream.

He rolls so I'm tucked under him, his weight on his elbows. It's somehow both tender and seductive at the same time.

His lips nip mine in playful kisses. "Good morning, beautiful."

I slide my hands up his chiseled torso and clasp them behind his neck. "Mornin'." I tilt my head and kiss him slowly. Just because I want to, and I can.

Davy groans. The sound shoots straight to my core, where his erection is teasing. "I could get used to this every morning." His lips tickle my throat.

As I snake my hand between us to give his hard cock a pump and guide him into me, a loud pounding shakes the door. We freeze and stare at each other wide-eyed.

"Bella? Are you in there?" Atty's voice booms just on the other side of the wood.

"It's Atty. You need to hide." I start pushing at Davy's shoulders, but the man is solid muscle and doesn't budge.

"Come on, Bells. Seriously?" His brows pinch. He looks confused and a little upset.

My stomach drops as I meet his gaze. I hurt him. It wasn't my intention, but the voice in my head is screaming that Atty finding us will be the end of the world. Right now, I can think of nothing else but avoiding this fight.

"I don't exactly want to broadcast to my brother that I had sex with his best friend. He said he didn't want to have to choose between the two of us. He also said if I did anything to mess up this wedding, he'd never speak to me again."

The knocking on the door intensifies. "Annabel! Open the door."

Davy searches my gaze. I'm not sure what he sees—probably desperation—but it's enough to have him sighing and getting off of me.

"Thank you." Then I yell at the door. "Hold on, Atty. Unless you want an eyeful." Davy raises a brow at me, so I give him a shrug. He looks around the room and holds his hands up—clearly asking what he should do now. "The closet," I whisper. Shaking his head and muttering to himself, he squishes his giant frame into the tiny space and shuts the door.

I throw my sleep shirt on from the floor. Halfway to the door, I notice David's boots and kick them under the bed. They land with a bang and I wince.

"What was that noise, Annabel?" Atty asks.

Davy opens the door, looking at me with concern, but I wave him off. "I tripped. Don't get your knickers all up in a twist. I just woke up." A soft snort sounds from the closet. I open the door enough to show only my top half . "What's up?"

Atty's brows pinch in worry. His blue eyes, so much like our fathers, scan me from head to waist—about all he can see as I hide behind the door. His body is practically vibrating with tension and it makes my hair stand on end. "What is it? Is someone injured? Grace?"

His eyes soften slightly, but he still looks troubled. "David's not in his room. Then I realized you weren't already up like you always are. I was worried you guys never made it back last night. If you're here, where the fuck is David?"

Ok, so at least no one is hurt. "He's probably out for a run."

"What? David runs?" Atty rocks back on his heels.

"Yea, he runs every morning. Helps him manage stuff."

The worry gives way to confusion and suspicion. "How the hell do you know that? You haven't spoken to the man in a decade."

"Um, yea I have. You told me to be friendly, remember? Heck, you saw us carpool here. You think we sat in silence for three hours?"

Atty rubs the back of his neck and smiles sheepishly. "Yea, ok. Sorry, Bug. You good? Tom said something went down at the club?"

I wave off his concern. Partially because I hate it when he worries, but I also need to keep him from finding the literal body in my closet. "Ran into a handsy jerk. Nothing I can't handle. I told him off, but got kicked out."

A devious smirk spreads on his face. "Glad you showed that micro-dick fuckwad who's boss." I lash out to cuff his head, but he dances out of the way.

"Thomas Sawyer!" I scream down the hall. "Just you wait until I get a hold of you." Atty clutches his stomach, laughing in the hallway. "Y'all will never be letting that go, are ya?"

"Nope! I think that story will be retold at every family gathering for the rest of time! I can't believe you actually said fuck, Bug."

I groan. I love my family, but brothers are seriously the worst. "If you tell Dad, I won't make your wedding cake." I cross my arms over my chest and wipe the emotion from my face.

Brothers may be the worst, but sisters are no angels.

Atty runs his tongue across his teeth, his eyes turning calculating. "What flavor?"

"Maple bacon chocolate." His eyes widen—wait for it. "With brown sugar frosting." He licks his lips. Gotcha! "And caramel filling."

He opens his mouth to answer, then his shoulders slump. "Aw, Annabel. I won't tell him, but I can't stop Tweedle Dee and Tweedle Dumb down there." His pout is actually adorable.

A twinge of guilt twists my stomach. "Oh fine. Promise to be my ally for the rest of the trip, take my side in all games or arguments. And go make me coffee while I shower."

"Deal." He smiles like a kid on Christmas, then leans forward and gives me a kiss on the cheek. "Love you, Bug."

I smile up at him, though my eyes sting with emotion. How would he feel if he knew the truth? That I wanted his best friend to myself. That said best friend is currently in my closet. Naked. "Love you, too, big brother."

My muscles tremble as I close the door and sit heavily on the bed. I stare at the patterns on the rug without seeing them. Warm hands cup my shoulders and pull me back against a familiar chest.

"Shh. It's going to be ok, baby. I really don't think he'll mind." His hand wipes my face and I realize I'm crying.

"He asked me not to ruin the wedding for Grace. And what do I do? I sleep with the best man. At the bachelor party. The party where all of my brothers happen to be. And a crazy bridesmaid who would absolutely cause trouble if she knew." I tick the items off on my fingers before dropping my head into my hands. "Oh god."

"Baby, I think you're exaggerating a bit." I glare at him over my shoulder. "Ok, you're right about Holly. But I don't think your brothers will care. Grace definitely wouldn't mind."

I shake my head. "Atty was serious, Davy. I can't chance it. Especially not with Holly here."

He searches my eyes, his lips forming a thin line. "Ok, Bells. We'll keep it a secret, at least for this weekend. But I'm serious, too, Annabel. You're it for me. I've known it for half my life. Eventually, we need to tell him." I nod, and he drops a quick kiss to my lips before finishing dressing. I play lookout at the door while Davy slips down the hall to change.

David seems so sincere. I know he loves me. He's always been my lighthouse in the storm. Is it because of nostalgia? The comfort of our childhood? Or is he right, and this is the forever kind of love?

I just don't know. My head and my heart can't agree.

CHAPTER TWENTY-FIVE

Running Away

DAVID - AGE 18

The gun fires and she takes off like she's racing the bullet instead of the other runners. Her long legs glisten in the sun as they pump. She gains on the runner in front of her.

"Go Bella!" Ace's yell and piercing whistle ring in my ear. He looks over to where Grace sits with a pissed-looking Holly. "Sorry about you and Holly, man."

I wave my hand at him, eyes still focused on the track. "It's fine. Wasn't anything serious."

Bella passes two more opponents, but then decelerates a bit. The 1300 meter isn't her strongest event, she's more of a sprinter, and it's the end of the day. "Come on, Bells. Halfway there," I shout. Her face pinches with renewed determination as she pushes herself.

That's my girl.

"What did you say?" Shit, guess I said that out loud. Ace gives me a weird look before returning his attention to the field. "Sun must be getting to me, misheard you for a second. Run, Bug!"

As the finish line approaches, Bella pumps her legs harder as she kicks up little puffs of dust. The ribbon splits across her chest and the crowd explodes. She did it!

Breathing heavily, she stumbles towards the fence, and I catch my breath. Blond hair sticks to her flushed face, but I can only see her ear to ear grin. Her teammates swarm her. Thanks to her, they've won the whole meet.

"Things weren't serious with Holly? That's not how it looked to me."

I spare him a slight look. Is he for real right now? "Whatever gave you that idea?" My eyes dart back to Bella, drawn like magnets. A runner from the boy's team hands her a bottle of water. He leans into her space as he smiles down at her. What the fuck?

"I don't know. You guys were always together." He squints at me as he lifts his cap to scratch his head.

"Yea, because our best friends are always together. Was just easier to go along with it. It's a small fucking town, man." He gives a thoughtful "huh" besides me, but all of my focus is on the fucker brushing a hair out of Bella's face. My fingers clench until my knuckles crack. "Who's that with Bells?"

Ace turns back to his sister. "Oh, that's Linc Hastings. He's Bella's year, been over a few times for school projects." The punk's been over? More than once? My lip curls as my cheek twitches. Ace laughs as he slaps my shoulder. "Calm down. Linc's a total puppy dog. Leave the girl alone. I don't think she's had a single date. She's always too busy."

I snort. Bella is too busy. If she's not in class or track practice, she's home looking after her little brothers. I've barely gotten to see her in months. Won't say I'm unhappy that little wild streak seems to have ended, but the girl needs to find balance before she burns herself out. A Bella with no fire is no Bella at all.

"Seriously, man," Ace claps my shoulder, "you're overprotective and I'm saying that as her actual blood brother. She's damn lucky to have you. We all are. You're a good friend."

Friend.

Bella's eyes rise as she sees us in the crowd and she smiles and waves. I can't help but notice it's not the same smile she gave Linc Hastings. That realization might as well be a bullet straight to the chest.

Friend.

Maybe that's all I'll ever be. Maybe I shouldn't admit how much more I wish I were.

Finding the break in the fence, Bella takes the stairs two at a time up the bleachers until she reaches us. "Hey."

Ace grabs her in a bear hug and lifts her off her feet. "You did it, Bella Bug! Best time yet!"

She laughs as she squeezes him back. "Wasn't sure I'd make it there for a sec." They part and she turns to me, wrapping her arms around my waist exactly as she did for Ace.

Friend.

My arms lock around her, savoring the contact. I breathe in her magnolia scent, still strong over her sweat. With effort, I release my hold before it lingers too long.

Bella returns to Ace's side and he slings a lazy arm over her shoulders, completely at ease. Completely unaware that I'm bleeding out in front of her. "I heard you both cheering, and it helped. Come on, let's grab the boys from school and get some ice cream." They continue chatting about the race as they step down the bleacher steps. My chest tightens with each step she takes from me.

I stand frozen in place.

My girl pauses and turns back to me, eyes bright and smile firmly in place. Everything else dims but her glow, and I don't care how cheesy that sounds. "You coming, Davy?"

"Yea." I'd follow her anywhere. Be whatever she needed from me. Even if it's only a friend. Because, Hell's Bells, a life without you isn't worth living.

CHAPTER TWENTY-SIX

Homecoming

DAVID - NOW

The rest of the weekend goes by with little fuss. Bella looks spooked, though. She's been quiet and a steady flow of food has been flowing out the kitchen since Ace's little wake up call.

Not that Ace has any idea about the stress bomb he's dropped on his sister.

He's sitting in an oversized chair nursing a coffee without a care in the world. Grace stares at me from her perch on the arm before jerking her eyes towards Bella, clearly asking what the hell is up. I jerk my chin at her, silently telling her to drop it.

Bella remains withdrawn as we pack up the cars and head to Hitchcock for our final day. I glance at her as we travel the empty country highways. She's leaning against the window, her forehead on the glass, staring out at the passing trees. I bet she doesn't see a single one.

Reaching out, I place a hand on her thigh, hoping to give her some comfort. She turns and looks at my hand for a beat, like she's surprised by it. When her smaller hand lowers onto mine, I'm half afraid she's going to push me away. Instead, she gives it a slight squeeze before turning her attention back to the view.

Progress, I guess.

As we pull up in front of the Bennets' house, I'm shocked how little it's actually changed. Sure, the paint could use a touch-up here or there. A couple boards on the porch warp, and there's an ancient frisbee stuck up on the roof. But it still feels like home.

My eyes scan to the house next door. It also remains largely unchanged, though where the Bennets' house has dimmed, my mother's is brighter. Mom started gardening after I enlisted, and her rose bushes are the envy of the street. She found a host of new hobbies to stay busy, including volunteering to work every holiday at the hospital to allow others to be with family. Even since I've gotten back, she's always on her way somewhere when I call.

Beside me, Bella still hasn't moved. She takes a deep breath and seems to steady herself. Hell, she looks like she's preparing for battle. But why? Is it because of what her brother said? Or does she feel this every time she visits her childhood home?

"You ok?" I squeeze her leg, trying to show her I'm here to support her. Whatever she needs.

Her fingers twist in her lap. "Yea. I just... it's hard coming back here... since Momma..."

She peers over her shoulder at me. Grief swirls in her chocolate eyes. My chest aches for her. I wish I had the words to comfort her. Before I can think of anything remotely appropriate, the front door swings open and a lanky man with messy strawberry blond hair ambles down the stairs.

The porch door slamming shut draws Bella's attention, and transforms her sadness to joy. Dimples wink on either side of Rhett's grinning mouth.

Bella sprints to him and throws her arms around his neck. He grunts as he catches her, pulling her tight.

I approach slowly, not wanting to interrupt the reunion. When I'm within reach, he holds his hand out for me to pump. I try to reconcile the young man in front of me with the little boy I remember. He was only eight the last time I saw him. Still obsessed with superheroes and race cars.

"What'd you do to my sister?" Rhett asks.

I freeze. Does he know? How would he know? He's still smiling, so it doesn't look like I'm about to get my ass kicked.

"We usually only see her at Christmas and Dad's birthday. An extra visit? And she turns up with you in tow? It's a miracle."

Bella leans back and smacks Rhett's shoulder as he towers over her. God, he's almost my height. "Har har. You can thank Atty and Grace. Why'd you skip the party?"

Rhett scoffs as he slings his arm around Bella and leads her into the house. "Gee, being the designated driver and responsible one sounds so fun. Love you guys, but most of my friends are heading off to school soon. Spent a last weekend with them instead."

"There she is. There's my baby girl." Mr. Bennet comes down the hall from the kitchen and pulls Bella into a hug. His eyes crinkle as he smiles at me over her head. "Come on in and have a visit. I just made a fresh pitcher of sweet tea."

As the three Bennets continue walking, a picture on the wall catches my eye. A blond woman with long hair and dark brown eyes smiles at the camera. Her arms wrap around a little girl no older than five or six. Freckles sprinkle the girl's face and she's missing a front tooth.

A warm hand lands on my shoulder, making me jump. I smile sheepishly at Mr. Bennet, embarrassed to be caught staring. "Annabel is the spitting image of my Lizzie." He's right. All the Bennets are blond, but Bella is the only child with Momma Bennet's brown eyes, though, I'd say Bella's sparkle with more fire. Mrs. Bennet was always gentle, serene. "Come on. It's good to see you two together. How's life after the Marines going?"

I let Mr. Bennet guide me into the kitchen, where Bella is already shoulder deep in the refrigerator. Rhett beams next to her as she tosses ingredients at him to add to the growing pile on the counter. We sit at the table and Mr. Bennet picks up the Sunday paper.

"Daddy, what happened to that meal subscription I got you? I'd say this fridge looks like a bachelor's, but even David has a better stocked kitchen."

Mr. Bennet winks at me over the pages as he chuckles at his daughter's nagging.

The front door opens and shuts loudly as a voice calls down the hall. "Hey! We're here." Grace and Atticus wander into the warm kitchen and start exchanging welcomes.

Bella organizes ingredients and barks out orders for Rhett, who's apparently filling the role of sous chef today. Ace leans against a counter and Grace grabs the chair across from me.

"So, David, you never answered my question. How's life, son? Your mom said you're putting down roots in Friendship Springs, like our Bella."

Clearing my throat, I sit taller in my chair. "Yes, sir. Buddy of mine and I started a security company there. Reasonable taxes, but close to several business hubs. It's a nice area."

"That's good. Now that Atty's settling down, are you looking to do the same?" My eyes widen as Mr. Bennet's piercing blue eyes study me. A loud crack draws our attention as Bella uses a bit of extra force with her knife.

"Come on, Dad." Atty grabs a chunk of apple Bella's been chopping, tossing it in his mouth. "The guy's been off fighting wars since he was eighteen. Let him live a little."

Rhett cracks eggs into a big mixing bowl next to his sister. "I always thought David and Bella would end up together."

The knife clatters on the counter. "What?" I'm not sure who's more shocked, Bella, Atticus, or me.

One eyebrow raised, Rhett looks around the kitchen. Like we're all the crazy ones. "Well, yea. You two were always a pair when I was a kid. Didn't realize y'all weren't a couple like those two," he jerks his chin at Grace, "for a long time."

Ace doubles over with laughter, holding his sides. Bella and I stare at each other, wide eyed. Recovering a little, Ace walks behind my chair and squeezes my shoulders with his hands. "That's ridiculous, Rhett. David is like another brother. He'd never betray me by going after my sister."

I watch the color drain from Bella's face. She turns back to chopping, but I don't miss the shimmer of tears in her eye. I shift my gaze to Grace, who's staring at her fiancé with a confused pinch to her brows.

"Now, Atticus. Don't you think you're being a tad dramatic, son?" Mr. Bennet doesn't even look up from the sports section. "Where are your brothers? They didn't want to stop in for a visit?"

Ace hooks his foot around the remaining chair, pushing it closer to Grace before flopping into it. "Huck was too hungover. Tom took them both straight back to their apartment."

Rhett huffs from the counter. "Sounds about right. Glad I stayed here." He glances over at the table where everyone sits. I follow his gaze and notice Grace's giant engagement ring glittering in the morning light, sending rainbows across Mr. Bennet's paper. "Why didn't you use Momma's ring, Ace? I mean, you're the oldest."

"I asked, but Dad said Momma left special instructions for it." Ace shrugs. "My girl deserved a big rock for waiting so long, anyway." He leaves a noisy kiss on her bare shoulder.

The oven beeps. Bella busies herself, putting a tray in and setting a timer. Her hands fly over ingredients as she whisks, chops, and blends. Rhett hangs on her every word as she tosses out orders. Exactly like when he was a kid.

The routine of cooking is her coping mechanism, but I can see her coming apart at the seams. Gotta be honest. At the cabin, I thought Bells was freaking out over nothing. But after that comment from Ace, maybe she's right. Maybe my best friend would disown me for loving his sister.

The real question is, do I care? Would I choose a life with Bella if it meant losing Atticus in the process? Hell yea, I would.

But would Bella?

CHAPTER TWENTY-SEVEN

Spill the Beans

ANNABEL - NOW

Saying goodbye to my father is painful. I don't regret leaving Hitchcock and building a life away from my family. Doesn't mean I don't miss seeing them more often. If I were a better daughter, I'd make it back more than once or twice a year. I'd face the ghosts in my mother's house and spend more time with my brothers.

As the miles speed by, the tension in my shoulders eases. It's like the further I get from Atty, the less I feel like there's a sword hanging over my head. His outburst in the kitchen is still heavy on my mind. Even though I predicted his reaction, a small part of me hoped I was mistaken. That Atty would have reacted more like Rhett.

I glance over at David as he silently drives. The dash lights reflect on his face, casting shadows under his eyes and cheeks. He is such a handsome man.

Feeling my gaze, David turns towards me. His lips quirk into an affectionate smile. "Penny for your thoughts, Hell's Bells."

"Thinking about Atty."

My fingers fidget in my lap until David's hand engulfs mine, forcing me to stop. "He'll come around. I'll talk to him."

I wish I had his confidence. "Davy…"

He squeezes my hand, then adjusts to entwine our fingers. "I get it, Bells. Although I'd like to shout it from the rooftops that Bella Bennet is finally my girl, I know you aren't ready for that. We won't say anything until after the wedding." He looks at me before turning back to the road. "I promise, Bells, nothing will come between you and your family if I have a say."

His firm tone helps to loosen the ball of stress in my chest. "Pinky promise?" I hold out my finger, which David immediately captures with his.

We pull into the employee lot at Pop around midnight. After eleven, we only serve a limited bar menu, so there's hardly anyone left in the kitchen as we walk in with the first cooler. I quickly send Asher and Tony out to grab the other.

"Anna, you have got to be the only person who brings their own groceries on vacation. These things are still full! Why'd you bring them?" Asher dramatically cracks his back, getting a laugh from the group.

"She re-filled them in Georgia." David chuckles as he steps closer and kisses my cheek. "I'll bring your bag up, Bells."

Asher crosses his arms and arches a brow at me. He makes a show of watching David walk back towards the stairs to my apartment. "Well, someone seems to have had an eventful weekend."

My face feels hot. I suck on my teeth and avoid Asher's knowing gaze. "Hope you're in the mood for peaches, y'all. I picked up twenty pounds on the way back. Tomorrow we'll have a bunch of specials. Asher, darlin', you think you could whip up some peach margaritas?"

"Sure thing, Chef. But don't think you're getting out of spilling the beans." With a grin the cat who ate the canary would be proud of, Asher swaggers back out to the bar.

"So…" I jump at the voice, suddenly realizing Ryan is standing next to me. He lounges against a prep counter.

The hair on the back of my neck stands on end. Yea, he's in my blind spot, but I must be out of it to not feel him get so close. The Atty situation has me more in my head than I thought.

"Am I supposed to come up with peach desserts now?" Ryan grabs a fruit off the pile and lightly tosses it into the air before catching it.

"Well, yes. That's the idea. I'm sure you have recipes that you can easily swap out peaches for something else. You can't go wrong with a classic cobbler. We also have that ice cream maker we hardly use. I can throw together some peach gelato and you can make those awesome biscotti. Don't overthink it. Now, if you'll excuse me, I'm still technically on vacation." I force a smile and laugh, my stomach feeling a bit like I swallowed Coke and Mentos.

Right before I pass through the kitchen doors, I glance over my shoulder. Ryan is still by the counter, watching me walk away. His white teeth flash as he takes a large bite of the soft peach flesh. As he pulls the fruit away, orange juice dribbles down the sides of his mouth.

I have to resist running up the stairs towards David.

Back in Friendship Springs, I happily crawl into the relationship bubble with David. The weeks rush by and before I know it August has hit hot and humid. With Atty out of sight—and out of imminent danger of discovering my secret—I can relax and fully enjoy exploring my re-emerging feelings.

Both of us have booming businesses keeping us busy. David secured four corporate contracts. It's fantastic for his growing company, but keeps him traveling all over the neighboring cities and out of my dining room.

I've cut back a bit at Pop. I still create all the menus and spend more hours in the kitchen than anyone else, but instead of closing practically every night, I've transitioned more dinner and night shifts to Tameka. Those evenings, I either visit Brianna, who is losing her mind on bedrest, or hang out at David's.

It's funny. The girls have been trying to get me to reduce my hours for years. It never made sense to me. Nic and Bree had interests outside of Pop—full-time jobs, other hobbies, sex lives. Pop has been my everything for so long. Heck, I live over the restaurant, for Pete's sake. Even if I'm "*off*," I'm on hand for the odd kitchen or management emergency. And those happen more often than you'd think.

Take tonight. Tony was flambéing a brandy sauce. He must have been heavy-handed with the booze, because the flame mushroomed up, scaring the living turd out of a new chef. Flailing, she knocked a vat of baked beans all over the floor. Then, rushing to clean it up, she slid and took out a second line cook in the process.

So here I am—on my night off—filling the spot of two line cooks who are getting checked up at the local urgent care. I'd rather be upstairs with David, but duty calls.

My cell vibrates in my pocket. Seeing Bree's name, I swipe to answer. Tucking the phone between my shoulder and ear, I continue to sauté garlic shrimp and get ready to get plates to the window. "Hey suga'. It's crazy here. You hear an update yet?"

"Yea." She sounds tired. "Sara has a slight burn on her wrist where she touched the pan. Heather sprained her ankle from sliding on the beans. They should be back to work tomorrow."

"That's good news." More loudly, I call out to the kitchen, "Sara and Heather are ok, folks." A cheer goes up around the room.

"I don't think either of them would sue, but can you get a copy of the surveillance footage from David? Just to be safe?"

"Yea, sure thing, Bree. You good? You sound stressed." I feel my eyebrows pinch as I transfer the pink shrimp to a waiting plate with a small nest of pasta.

Bree sighs in my ear. "I'm fine, but fucking uncomfortable. This kid thinks she's the next Conor McGregor and is using my bladder as a punching bag lately."

I chuckle slightly. "Well, that was an actual Irish reference this time, so good job! Anything I can do to help?"

The sounds of rustling fabric and another panting groan from Bree filter through the call. "You're already doing so much at the restaurant. I have been craving your mom's ginger cookies, though. This heartburn is no joke."

"Consider it done. I'll drop them off in the morning after my run. Love you."

Hanging up, I arch my back to work out a twinge. It's been ages since I took a break, might as well take one now. I can pull out the butter to soften and maybe get a little back rub. With a smile on my face, I call for someone to take my place and head upstairs.

I find David at my kitchen counter. Laptop open, papers spread across the surface in front of him. Walking up behind him, I wrap my arms around his waist and lean my head on his shoulder.

He reaches up and cups my hands in his much larger one. "Hey, baby. How's it going downstairs? Anything I can help with?"

"Bree called. Everyone's been checked out and cleared to return to work tomorrow. She asked if you'd send the video of the accident though. Also, she's craving Momma's ginger cookies."

He chuckles as he turns the chair to cradle me between his thighs. His lips capture mine. I still haven't gotten used to it. Every kiss feels like the first and last time.

"Don't you start something you can't finish. I gotta get back down in a minute." I tug out of his grasp easily and head to the kitchen to pull out the butter. If I take it out now, it'll be soft by the time I get off work. Was it one stick or two, though?

I scan the counter for my mother's antique recipe box. The little yellow crate isn't standing out against my white counters like it normally does. Brows creased, I twirl in a slow circle, trying to find it. Funny, that usually works. Let me spin again.

"What are you doing, Hell's Bells?" Papers abandoned, David is full-on watching me with a quirked brow.

"Have you seen Momma's recipe box? Yellow, about this big, white flowers painted on it. It should be right here." I point to the left of the stove where I always keep it on display.

I'm still staring at the empty spot when David comes up next to me. He casually palms my hip bone, like it's the most natural thing in the world. Butterflies start a conga line in my stomach at the way his hand engulfs my side. I was never a girly girl, but David has a way of making me feel feminine.

"Can't say I have. I can't remember seeing it since we got back from Georgia." I glance up at him over my shoulder. His brows pinch as well.

"Pull out more than you think you need to be safe. You got a kitchen to run, I'll keep looking for the box."

Turning fully into him, his hand skates over my hip and butt as I push up on my toes to peck his cheek. "You're the best."

"You can thank me by baking naked." His eyes heat as he looks down at me. David's free hand cups my face and he leans down for another sensual kiss. As I break the embrace, I lean back to study his face. With his beard, rippling muscles, and tattoos, he still doesn't resemble the boy I fell for, but I'm finding traces of him left. His strength and determination. His protectiveness and loyalty.

Who am I kidding? I gave my heart to him two decades ago, and I never got it back. As I look into his eyes, my breath catches at the love I see shining there. A look I'm sure I'm wearing right now too, because I love this man. And after I bake some cookies for my best friend, I'm going to tell him tonight.

CHAPTER TWENTY-EIGHT

Christmas Surprise

ANNABEL - AGE 11

The sound of sizzling bacon is music in my ears. It helps drown out the crying baby, anyhow. My nose curls as I push the bacon around the pan with a pair of tongs. Why did Momma have to go and have another boy, anyway?

The yellow box in my hand feels cool in the warm kitchen. I flip through the stained edges of the cards until I find the one I need. Carefully, I slide the card out and place the recipe box back on the counter.

When they first told us we were going to have another sibling, I was so sure it'd be a girl. I prayed every night for a baby sister. Even put it on my Christmas list! Both Jesus and Santa let me down.

I heard Momma tell Mrs. Hawthorne that the baby was a surprise. He wasn't due until January, but decided to come just in time to ruin Christmas. I guess that's a surprise? The cries quiet as Momma sings a lullaby in the front room.

Bacon crispy, I move it to a plate and add mushrooms and scallions into the pan. A timer dings. I scramble to silence it before the baby wails again. Footsteps enter the kitchen behind me.

"Smells good, Hell's Bells. Whatcha cooking?" Davy stands next to me, a Jack Reacher novel in his hand. His mom picked up some overtime at the hospital, so he's spending Christmas with us. Most holidays include one or both of the Hawthornes since they moved in.

"Shrimp and grits. Can you pull the sweet buns out while I flour this?" I hand him the mitts and get to work seasoning and coating the raw seafood.

Davy pulls out the pan from the oven and moves it to a waiting cooling rack. He leans close to get a good whiff of the dessert. "Mm, you make the best food, Bells. Need anything else?"

I use the back of my wrist to move my sweaty blond hair out of my face. Winter in the south never gets cold, especially when you spend hours over a stove. "Give the veggies a toss?" One flour-caked finger points to the nearby tongs.

"Yes, Chef." Davy winks and carefully stirs the mushrooms to keep them from burning.

We work together. Davy has no idea how to cook, but he's happy to fetch things for me and take casseroles in and out of the oven. It's a routine we've perfected. Davy learned early that being my helper means taste testing, and the boy likes to snack. As we're finishing up the last dish, Atty wanders into the kitchen.

"Dinner almost ready, Bug? I'm starving." He scratches his belly as he opens the fridge.

"Don't you dare eat now, Atticus Finch Bennet! Take this plate to the dining room and get the twins to set the table. It's just about finished."

Shouts of excitement echo in the next room as Davy brings the dishes out one at a time. I climb up on the step stool to get the gravy boat from the cabinet as a big hand reaches past me to grab it. Daddy scoops me up and plants a kiss on the top of my head. I thank him and start pouring my bacon cream gravy into the dish.

"What's all this, baby girl? I thought y'all were warming the casseroles for Momma? Did I see grits go by?" I turn to him. The hair at his temples has lightened from his normal dark blond, and new creases line his blue eyes. Daddy looks tired.

"Yea. Momma's been busy with the baby, so I wanted to do something special. I made her favorites for Christmas."

His eyes glitter in the low light of the kitchen. He clears his throat and hugs me closer. "You're such a good girl. You just keep on looking after Momma, baby girl. She's too proud to ask, but I know she's real grateful for your help. What'd we do to deserve an angel like you?"

I beam up at him as we walk into the dining room, hand in hand. In an effort to stop the twins from fighting over a roll, Atty positions his chair in the middle.. I slip into my seat between Davy and Momma, the baby still in her arms. Davy serves himself mashed potatoes, then winks at me and drops a spoonful on my plate. Dishes are passed and plates filled. I make sure Momma gets plenty of her favorites.

Daddy clears his throat and the room quiets as everyone settles in and joins hands for grace.

"On this holiest of days, I want to thank Our Lord for his many blessings on this family. For our friends who join us at this table and bring our lives joy. For Momma's safe delivery of our newest blessing, and his continued health. We thank you, Lord Jesus, for guiding our children as they walk your path. That they may experience peace and the comfort of helping others. Lastly, I thank you for this amazing food delivered through our daughter, Annabel. For all this and more, we thank you, Heavenly Father."

My mother squeezes my hand and beams at me. "Amen."

Dinner is an endless stream of stories of Christmas past and dreams of Christmas future. As I scoop up my last forkful of cornbread stuffing, the baby stirs. I look over as Momma tries to soothe him—her plate still full.

"Here, Momma, I'll take him." I reach over and lift him like a bomb about to explode. His little face turns up to me and his eyes widen.

"Thanks for making dinner, Annabel. You even remembered the secret ingredient." Momma reaches out and smooths one of my braids. Her eyes are tired, but her smile is bright.

"Twice the sugar, to sweeten the heart. Half the salt, to dry the tears." I easily parrot back the phrase I've heard hundreds of times from my mother.

"That's right. Tears may be salty, but love makes even the most bitter pill go down easier." Her eyes twinkle and she squeezes my knee before lifting her fork to eat.

"Merry Christmas, Momma." As I adjust the blanket around the baby, he grabs for my finger.

"Merry Christmas, Annabel." Momma finishes her meal. Atty and Davy clear the plates while Momma recites her favorite Christmas poem.

I stroke the baby's tiny palm with my finger, and his fingers weakly lock onto me. A wet gurgle forces me to smile. Maybe he's not so bad. "Merry Christmas, Rhett," I whisper.

Still would have rather had a sister, though.

Chapter Twenty-Nine

Lost and Found

As soon as Bella heads back down to the kitchen, I pull up the video database. Those recipes are all she has left of her mother. Most of them were hand copied by Momma Bennet. There's no way Bells would misplace them, so no point wasting time searching the tiny apartment.

Jumping back to before the bachelor party, I find the yellow box sitting clearly in view on the counter. As I fast forward, there's little of interest. Once, Asher enters and waters some plants, but the box is still visible when he leaves. Just as I'm about to give up, a figure enters the screen.

He is wearing a boxy sweatshirt with the hood pulled up, casting his face in shadow. At least I think it's a "he." Based on the recording, I believe the suspect is a man of average height and build. He's obviously unfamiliar with the layout of the apartment, his movements frantic and disorganized.

When he approaches the counter with the recipe box, his hand is a flash of white as he grabs it. I pause the video, then rewind and watch it in slow motion. As his sleeve pulls back with the gesture, a smudge of darkness is clear on the inside of his wrist. I take a screenshot, then resume the playback. With the box now shoved in the pocket of his hoodie, he heads back towards the door.

"Come on bastard, look at the damn camera," I mutter to myself. As if he can hear me, his head jerks up and for a split second, more of his features are visible. It takes a few tries, but I capture the still and send both images through our enhancement program.

As I wait for the software to process, I pull out my cell.

Me:

> Do you have Momma Bennet's ginger cookie recipe?

Grace:

> Of course, they're Ace's favorite. When did you start baking?

> It's for Bells. Her recipes are missing and her pregnant friend is craving them

> That's not like her. Give me a couple, I'll text you a picture of it.

I shoot a thumbs up emoji before placing the phone back on the counter. Checking the program, it's still only fifty percent complete. Who the fuck is this guy? My cell vibrates, breaking my concentration. Ronnie's name flashes on the screen, so I swipe to answer. "Hey man, what's up?"

"I got an alert of someone accessing recordings of Annabel's apartment. That you?"

Scraping my hand down my face, I sigh. "Yea. Her mother's recipe box is gone, so I was combing through the footage. I found a video of an intruder, but the software is still processing the figure. Not sure why the alarm didn't trigger, though."

The clicking of a keyboard comes through the speaker. "Looks like the system was disabled on July 2 and wasn't reset until a few days later."

Flipping through the recording to that day, I watch again. "That was when Asher watered the plants. Dammit. He probably forgot to rearm it." The computer chimes, telling me the enhanced image is ready. Switching over, my brows pinch in confusion. "You still have that facial recognition software?"

"Yea, why?" I hear the crack of a soda can. The man seriously needs to work on his sugar addiction.

Guess I shouldn't judge. I've had two helpings of Bella's peach bars. What can I say? She's a stress baker and I'm quickly turning into a stress eater. "I got a still of the bastard. He's familiar, but I can't place him. There's a tattoo on his hand too. A skull with a knife and... oar? The images are on the server now."

"Got them." The silence is heavy and only interrupted by the odd click of a mouse or keyboard. "An oar? Maybe he's a sailor? You think this is connected to the attack? Did you piss off anyone in the Navy lately?"

My gut drops. I'd never considered the attack might be about me and not Bella directly. Sure, I helped bring down some truly evil men while in the Marines. But I was surveillance, not tactical assault. No one ever saw my face or knew my name. "Not that I can think of. Something is bothering me about that tattoo." It's like an itch at the edge of my mind, but the closer I get to answers, the farther they slip away. I know I've seen this guy before. But where?

"Yea, weird, but should help nail him. You staying at Annabel's tonight?"

I pause with the bar hallway to my mouth. "Um, yea."

"Bring me one of those bars tomorrow. They look amazing." I jerk back and look up at the security camera by the front door. Ronnie barks a laugh in my ear. "Just keep the sex out of the kitchen. I don't need to be seeing your ugly ass buck naked. Bye."

Shaking my head, I go back to work and waiting for Bells.

"**W**hat's this one for?" Bella's cool fingers trace the trailing flowers inked on my shoulder and upper arm. A playful flour fight while baking cookies led to a sensual shower and now cuddling in her bed.

"Hitchcock. You. It reminds me of the tree in front of our houses back in Georgia and the day we met. You also always smell like magnolia blossoms." I bury my nose in her hair as if to prove the point.

Bella smiles against my skin, her fingers continue to trace the black sweeping lines. She rotates my arm to expose the tattoo of a whisk surrounded by stars. "And this one?"

"Your home cooking. Something delicious to look forward to when I got out." I playfully nibble on her neck.

She giggles and pushes me away. "What about the one on your back?"

"Actually, your namesake inspired the angel. The part of the poem where the angels were so jealous, they took his Annabel Lee away. It also kind of made me think of your mom. Like she was looking out for me over there."

Bella props herself up on her elbow. As she looks down at me, golden strands slip over her shoulder, shadowing her face. "So, all your tattoos are about me?"

I spear my fingers through her hair and push it off her face so I can see her better. "Yea, Bells, it's all about you." Her eyes glisten and she catches her plump lip between her teeth. My thumb traces her mouth and frees it from the pressure. "I'd say letting go of you killed me, but I never really let go. You were always with me. I was stuck in the shadows, waiting until I could find your light again. I love you, Annabel. Always have, always will."

A single tear trails down her cheek before I catch it. She leans down over me, her long fingers cup my face as she stares into my eyes, sending tingles across my skin. Her lips touch mine in a soft kiss. This isn't about sex, this is about a deeper connection.

Bella drops her forehead to mine. "I love you, too."

My cheeks hurt from the face-splitting grin I'm sure I'm wearing. I've waited half my life to hear those words, and fuck, are they ever sweet. "Pinky promise?" I whisper, holding up my finger.

Her smile is radiant as she sits up to entwine our pinkies. "Pinky promise."

I pull her down to me by our linked hands. The kiss starts gentle but grows more charged as we both pour two decades of emotion into it. My fingers glide down her back and urge her hips on top of mine. Our bodies cling to each other, and as we tumble over the edge of oblivion, it's while staring into the other's eyes. I drift off with her in my arms, and like every night we've spent together, I sleep without dreams haunting me.

A loud buzzing wakes me up. It takes a few repetitions for me to realize it's a cell vibrating across the nightstand. I nuzzle closer to Bella. Whoever the fuck it is can wait.

She groans from underneath a cloud of blond hair. "Answer it already. Make them go away."

With a husky chuckle, I drop a kiss to her shoulder before reaching blindly for the offensive device. Squinting my tired eyes against the harsh light, I stab at the bright green circle. I settle back in behind Bella with the phone to my ear.

"Hello?" The line is silent. "Hello, anyone there?"

"David?" I crack my eyes open at the sound of Ace's confused voice.

"Yea. What's up, man?"

"Shit. I thought I called Bella, must have hit the wrong button. Sorry I woke you."

"No worries. Talk to ya later."

As I end the call, the phone returns to the lock screen—a familiar logo of a pink champagne bottle with bubbles and the word Pop. Bella smiles at me, surrounded by her brothers and father. I sit straight up in bed. "Fuck."

Next to me, Bella grunts and kicks me to be quiet. "What is your major malfunction? I'm sleeping."

The phone in my hand vibrates and lights up with a picture of Atticus. "Double fuck."

With a half snarl—my Bella isn't a morning person—she sits up, pushing tangles away from her face. "What?"

"That wasn't my phone." The phone in question keeps vibrating in my hand.

Her eyes are bleary, her hair rumpled, and her lips pouty. If I wasn't freaking the fuck out, I'd tell her she is adorable and kiss the shit out of her.

"So?"

"So... Atticus called you and I answered at seven a.m., obviously still asleep."

Her eyes widen, the freckles standing out against her suddenly pale skin. "Maybe he won't figure it out?" Her lip quivers as her eyes dart between the phone and me.

"Baby, he may not be the most observant man, but he's not stupid."

Pulling her knees to her chest, Bella rakes her hair out of her face. "Maybe I can tell him we were going for a run?"

"Asleep? Bells, time's up. We need to tell him. We owe it to him." I hold the phone up as it vibrates yet again. "Do you want to do it, or me?"

She swallows, looking like she might vomit. "Put it on speaker."

Phone in my opposite hand, I wrap my arm around her shoulders and draw her into my side. I've been the one wanting to come clean since the beginning, but the way this is going down sucks. This is her worst fear come true and I wish I could simply make it go away.

Electric silence fills the room as I answer the call.

Bella gulps before speaking. "H-Hey Atty, what's up?"

"What's up? Seriously, Annabel? What's up? I should be asking you that. What the fuck have you done?"

Bella trembles under my arm and my stomach clenches with anger. "Don't you fucking talk to her that way."

A bark of humorless laughter crackles through the speaker. "I'll get to you in a minute, you fucking traitor. This is between Annabel and me and none of your fucking business."

"Bella, and my relationship with her is my business. I'm sorry you found out like this, truly I am. We were going to tell you after the wedding to avoid exactly this drama. I get you're pissed, but you are the one out of line here, brother. Calm down before you say something you regret."

"Brother?" Another bark of laughter. "A brother wouldn't sleep with my only sister! We're fucking done. Don't bother coming to the wedding or ever calling me again. Annabel, call me back after you take out the trash." He hangs up.

Bella sits frozen under my arm. Tears stream freely down her face as she stares straight ahead. Her eyes are dim, her complexion slightly green. I haven't seen her like this since the day her mother died and it's scaring the fuck out me.

Shifting so I am kneeling in front of her, I cup her face in my palms and tilt her eyes up to mine. "Annabel? Baby? Talk to me."

"This is what I was afraid of. He's so mad. He'll never forgive me." Her chest is heaving in quick breaths. She's going into shock.

"Baby, breathe. Slow, deep breaths. You need oxygen to think. He is mad. He's allowed to be mad. We hid this from him. He isn't allowed to speak to you that way, though."

"He's right. I did this. I betrayed him."

My hands grip her shoulders. I want to shake her as a pit of fear opens in my stomach. "No. We did nothing wrong. We're consenting adults. He doesn't get to decide if we can love each other or not. Ace has always had a temper and a selfish streak. He'll calm down."

She only shakes her head harder. "He won't. Not about this." Tears still pour freely down her face, soaking the sheet pulled tightly around her.

She looks so broken.

I've brought down terrorists. Rescued hostages. Uncovered threats to national security. But fixing this for her, it's not something I can do. As much as I'd like to. I try to pull her into my chest to comfort her, but she stiffens and pulls away.

"I think you should go." She sniffs and won't meet my eyes.

"Annabel. Please don't do this to us." My voice cracks as my throat burns with unshed tears. I don't give a fuck if I cry in front of her. She's breaking my fucking heart.

Again.

She squeezes her eyes shut, and when she speaks, it's barely a whisper. "Not for forever. I do love you. I... I just need some time." She meets my gaze and the pain in her chocolate eyes is my undoing. "Please."

Sniffling, I nod once. My hand cups her cheek, and I drop a kiss on her forehead. "Ok, Bella. Whatever you need."

I get dressed and grab my shit despite the crater in my chest. At the bedroom doorway, I pause. She's still sitting in the same spot, looking small and alone. I will do fucking anything to make this ok for her.

CHAPTER THIRTY

Family Recipe

ANNABEL - AGE 9

"Hey! Wait up for me, guys." I scramble over the rocks by the creek, trying to keep up with Atty and Davy. It's summer vacation. Instead of books and math problems, chasing frogs and catching fish fill our days.

I was right, Atty and Davy are in the same class at school. When the boys hang out at our place after school or on weekends, they always include me. Well, Davy does anyway. Atty can be a real jerk.

My favorite times are when Atty is at baseball practice. Those afternoons I get Davy all to myself. Well, sometimes I need to share him with the twins if Momma needs to rest. They're five now and think they're big boys, but they still need naps, too.

"Hurry up, Bug! Or next time, stay home."

Pebbles tumble loose as I rush over the sloped bank. As I step on a particularly large rock, it shifts under my feet. My arms flail out, looking for something to grab onto. I shriek as I skid to the creek floor.

Wincing, I sit up. Beads of blood appear on my knee. A rustle in the brush above draws my attention. Davy bursts through the green, face red and chest puffing. His eyes scan the creek until they find me. He stays upright as he easily slides down the rocks. How'd he do that?

"Hell, Bells, that looks bad. Can you stand?" Davy wades into the shallow water to help me up.

I clasp his hand and give him a toothy smile. The back of my overalls is sopping wet, and my knee stings when I walk. With Davy's arm around my back, I limp to the bank.

Atty comes marching up a solid five minutes later. After Davy had to half carry me up. How does he manage to always miss the hard work? His fists sit on his hips and his face turns red. "Dangit, Bella, why'd you do a dumb thing like that?"

I glare up at him. "Well, who's the one who told me to hurry, Atty? Wonder what Momma will say."

Davy laughs next to me. "She's got you there, Ace."

"Oh, shut up, David. Whose side are you on?" Atty scuffs his sneaker on the loose dirt. "How did you fall, anyway?"

"I was looking for a shortcut. Figured if I jumped across there," I point to where the creek narrows and large rocks sit on either edge, "I could catch up faster. You think I want to stay home with the twins?"

Atty's eyebrows wrinkle as he follows my finger. "How the heck were you going to do that? It's got to be four feet across!"

"Running leap, but the last rock tilted and I fell." I shake my head like the answer should be obvious.

"Ugh, Bella! What am I supposed to do with you? Momma is going to kill me."

Davy helps me limp forward. "Come on, Bells. Ace, go distract your mom. I'll take Bells to get cleaned up."

Together, the three of us make it back through the woods behind our houses. Atty goes first, to draw Momma away from the back kitchen window. Davy and I count to one hundred and then stumble to his back door. He pulls out a chair and I sit down, wincing.

Davy squats down in front of me and inspects my knee. He whistles. "Hell's Bells. You did a number on this one." He gets a towel and wets it at the sink before handing it to me. I dab at the scrape, trying to dislodge the little rocks stuck in my skin. Returning with a first aid kit, Davy pulls the cloth from my hand and takes over, cleaning my wound.

"You gotta be more careful, Bella." His face scrunches up in concentration as he gently dries and applies ointment to the cut.

"Would you tell Atty to be more careful? I don't want to stay behind just because I'm a girl." I pout and cross my arms. It's bad enough Daddy leaves me home when the boys get to go.

A rueful smile crosses Davy's face. "That doesn't matter. Hell, Bells, you have more balls than most of the boys in my class." He laughs. "That's what I'll call you. Hell's Bells. 'Cuz you're always surprising me." I grin down at him as he secures an extra large band-aid over my knee. "There you go. All better."

All evidence of our adventure is now hidden. "Thanks, Davy." Our stomachs grumble in unison and we laugh. "Come on, I'll make lunch."

We head out the back door and across the yard to my house. As we enter the kitchen, I hear Atty talking with Momma while the twins run around the living room.

"Grilled cheese?" Davy's head perks up and he sounds eager.

"Duh!" I punch his arm gently.

Davy smiles at me, a missing tooth making him look silly. "I'd do anything for your grilled cheese, Bella! How do you make it so good?"

"No way. It's my secret recipe. You can only give secret recipes to your family." That's what my nan says when someone tries to get her peach cobbler recipe. I look at him, forcing a serious expression.

"Come on, Bells, aren't we sorta family?" He pouts.

I suck on my teeth while I think. "Nope. Won't even tell my brothers."

"Well," he scrunches his nose in thought, "will you still make them for me when we're old?"

I've never seen Momma make anyone else sandwiches. "I'll probably be too busy making them for my husband and kids by then."

"Guess you'll just have to marry me then." Davy hands me more bread.

I expertly slather butter and layer cheese. "What about Atty? Won't he feel left out?"

He grins down at me. "Ace can live with us, too."

We laugh and cook our grilled cheeses. Davy Hawthorne is my best friend, and I don't think that'll ever change.

CHAPTER THIRTY-ONE

Anna Decides

ANNABEL - NOW

The sound of the front door closing might as well be a bomb going off. Everything I was afraid of just blew up in my face. I don't know what I'm going to do.

I should call Atty back. Probably beg for his forgiveness. Tell him I didn't mean for this to hurt him. Explain that this wasn't a whim. I love David.

There's so much here that Atty doesn't know. I don't blame him for being mad. David was right, we should have told him right away. Not that I'm convinced it would have helped, but telling him instead of getting caught would have been an improvement.

Well, one thing's for sure, I'm in no state to talk to him now. I'll take a shower, make some tea and toast. That's it. Food makes everything better. When my head is on straight, I can make a plan.

I feel clean but not particularly calmer. I read a meme once about how women have four types of showers: body only, body and hair, everything, or rock in the corner as your tears flow down the drain shower.

It was the last kind.

I'd like to say I cried myself out, but getting dressed inspires a fresh wave when my eyes land on David's sweatshirt.

The familiarity of the kitchen helps. The sounds, the smells. As I nibble on my toast and sip my tea, I try to formulate a plan. My mind is blank, though.

How do I choose between the man I've loved my entire life and my brother? David makes me happier than I've ever been. He is my rock. Atty is my family, my blood. We share a lifetime of memories and matching scars from the loss of our mother. If I lose him, do I lose the rest of my brothers too? My dad?

The buzzing of my phone interrupts my emotional spiral. My heart drops. I'm really starting to hate this thing.

It's a FaceTime request from Grace. I decline, but it immediately buzzes again. Swallowing the lump in my throat, I reject the call again, only for a message to appear.

Grace:

> **Pick up or I'm getting in the car right now.**

My stomach twists, making me regret the little toast I've gotten down. This time, when the request comes in, I answer. No words form, no idea what I'd say even if I could.

Grace's pretty face fills the screen, her eyes tight with concern. At least she isn't scowling. "I'd ask how you are, but you look like shit." I sniff and look up at the ceiling as fresh tears brim. How am I not dried up by now? "Oh, honey. I may love your brother, but he is a stubborn ass sometimes."

Gasping, I blink to refocus on her. "You're really not angry?"

She scoffs. "Honey, you and David have been stuck in this dance since high school. Only an idiot would miss it—like your brother."

"Don't blame him, Gracie. He has a right to be mad. I hid this. He's only asked one thing of me, and I let him down." I poke my toast on the plate, no longer interested in eating it.

"Ok, yea, probably would have been better if you told him. But he doesn't get to tell you who to love. If you didn't like me, would you tell him he had to choose?"

"No, of course not."

"If Nic and Huck slept together, would you stop talking to either of them?"

I wrinkle my nose at the mental picture. "No... but it'd definitely gross me out."

Grace smiles. "Yea. I think he's more shocked than mad, honey. He doesn't like thinking of his baby sister as all grown up and having sex. Give him time to calm down."

Closing my eyes, I voice my inner fears. "What if he doesn't, Grace? I can't lose him. Any of them. Not again. Not after Momma."

When I open my eyes again, Grace's expression pinches. Her lips are tight and her eyes glisten. "I'm so sorry, Bella. This isn't fair to you. I honestly don't think any of the other boys will care, though. You heard Rhett. Atticus is being an idiot, and he'll be sorry when he's sleeping on the couch tonight. See how quickly he changes his tune after days with no sex."

"Ew." I chuckle despite myself. "I appreciate the support, but not sure that'll help."

"Just give it time. I'm on summer break, so say the word and I'll drive down for a visit. I know you have Bree and Nic there, but sometimes you need a sister." She blushes slightly and worries her lip.

"Sister time might be nice. I'll think about it. Love you, Grace. I'm glad Atty brought you into our lives."

Grace blinks repeatedly, widening her eyes and looking up. "Fuck. Love you too, Bella. Call if you need anything."

I'm so lucky to have Grace. For how long, though? What if Atty doesn't come around? What if he makes both of us pick a side? I'll never forgive myself if I come between them.

What am I going to do?

Hours later, I still have no solution. I have seventy-two cupcakes, four dozen lemon squares, five loaves of bread, and fifteen pre-made crock pot meals. But no solutions.

It might be time to accept I can't have my cake and eat it too.

Or I can pop on downstairs, lose myself to the distractions of the kitchen, and run from my problems.

Definitely the second one.

The dinner rush is in full swing, I'm not supposed to be working today, so every station already has a person on it. Over at the grill, white tickets are piling up. Whatever the lunch special is, it's impacting the line and we need another set of hands.

"Hey, Heather, looks like you can use some help. Where should I start?" I try for a sympathetic smile, but her eyes widen a little. Must have come across more of a grimace.

"T-Thanks, Chef. It's this special grilled cheese! That's why..."

All sound in the kitchen fades away as Heather's words hit me like a ton of bricks. My chest squeezes. My ears ring. Special grilled cheese.

David.

"What did you say?" I turn to Heather, but it's not her face I'm picturing.

"I said this grilled cheese special is super popular, so I'm falling behind."

Tony snorts out a laugh. "Ha! Falling! Everyone hide the beans."

"Oh, shut up, Tony." Heather is glaring at him, but I stand frozen.

"The secret family recipe." That's it. That's my answer.

I want a lifetime of special grilled cheese sandwiches. I don't want to imagine a future without my brother. Atty is my hero, but he's moving on. He's marrying Grace. Before we know it, they'll have kids and split holidays between grandparents. Coaching baseball games on the weekend. Atty gets to move on with the love of his life. Why can't I?

The past decade has shown me I *can* live without David Hawthorne. The past months have taught me I don't *want* to.

"Uh, Chef? What recipe?" Heather's words startle me from my trance.

I shake my head to clear the last cobwebs. "Tony, come help Heather catch up. Even if you only prep the sandwiches for her to grill." I turn to the joker in question with a raised brow. "I trust you are capable of making a sandwich?" Heather snickers beside me.

Tony's ears redden. "Yes, Chef."

"Good. I gotta go." I feel their eyes on me, but I don't stop to explain as I rush through the back door and across the employee lot.

My legs burn as they eat up the distance to David's house. After months of running this route together, I move on autopilot while I mentally work out what I want to say.

I slam through the white gate in front of the house and speed up the walkway. My knuckles sting as I rap them against the blue door. The light turns on over my head as I wait. Chest heaving and lungs burning, I struggle to catch my breath.

The door opens, and there stands David. His broad shoulders fill the doorway as he stares down at me. Tousled dark hair and disheveled clothes give the impression that he rolled out of bed. His comforting spicy smell wraps me in a warm embrace. I close my eyes and breathe more deeply to take it in.

"Davy, I..." I step closer so I can better see his face. The words sputter out as I look into his eyes, which lack their familiar warmth. His lips form a straight line, no hint of his usual smile.

Something is very wrong.

Well, I did kick him out of my apartment this morning. That was hours ago. I shouldn't have waited so long. He's understandably upset, but we'll get past this.

"Annabel, I was going to call you later. I've been thinking a lot about this, and maybe Ace has a point."

"What?" I rub my chest, his words tearing through me. This can't be happening.

David's jaw muscle spasms, the only reaction on his face. "Look, you'll always be my first love, but I can't do this anymore."

Thunder booms in the distance.

"No. I love you, what are you saying?" Hot tears trail down my cheeks. I don't bother to wipe them away. This isn't David. My David wouldn't do this. "You don't mean it."

Before my eyes, all traces of the man I love disappear. His brows lower over his eyes as he stands taller and wider. The intense man in front of me is Sergeant Hawthorne, a complete stranger. "This is too much drama. I should have considered the consequences. It's over."

"You promised." The words are barely a whisper. The pain in my chest is overwhelming, like I can physically feel my heart break. My throat burns with repressed sobs.

What just happened? I came here to tell David I want to spend my life with him, and instead I'm leaving with a piece of my soul missing.

A flash of lightning highlights the planes of his face, adding to the harshness of his expression. Shaking my head, I back away. I hold my hands in front of me, unsure if I'm reaching for Davy or trying to push this stranger away.

As the first wracking sob escapes, I turn and run back to my apartment. Half a block away, the skies open and rain pours down on me. Almost as if the angels share my heartbreak. The lights of Pop shine in the distance.

I. Keep. Running.

My sneaker skids on the wet asphalt, and I go down hard on my knee. Instead of getting up, I half lay in the parking lot. The ground is still warm from a day of soaking up the sun. The rainfall bounces off every surface and reflects the bright lights into starbursts.

I bow my head and let it all out. The pain. The irony. My shoulders shake as wave after wave of sobs rack my body. My worst fears came true, yet I was still willing to pay any price for a life with David. With the boy next door.

A keening wail echoes over the pounding rain. It takes me a minute to realize the noise is coming from me. My head hangs almost to my knees. The water has soaked through everything, my clothes and hair cling to me.

A heavy fabric drops around my shoulders. "Jesus Christ," a male voice mutters.

He came after all! But as I look up, I find Asher wrapping a towel around me instead of David.

"Can you stand?" Asher shouts over the downpour. With his hands under my armpits, it's a near thing, but I rise without knocking us over again. Numbly, I let him lead me through the back door and up the stairs to my apartment.

Before I know it, I'm sitting on the edge of the bathtub, shivering as Asher pulls off my ruined sneakers.

"I need to get some newspaper in these. Take a shower to warm up. There will be sweats waiting on your bed and tea in the kitchen." His brows pinch in a frown as he heads to the door.

"Cocoa." My voice cracks.

Asher jerks back. Maybe he didn't expect me to speak? "What?"

"Cocoa, please," I say.

"With water or milk?"

That shocks a snort out of me. I may be heartbroken here, but I'm still a foodie. "Milk. And thank you, Asher."

His lips twitch into a sad smile. "What are friends for? Get warm. We can talk—or not talk—after."

I crank the temperature hot enough to scald, wanting to feel something other than the aching numbness that has settled upon me. My knee stings as the water slides over it, turning pink before heading to the drain. I pick gravel out of the gash and scrub every inch of skin until it's red. As I slather cream on my knee, memories of the many times Davy had done this for me as a kid bombard me.

No one would have called me graceful as a child. I was constantly getting into mischief and owning up to my Hell's Bells nickname. With a doctor for a brother, you might assume he was the natural caregiver when we were kids. Not the case. Atty had no patience for his clumsy baby sister, it was always Davy that patched me up before Momma could worry.

Bundled in sweats, my hair in a towel, I pad out to the kitchen. A steaming mug waits for me. Asher stands on the other side of the counter with a matching cup. "Do you want to talk about it?"

Biting my cheek against a fresh wave of tears, I shake my head. The cocoa tastes rich on my tongue as I sip.

Asher lowers his mug with a soft click. "Are you going to be ok?"

With a sniff, I nod. I learned to live without him once, I can do it again. It'll be so much harder this time, but I will stay strong.

"Call me if you need anything. I'll stick around and keep an eye on things until we close." Asher hesitates by my stool, then pulls me into a brotherly side hug.

Physical contact isn't really our thing, but I appreciate the comfort. I lean into him and rest my head on his shoulder for a moment. My support network is stronger than last time. I'll get through this fine. After a brief kiss on the top of my head, Asher heads back out.

Before I can wallow too deeply in my grief, my cell rings in the bedroom. Atty's name flashes on the screen. I perch on the bed and answer with trembling hands. "Hello?"

"Hi. Haven't heard from you all day, so I figured I'd check in." The tension hangs heavy between us. I've never felt more awkward with my own brother. Atty clears his throat, breaking the silence. "Listen. I was a little harsh this morning. Whether or not I had a right to be mad, I shouldn't have said what I did. I'm sorry."

I squeeze my eyes against the welling tears and pinch the bridge of my nose. "Me too," I whisper.

"I hate the idea of the two of you. I wasn't kidding, my friendship with him is over. He broke the bro-code, but you're my sister and family sticks together. So..."

My stomach clenches. I'm going to be sick. Unable to hear another word, I rush to interrupt. "It doesn't matter anymore. We split up." My body spasms as if the words are a physical blow.

"Oh, well... I think that's for the best."

"Yea. I.. I got to go. I'll talk to you soon." I hold my breath, praying the ground swallows me whole.

"Sure, probably busy at the restaurant tonight. I love you, Bella Bug."

"Love you, too."

I end the call and curl onto my side on the covers. As tears silently bathe my cheeks, I reach for the pillow and clutch it to my aching chest. David's smell lingers on the sheets, taunting me. I don't know how long I lay there before I drift to sleep.

When I wake, the apartment is dark. The only light I find on is the one over the stove. A note sits illuminated on top of the surface.

Anna,

Didn't want to disturb you. There's a sandwich in the fridge for you. Please eat something. I don't want to see you downstairs until the dinner shift.

Asher

The microwave tells me it's almost three in the morning. My stomach grumbles, reminding me I haven't eaten in over twelve hours. I pull out the covered plate, and without bothering to sit, I eat over the sink.

Tonight I'll mourn the loss of what could have been. Tomorrow I'll get back to my regularly scheduled life. Starting with scrubbing every memory of that man out of my house. And my sheets.

CHAPTER THIRTY-TWO

Surprise Visits

ANNABEL - NOW

"**O**rder up." I bring the plate of perfectly golden scallops to the pass, double checking the amount of lemon butter sauce and sprinkle of chives. It looks perfect. I only hope it tastes good. Momma always said my cooking is so good because it's made with love, but today all I feel is emptiness.

"Tony, how's that sauce coming?" I barely spare a glance at him as I move on to the next ticket. All day, I've been going through the motions, hoping to feel like me again.

"Almost ready, Chef." Tony's voice is lacking his usual playfulness. I must be hiding my hurt worse than I thought.

"Um, Chef." I look up as Chrissy calls me from the pass. My brows pinch at her flushed expression. "There's someone here to see you. A man, blond, and in a suit."

Tony perks up from his station. "Inspector?"

We're not due for any checks. It's not tax season, and auditors would be asking for Bree.

Chrissy's blush deepens. "He said it was personal."

"Someone's sure popular lately," Ryan mutters.

"Ok, Meeka take over." I remove my apron and chef coat. I don't have cooking in me today, anyway.

As I follow Chrissy to the hostess stand, I look around the restaurant I've built. Lively chatter fills the space. Couples, families, business meetings. It's a mixing pot of purposes but everyone leaves full and happy. I try to feel my usual sense of accomplishment, but my bruised heart is subdued.

More people congregate in the waiting area, among them a familiar blond man. He stands apart from the crowd, looking unbelievably handsome in an expensive suit. As our eyes meet, his lips spread into a grin, and I break into a sprint. He catches me in his arms and holds me close as I fight my brimming tears.

"Woah there, sis. I got you." Tommy's voice rumbles in my ear and his big hand rubs my back.

I squeeze him tighter, soaking in his comfort. "What are you doing here? You should have come around the back."

"Had a meeting in Jacksonville, decided I'd drive the rest of the way to surprise my favorite sister."

"Are you hungry?" I lean back and give him a watery smile.

Tommy drops a kiss on my forehead. "For your cooking? Always."

"Would you like a seat in the restaurant, Chef? Ms. Chance's table is still available." Bree has a standing Friday reservation in her favorite booth.

"That would be great, Chrissy, thank you." She's blushing again as she eyes my brother. Goodness gracious, that's going to get old fast. I'm so not used to seeing my brothers all grown up.

We sit and are quickly served—just one of the perks of being the owner. My mind whirls with all the reasons Tommy might be here. In five years,

Daddy has come a couple times, but my brothers haven't seen it since that first day.

Did he hear about the blowup with Atty? My cocktail napkin turns to confetti in my fingers as I shred it. Is Tommy going to yell at me, too? I sneak a look at him, but he's looking around the restaurant instead of paying attention to me.

"This is amazing, Bella. You've created something special here." His blue eyes are full of sincerity and affection as he looks back at me. He reaches across the table and grabs my icy hands, still clutching the mutilated paper. "I'm so proud of you. This is where you're meant to be."

My shoulders relax. The guilt I've felt about running from Hitchcock lightens at his words. I was worried I'd missed too much of my brothers' lives. That I'd abandoned them when they needed me. Seeing the confidence and pride on his face reassures me I wasn't selfish, but I can't help the twinge that remains. "Really?"

"Of course! You're the one who inspired me to go into business. Showed me there was a world beyond Hitchcock full of riches to be found." His lips twist into a grin. "Speaking of which," he shifts and pulls an envelope out of his suit jacket before sliding it across the table, "this is for you."

I lick my lip as I pick up the simple white rectangle and open it. Inside is a check for a quarter of a million dollars. "What is this? I can't accept this."

"That's yours. It's the investment we discussed."

"But I only gave you ten thousand! How did you possibly turn that into this in two months?"

His smile is practically feral as he lounges in the booth. My intellectual, awkward little brother completely morphs into a killer businessman. "I told you, I've been trading for a while. I know what I'm doing."

I blink at him in shock. Our food arrives, saving me from having to respond right away. Looking at the check one more time, I carefully fold it back into the envelope and tuck it into my pocket. "Thank you, Tommy."

He waves a fork at me with a scallop on the end. "I was serious at the cabin, Bella. You've always been there for us. This was literally the least I could do. Is it enough to do what you want?"

"Yea," I need to swallow to clear the emotion clogging my throat, "I think it is. Bree is more of the numbers and planning person, but I really think I can make the expansion work now."

He squeezes my hand one more time before we dig into our meal. We catch up a bit on fairly innocent topics. He talks about Huck's upcoming gig at a club in Atlanta and helping Rhett buy a new car for college in the fall. It is a wonderful visit and I am so very blessed to have my brothers.

I walk with him to his jeep, wishing he didn't have to go so soon. Worried about the long drive he has ahead. I'm so distracted I don't see the mood shifting.

He pulls me into a tight hug, his height and broad shoulders still feeling foreign, and then whispers in my ear. "Atticus is a selfish asshole. Huck and I chewed him out and Rhett isn't talking to him."

Freezing in his arms, I don't know how to react. Conflict within my family makes me uncomfortable. My role has always been to smooth out any ruffled feathers, so being right in the middle of this drama? Yea, that's churning me up inside.

"No, y'all shouldn't be mad at him. It doesn't matter, we broke up, anyway." My voice cracks and I will the tears to hold.

His penetrating gaze studies me. I struggle not to fidget under its weight. "Did you break up because of Atticus?"

I catch my lip between my teeth slightly as I look away. "It's for the best. Now I don't have to choose."

Tommy cups my cheeks in his hands, turning me to face him. His serious blue eyes pin me in place. "You get to live your own life, too, Bella. Go find your own happiness. Put yourself first, for once." A single traitorous tear rolls down my face. He catches it with a thumb before pulling me back into a hug, stroking my back and telling me it'll all be ok.

Once I've calmed down, I watch him drive away, then trudge back to my apartment. I let the tears fall. When I'm cried out, a little peace finds me.

Find my happiness. What does Annabel want?

With new determination, I boot up my laptop and get to work figuring that out.

Two grumpy faces stare back at me on my screen the next day.

"Why the fuck did we have to meet so goddamn early?" Nic is still in her pajamas, complete with a sleep mask pushed up on her forehead and dark circles under her eyes.

Bree looks more awake, but then again, she's always been a morning person. "It's nine a.m. lazy bones."

"Not all of us work nine-to-five, asshole. Some of us just got to bed four hours ago. New York stays up late." Nic picks up a steaming mug, cupping it between her hands more than drinking it, as she continues to grumble.

Completely used to Nic's grumpiness before noon, Bree goes on, "I'm wondering why the hell we're having a meeting without baked goods! Isn't that a rule? The baby wants lemon bars."

I smile at my friends and partners. "Sorry, Bree. I'll swing by later with some, but I need to share visual aids." I hit a couple keys so my laptop displays the proposal I put together last night.

Bree immediately perks up. The girl goes nuts for bar charts for some reason.

"I want to reopen the discussion of expanding Pop. Speed dating has a waiting list a mile long. Now with the book club meetings and women's business lunches, it's taking resources away from the already busy restaurant."

Nic opens her mouth, most likely to object, so I plow on before she can interrupt. "The space next door is coming available for lease in a month. There are separate entrances for the front and back, and we could open the wall in the kitchen so we can serve both the restaurant and event space. As a corner property, there's more street parking, combine that with the public lot down the block, and I don't think there will be a problem. But I've also looked into a second location we can use for valet down the road."

I switch slides. "This is what I think we could make based on the catering orders I already have requests for, and this is what I think it will cost. Bree, you're welcome to rerun the numbers to confirm."

She squints at the screen, the gears clearly whirling in her beautiful brain. "That looks about the same as the last time we talked."

"Anna, babe," Nic sighs. She sounds stressed, "I know you want to do this, but where is the $300,000 coming from? I could try to get it from my trust fund, but I won't have full control for months still."

"I'm glad you asked." A knock at the door interrupts me. Perfect timing. "Come in."

Asher strides into the Pop main office, eyes darting between me and the screen in front of me. "You wanted to see me? I can come back if you're not ready." His brows pinch in confusion.

"No, come in and shut the door. To get the capital for expanding, I propose we let Asher buy in as a fourth partner. We already lean on him to share responsibilities, he should share the profits as well." Three pairs of wide eyes stare back at me.

"I agree he deserves a bigger role," Bree starts, "but that's more than any of us invested. He'd be the majority holder."

"Woah, I'm honored, Anna," Asher's eyes widen at the number on the screen, "but I don't have that much cash."

"Asher wouldn't be the majority owner. I would. He would buy in at $50k, I would provide the other $250k for the expansion. I love you all, and I am so grateful that you believed in my dream. But you both have lives and careers outside of Pop. This is my baby. I'm here every day and I want to make this happen." Shocked silence follows my speech.

Then Bree bursts into tears.

"Jesus, Bree, what the fuck is your problem?" Nic's lip curls up like she's eying a ticking bomb.

"I'm sorry. I'm just so proud of you. Damn these hormones." She pulls a tissue from somewhere I don't even want to guess and blows her nose like a foghorn. "I think this is a wonderful idea. Of course, you should be the majority owner. I love doing the books and planning the events because I get to spend time with you girls, but between work and the baby, there's no way I can put as much time in as you."

"Moaning Myrtle is right. I'll be traveling even more soon. Doing the artistic aspect and working together is fun, but I don't deserve one third or even one fourth vote over anything. Your dedication has already paid back my initial investment tenfold. I trust you."

Hearing their immediate support and compliments fills something I didn't fully realize I was lacking. Sniffling back happy tears that spring to my eyes, I turn to a still silent Asher. "So what do you say? I know it's a big chunk of cash up front, but you'd get more salary than you do today. Are you in?"

"Do I still get to tend bar? Or do I need to do more managerial stuff?" He looks unsure.

"Nothing else would change. The staff turns to you if I'm not here, and we already bring you in on major discussions, anyway."

His handsome face splits into a cheery grin. "Let's do this!"

This is it. I'm getting my happiness, what I've wanted for years. My smile dims slightly as I realize I can't call the two people I want to tell the most.

CHAPTER THIRTY-THREE

Grief Casserole

DAVID - AGE 17

I watch and wait. I wish I could do more, but as a teenager myself, her grief is an enemy I don't know how to fight. It's a tangible thing, I see it on her shoulders, like a demon where an angel should be.

The Bennet house is eerily quiet for how many people cram in. It seems all of Hitchcock has turned up to pay their respects. Tom and Huck sit on the loveseat in the living room. For once, the pair of troublemakers are reserved and still. They simply stare ahead, sides pressed together.

Rhett tugs on his father's jacket. Mr. Bennet's eyes look lifeless as he stoops, and whatever his son says has him quickly mask his overwhelming grief. I take two steps to intervene, but Grace is quick to scoop up the boy as Ace comforts his father. As they pass, I hear the kid cry for his mother. It hits me right in the gut.

I make my way through her friends and family, searching for our girl. Of course she's in the kitchen. When the going gets tough, our Bella gets cooking. She's wrapped a faded blue apron around her black dress. Her eyes are red-rimmed and her nose is the slightest pink.

"Such a shame. Lizzie was so young," says a nearby woman with gray kinky hair and a black shawl.

Her friend eyes Mr. Bennet where he sits with Ace, shoulders shaking. "What's Clay going to do alone with all those kids?"

"Well," the first says, "the girl is still home, thank the Lord. I hear the oldest boy is going to defer college a year to help out."

I leave the gossipers behind, eating up the distance until I can put my arm around her shoulders. "What do you need, Bells?" Her head leans on my shoulder, wearing flats she just reaches. I drop a kiss on her head and give her a little squeeze of support.

"Those three casseroles are all set. Can you swap them out on the table, please? Grab any half-empty platters and I'll consolidate. Did your mom send those to-go containers from the diner?" Her voice is flat. My hellfire is barely a spark today and my heart twists to see it.

I turn her by her shoulders and force her chin to look up. "No, Bells, what do *you* need?"

Tears well in those dark chocolate eyes. Her nostrils flare as she fights the emotion. "I need to get through the next few hours." She sniffles and blinks, all signs of sadness disappear. "I also need to get these dang grief casseroles out of the house. They're just doubly depressin'. Who in Sam Hill puts cheese with tuna?" Her lips curl in disgust.

Bells is the most giving person I know. For years, Bella has silently picked up the pieces, the transition so seamless, I'm sure even Ace didn't realize it until their momma was bedridden. I've watched Bella take Rhett to school, teach him to tie his shoes, and read him bedtime stories. If taking care of others is the distraction Bells needs, so be it. But I am circling back to her later.

Eventually, the crush of bodies trickles out, leaving only the grieving Bennets, Grace, and me. Mr. Bennet takes a sniffling Rhett upstairs for a bath and bed. The twins wordlessly clean up cups and plates without being asked. Grace and I wash and dry the dishes as Ace resets the furniture. As the clock ticks away, even the Bennets dissipate and the house is still.

I find her in the study. Long ago, Mrs. Bennet declared this a kid-free zone. Bella runs her hands over the spines of books as she wanders the room, still in her funeral dress. I close the door a bit—sounds carry too easily in this house. Before I can approach her, she speaks.

"These were Momma's pride and joy. When she got too sick to come in here herself, she'd send me to fetch her one. Near the end, she was too weak to even hold the book, so Atty would read her poems. Poe, mostly."

On the desk in the center of the room, I put down the plate I've brought. In two strides, I have her in my arms in a tight hug. Her fingers grip my shirt as she buries her face into my shoulder in wracking cries. Pivoting our bodies, I pull her into my lap on the nearby window seat.

She turns into my body and clings. One of my hands strokes the back of her hair, while the other holds her secure. I rock her, my lips against her forehead, murmuring comforting words until she's cried out. As her sobs turn to sniffles, I move her next to me and grab the plate and a box of tissues.

Bella blows her nose as she eyes the brown and tan square. I look away to hide the warmth of my cheeks, feeling self-conscious. "You didn't eat much at the funeral. So I made you something." Once she finishes the grilled cheese, I clear the dish and swing her legs over mine so I can see her face.

She stares down at her hands clasped in her lap. "Thanks, Davy. You always seem to know what I need."

"That's what friends do. Was it any good?" I ask and wait while she nods. "Now, can I learn the secret recipe?"

That earns me the faintest curve of her lips. "I can't stand the quiet, and it's only going to get quieter." She leans her head on my shoulder, and I wrap my arm around her back in a comforting hug. "What am I going to do next year?" Her voice ends in a near whisper.

"That's months away. You'll still have Atty—didn't he switch to online classes? Plus, watching the twins navigate high school should be entertaining. You'll have to tell me all about how Huck runs the place and Tom drives the teachers nuts."

"Nothing is ever going to be the same again." Her fingers fist in my shirt and I hear her sniffle.

"No, can't say it will. But different doesn't have to mean worse." I feel Bella stiffen in my arms and rush to continue. "Right now is going to suck. You gotta grieve, but you also gotta keep going. If we don't adapt, we die. It's the nature of life, and, Hell's Bells, you got a lot'a living left to do."

"How do I live in a world without her in it?" Her voice is small as she burrows deeper into my chest. Her breath catches on the beginning of another sob.

I wedge myself tighter into the corner of the window seat and cradle her more securely. "One day at a time. Live your best life, and remember, she's always watching." My eyes burn with tears as Bella's slim body wracks with grief. I hold her in my arms and gently press my mouth against the top of her head, murmuring words of support. Eventually, the sobs fade to hiccups. Then the hiccups to even breaths.

I chance a peek at her face and see her fast asleep, still clutching at me like a lifeline. Droplets cling to her long lashes like diamonds. It's probably the first sleep she's gotten in weeks and I don't want to disturb her. I'll let her rest for a bit.

Hours later, I stir, still holding Bella as the first rays of sunshine filter through the window. I must have dozed off. Praying I don't wake her, I stand with Bella in my arms and settle her more comfortably on a small reading chaise. After covering her with a nearby blanket and dropping one more kiss on her forehead, I slip from the dark house.

CHAPTER THIRTY-FOUR

Mission Mode

A sharp cracking reaches my ears seconds before I feel the slight impact against my cheek. "Fuck!"

"What did that computer do to you?" Ronnie rolls his chair back to catch my eye around the monitor.

I look down at my keyboard, which is now missing a backspace button. It's possible I took my frustrations out on the keys—and the coffee pot I'd shattered this morning. Not trusting my words, I grunt at him.

Everything feels wrong. The sun shines less bright. Food tastes less flavorful. Nightmares plagued what little sleep I'd gotten, and every inch of my skin stretches so tight it's about to split open. Not even the ten-mile run helped the tension.

"Woah, there. Who pissed in your cereal? Do I need to call Bella for some stress relief for you?" He waggles his dark eyebrows at me suggestively. "Either baking or banging, you can choose."

The copper taste of blood hits my tongue as I bite my cheek. I carefully keep my face blank. Mission mask. "That would be a waste. We broke up."

"The fuck? What do you mean, you broke up?"

I shrug and turn back to the email I've read a dozen times and still have no idea what it says. Come on, Ronnie. Just drop it.

Of course he doesn't.

"What did you do? You've barely looked at another woman in the time I've known you. There's no way you ended things."

"Ace found out and didn't approve. Shit got ugly. He told her to choose."

"And she chose him? That's cold, brother." I swallow the lump in my throat, but don't correct him. Let him think it was her decision. It'll keep Ronnie from digging. "I thought she was better than that." He scoffs.

My stomach twists with guilt, but he can't know the truth.

"Guess we don't need this surveillance report, then." Ronnie moves to toss a manilla envelope into the trash but I reach for it.

"Pop is still a client, even if Annabel and I aren't dating." I flip through the photos and swear under my breath as a familiar face appears. That tattoo isn't a damn oar. The file includes two pages of known aliases and a string of crimes. This is Bella's attacker.

Abandoning the email yet again, I lock my computer and walk out the door. Folder and keys in hand.

Friendship Springs's police station is empty when I stride through the ancient double doors. It resembles mall security more than an official station—the joys of a small town. The library, town hall, DMV, and post office all share a building on the edge of downtown.

Deputy Ramirez looks up and sneers at me as I approach the main desk. "What do you want?"

"I have new evidence on the Pop attack." I toss the file across the wooden surface so it lands in front of the other man.

Ramirez flips through the pages. His scowl deepens with each page. "How did you get this?"

"Smith and Hawthorne provides security for Pop and Miss Bennet's apartment above. Miss Bennet came to us when her recipes went missing and this is the footage we found."

He gives a dry laugh. "Miss Bennet? You mean your girlfriend?"

"Not that it's relevant to this conversation, but I am not currently in a relationship with Miss Bennet."

A gleam of interest lights in his eyes. "Is that so?"

It was only a matter of time before the smug bastard figured it out and tried to shoot his shot again. The way Colin tells it, Ramirez has been sniffing around Bella for years. Almost feel bad for the guy that he's failed so utterly.

Almost.

Taking a deep breath through my nose, I tower over the man and tap the open file. "I believe this is the same perp as the original attack."

His lip curls as he closes the folder and pushes it back to me. "Belief and feelings may have been enough in the Marines, but in the justice system, we need proof. This proves nothing."

Son of a bitch. I clench my jaw and breathe to calm down. "What would be sufficient, Deputy Ramirez?" I aim for respectful, but it probably comes out more sarcastic based on his expression.

"Recorded confession. But as Florida is a two-party consent state, good luck with that."

Grabbing the file off the desk, I leave without another word. I know all about surveillance and consent laws. There's a simple workaround, it just needs a little strategy.

An idea forms in my head, but I'll need a little help. Pulling out my cell, I shoot off a quick text.

A response flashes on my screen almost immediately. It simply says, "When and where." A sense of calm washes over me as I drive back to my house. I can feel myself slipping into mission mode. Emotions clicking off and cold logic turning on.

This is what I need to get through today.

As the designated time approaches, I pace my kitchen. Ronnie eyes me from his perch on the counter, sipping a beer. His typical humor is absent as he awaits orders. Finally, the doorbell rings and I take off, my boots echoing in the silent house. It's been too quiet without Bella, like she's taken all the sound from my life.

Focus, Marine.

I open the door to reveal Asher on the front step, as expected. What I don't expect is the dark head behind him. "What's he doing here?" Stepping back, I let the two men in.

Asher's shoulders lift slightly, making his man bun bounce. "He's good at planning." Shaking my head, I follow them into the kitchen. I pass out beers as I make quick introductions.

Ronnie lifts an ebony brow at the two men. "I get why the bartender is here—we need an inside man—but what's the pretty boy going to do?"

I snort. He's not wrong. Even in a black tee and jeans, Johnson looks more model than Marine.

Crossing his arms, Johnson levels Ronnie with a deadpan look. "Didn't your mama ever tell you not to judge a book by its cover? I helped Colin and Bree take down the asshole leaking corporate secrets last year. Anna is my friend, and I want to help."

A harsh, humorous laugh comes from Ronnie. "So you think because you Hardy Boys took down a white collar schmuck you are ready for a violent serial criminal? Leave it to the professionals, pretty boy."

"This isn't helping. He's already here. Let's just get started," I growl. Both men nod but continue to glare at each other.

"Here's what we know." I spread papers neatly on the counter. "We have evidence of this man breaking into the apartment above Pop and taking Miss Bennet's personal recipe box. Facial recognition and prints match a Bruce Hayes, age twenty-eight, from Houston, Texas. A conman, Hayes has a dozen known aliases, and we can link him to a slew of open cases across the country. We believe he is the same man behind the attack in June."

Asher scowls at the photo in his hand, no doubt feeling betrayed by the familiar face he never suspected. Johnson studies the rap sheet. "None of these are violent crimes. Why did his pattern change?"

"That's true," Ronnie sounds surprised, "the other charges were embezzlement and credit fraud, typically against women he dated. Miss Bennet fits the victim profile, but not the crime."

"Anna doesn't date." Asher winces as his gaze darts to me. "Well, didn't, and especially not someone from Pop. His usual angle wouldn't have worked. Maybe he got desperate. One thing is bothering me though, why didn't he take the bank bag? It was still in the office when I arrived the next morning."

"Colin said the cops got there pretty fast. He probably panicked and ran out without the cash." Johnson tosses the papers down and turns to Asher. "All the crimes fit an identical structure. That doesn't say criminal mastermind to me. If he wasn't expecting Anna to be there and shit went sideways, he could have gone full Leeroy Jenkins." Johnson looks at each of us, but the room stays silent.

I grit my teeth. "What the fuck are you talking about?"

Johnson leans on the counter and stares with wide eyes. "Come on. Leeroy Jenkins? Seriously? So none of you game? It's when someone just charges in without a plan and royally fucks the mission up." He shakes his head and I notice his ears turning red.

Asher clears his throat. "So I'm assuming you brought all this to Ramirez, and he said it was all circumstantial and he needed more." My head snaps towards him. "What? I listen to true crime podcasts. I know things."

Ronnie groans behind me, but I keep my eyes on Asher. "Cops want a confession on video. Our best bet is to get him talking by a security camera at Pop. That's where you come in, Asher."

He shakes his head. "Naw man, he knows I'm loyal to Anna, he'd never open up in front of me. The man's a narcissist, and judging by his victims, a sexist. We need to appeal to his hurt ego." Asher looks me in the eye. "You got to do it."

"Do you listen to psych podcasts too? Jesus." I ignore Ronnie's mutters behind me.

"All criminals want credit deep down. They're proud and want you to know it was them." Asher takes a swig of his beer.

"Oh yea," Johnson's lips spread into a grin, "with a little encouragement you can get their whole villain monologue on camera. Trust me."

I look back and forth between the two men in front of me. How the hell did they do in minutes what two highly skilled Marines couldn't do in days? Granted, Ronnie and I are used to having a bigger team with other specialties. We should have pulled these two in ages ago.

"Well, fuck, chalk one up for the junior detective agency." Ronnie jumps off the counter and joins us at the island. "So how does David get him talking, then?"

Asher stares me down, his mouth a hard slant. "I have an idea. It's going to be tough, but if you want to get the bastard, I think it's the only way."

My stomach turns to lead. I can tell I'm not going to like what he says next. Can I do this?

For Bella, I'd do anything. Even carve out my own heart.

T he USB drops to the desk with a satisfying clatter. Deputy Ramirez jerks at the noise. Some cop, he's too busy on his phone to notice me coming in.

As he realizes who disturbed him, his surprise morphs to anger. "You again? What now?"

I nod at the hunk of plastic. "There's your confession."

Ramirez heaves a sigh, then picks up the drive and plugs it into the nearby PC. The video automatically starts playing.

"What's got a guy like you so down?"

I know I'm not visible in the clip, but my voice is clear on the recording. "What else? Women trouble. A man can do everything but one thing, if you know what I mean?"

A hearty chuckle crackles on the speakers. "Oh, I know. Nothing is as satisfying as the real deal. You bagged Chef Bennet, though. She can bake you biscuits and then butter them for you, too. Lucky man." He laughs at his own joke.

"Yea, she's hot alright." I give an exaggerated sigh. "Didn't work out. Guess it's true what they say about nice guys."

"Damn, successful women are heartless. Bet she was a good fuck." He stubs out his cigarette and looks around before lowering his voice. "You should thank me. If it wasn't for me, she never would have run into your arms in the first place."

"What are you talking about?"

"Figured I'd take my due out of the office safe, didn't expect her to still be in the kitchen! Whole thing went sideways. Bitch hit me with a pan, but I got my own in the end."

"Oh yea?"

His lips spread into a malicious smile. "Yea. Kicking her wasn't nearly enough, I'm going to make the Bennet bitch pay."

As the recording ends, Ramirez looks at me appraisingly. "This could easily get thrown out as entrapment."

I cross my arms over my chest, expression even. "Except I'm not a cop, I never lied, and he'd already committed the crime beforehand."

"Still doesn't solve the consent issue."

Prepared, I drop an envelope on the desk. "When we installed the security cameras, Miss Bennet had all employees sign a consent form. Idiot signed it and had this conversation clearly within view of the back camera."

Sucking his teeth, Ramirez nods slowly. "Ok. I'll give it to you, you thought this one through. I'll draw up the paperwork for a warrant and bring the scum in." With a curt nod, I turn back towards the double doors. As my hand grips the handle, Ramirez calls out to me. "How'd you get through all that without punching him?"

"If I lost it, we wouldn't get the bastard and Bella would still be in danger." I leave a stunned Ramirez still staring after me as I head back to the office to catch up on work.

CHAPTER THIRTY-FIVE

Pasta and Procrastination

ANNABEL - NOW

I'm the only one to blame. Why do I do this to myself? There's a heck of a lot of better ways to get some excitement in one's life than procrastination.

As I survey the nearly empty kitchen around me, my stomach churns. Weeks ago, I agreed to this catering job, but that was before—well, before everything. Now it's Tuesday, our early close night, and instead of avoiding my emotions with a tub of Ben & Jerry's and Netflix binge session, I'm staring at a $5000 order due tomorrow.

It's going to be a long night.

I meant to start this ages ago. First, I was too busy with my love bubble. Then, too distracted by the emotional aftermath of Atty and David. Then, just too dang depressed to cook.

That was new for me.

Today, I even ran off to visit with Bree for a few hours to escape reality. She was grateful for the freezer meals.

Bree is the most capable woman I've ever met. The woman can pick apart complex problems in her head and implement solutions effortlessly. It's why she's the Chief Product Officer of a major engineering firm. Even she is human, though. So I'm happy I can take one thing off her plate when the baby comes.

It was great until Colin came home. I love him like another brother. Seriously, he is perfect for Bree, and I'm so glad I helped them work through their crap. But seeing the two of them so crazy happy with this amazing new phase of life starting made the broken bits of me feel, well, more broken.

Slowly, I lose myself to the monotony of cooking. I focus on each tomato as I prepare them for the pot. The scent of onion and garlic overwhelms the senses, bringing back comforting memories of my mother's kitchen growing up. As I find my groove, I hum along to the Top Forty music streaming from my phone.

I mentally tick through my to-do list. Chicken prepped and ready to be cooked through. Coffee cake just needs to be cut. Fillings for finger sandwiches prepared, waiting for assembly last minute so they don't get soggy. I'll have one of the line cooks prep the salads tomorrow. Almost everything else can wait, it's really just finishing this alla vodka sauce, and I can reward myself with a bubble bath and a glass of wine!

As I turn to grab the bottle of vodka next to my phone on the counter, a looming shadow startles me. With a half-shriek, I find Ryan standing nearby. "Heaven's to Betsy, you scared me." My chest heaves as I try to slow my pounding heart. "What are y'all still doing here? I thought everyone left."

"Forgot something, so came back for it." His gaze is intense, but his face is otherwise blank. He runs his fingers through his dark hair. A tattoo near his wrist catches my eye. A skull with crossed knife and spatula.

"Oh, o-ok. Did you get it?" The hair on the back of my neck stands. Picking up my phone, I pause the music and launch the panic app. Moving closer to the counter, I keep Ryan within my line of sight and my phone in hand behind my back. After the last attack, I'm probably being paranoid, but I'd rather be safe than sorry.

"Not yet. What are you cooking?" He steps to the right, so he stays directly across from me in the narrow aisle. He crosses his arms and muscles flex his short sleeves. I'm not sure I've seen him outside a chef coat before.

"Penne alla vodka. The women's business association hired us to cater a brunch." I try to keep my voice even.

Ryan scoffs, and his lips twist into a sneer. "Typical."

Warning bells go off in the back of my mind. I wouldn't say I've been close to Ryan, but we got on fine in the kitchen, though without the same banter as the other staff. There's always been something slightly off about him, and keeping professional barriers in place seemed best. Especially after he hit on me a few times.

My fingers search the side of the phone case for the volume switch. Finding it, I push and hold it all the way down so it won't give me away. Got to keep him talking. "How so?"

"Women needing a special association because they can't hack it in the real world."

"And that upsets you?" My thumb slides along the edge of the phone.

"Of course. Some of us have to actually work and earn everything we get, not have it handed to us. Women have it so easy."

When I find the power button, I hit it five times. "And that makes you mad."

"Damn right. Though I figured in this case I could make feminism work for me. If women can marry for money, why can't I? Two single business owners, thought I could cash in. You're both attractive enough it wouldn't have been a burden. But that mixed bitch is never around and once Soldier Boy showed up, you wouldn't look at me twice."

I gulp at the acid rising in my throat. This guy is unhinged. My hand trembles as I let go of the phone and feel for something I can use as a weapon. It takes everything in me not to turn and check the panic app.

"Then I figured I'd just take your recipes and sell them. Maybe a publishing or tv deal. Good thing I tested them first. You may be a successful chef, but you are a shit baker. They were awful."

My fingers brush cold glass and I shift for a better grip. "That's 'cuz Momma always left something out. Without a secret, they aren't family recipes."

Sirens echo in the distance. Please hurry.

"That's dumb as fuck. What are you doing?" His hand lashes out to grasp my throat.

The instant pain is distracting, but my fight-or-flight instinct kicks in and the adrenaline spurs me on. I swing with all my strength. A crash sounds as the vodka bottle connects with Ryan's head, followed by the tinkling of falling glass. Cold liquid splashes and I turn away, raising my arms to protect my face.

"You fucking bitch! You'll pay for that." Blood drips from an open gash on his temple. The red trails make his manic expression more sinister.

As he lurches forward, hands ready for another strike, I dive towards the stove. The burner dial clicks in my hand. I crank it up as I curl into a tiny ball against the tiles. A whooshing sound and a terrible scream echo over me. The sirens grow louder.

When the blow I expect never lands, I chance a peek up. Ryan is slapping at his still smoking shirt as blisters form across the exposed red skin.

Villain a la flambé. You'd think a pastry chef would understand the dangers of vodka and open flame.

Two officers burst in through the back door, guns drawn. I remain on the floor as they recite his rights and slap cuffs on him. Even as they drag a cursing Ryan out, I stay still. Warm hands cup my shoulders.

David!

I push off the ground and leap into waiting arms, gripping his shirt tight. The material is stiff under my fingers and smells unfamiliar. I lean back, finding brown eyes where I expect hazel. With a gasp, I step back out of Billy's embrace.

His brows pinch and as he reaches for me again, I retreat, nearly slipping in the mess on the floor. "Careful."

Avoiding his eyes, I busy myself canceling the panic alarm on my phone. "Guess this app works."

"Good thing you got that security system or we might not have caught him in time. Though you seem to have handled it well enough on your own. You feeling up to a statement now? Or do you want to come by the station tomorrow?"

Might as well get this over with. As succinctly as possible, I go over the events with Billy. From realizing Ryan was behind me all the way to the vodka and fire. He takes notes and asks the occasional question, but the whole thing is straightforward.

"Anna!" I look up as Asher runs through the doors and pulls me into a hug. "Are you ok?"

"Asher? What are you doing here?"

"I got a text when you hit the panic button, but didn't read it right away. I'm so sorry, Anna. Are you ok?" He pushes me back and looks me over, his handsome face marred with stress.

"Yea, I'm fine. I need another bottle of vodka so I can remake the dang blasted sauce."

With a groan, Asher gives me a small shake. "Would you worry about yourself for one goddamn minute? I'll have Tony make it in the morning and Meeka can take care of the rest of the order." He pulls his cell out of his back pocket and starts typing.

Billy clears his throat. "If you think of anything else, give me a call. If you'll excuse me, I'll go check on things back at the station." With a tip of his head, he leaves.

Asher looks up from his flying fingers to pin me with a look, his eyes still tight. "You aren't staying here tonight. If you need to, you can stay with me, but I don't have a spare room."

I try to wave him off. "I'll crash at Nic's for the night, but honestly, I'm fine. They caught the guy and all the security doo-dads worked." Asher frowns down at me, his forehead wrinkling. "What? Seriously. I'm ok."

Asher continues to hover like a mother hen while I pack a bag. Finally, I snap at him to go clean up if he wants to be helpful. I check my phone for the hundredth time. Nothing from David. Can't say why, I've just come to expect him to be there when I need help.

The kitchen is spotless when I come down with my stuff. Asher locks up and leads me to my car. I see a familiar tall shape from the corner of my eye, but when I look, only shadows stand at the edge of the parking lot.

I could have sworn I saw Davy, but it must have been a trick of the light.

I force my lips into a smile as I thank Asher. He stays by my door as I turn the key. When I check my mirrors and pull out, he still hasn't moved. As I drive through the silent night, one thought repeats in my head.

It's really over. He didn't come.

Chapter Thirty-Six

Lucky Charm

David - Age 20

Seven blissful days. That's how long I got to know what it feels like to be loved by Annabel Bennet. Seven days of rides to nowhere, just talking and holding hands. Seven nights making love under the stars.

The night before I ship out, I hardly sleep. Bella cuddles beside me in the bed of my truck. I smooth her hair and admire how perfectly she fits in my arms. I commit each detail of her to memory. The sound of her voice, the smell of her shampoo, every freckle on her precious face.

It feels so damn right. I barely remember a time before Bella, she's so rooted into my life, but this blossoming thing between us, it's like waking in color after a lifetime living in black and white. Still my life, only infinitely richer, and I don't want it to end.

I'm not a fool. The next few years are going to be tough as hell. Months apart, maybe only days together. Loving each other through letters once a month and the odd video call. I signed a six-year minimum contract. Bella will already be a year out of college by the time I'm free to settle down. And Bella better be going to college—I'm not dragging her from base to base.

My lips curve into a smirk as I realize I'm planning our lives together. It's a dream that will keep me going as I leave the only life I've known. As dawn breaks, I gently wake her. She's somber as we pack up the truck and sneak back home.

Tears roll down her cheeks as she looks up at me next to her kitchen door. I dry her eyes with my thumbs as my lips capture hers. Her breath catches as she opens for me, her hands clutch mine still on her face. I pour into the kiss everything I feel for her, the words I dare not say out loud. Her eyes fill with longing as I pull back.

"Davy, I…" her voice falters.

I lower my forehead to hers. "Shh, baby, me too." I squeeze my eyes and drop one more peck to her crown before pulling away. If I don't leave now, I can't guarantee I won't go AWOL to stay with her. "Be good, Bells. Keep out of trouble for me."

A touch of sass fires in her gaze. There's my girl. "Look who's talking. Don't you go being a hero now, David. Get your butt back home in one piece, ya hear?"

She always makes me laugh. "Yes, ma'am." I back away, my eyes on hers until the last possible second. As I turn the corner, an ache spreads in my chest. Miss her already.

"Hey, man." I jump a solid foot in the air. So lost in my own thoughts, I don't see Ace sitting on his front porch.

"You scared the shit out of me, brother." How long has he been there?

Ace smiles and pats the steps next to him. Did he see me and Bells? Is he going to kill me? I study his face as I sit down. Dark circles mar his face. His hair is shaggy and stands in a halo around his head.

"So much for super soldier." Ace bumps me with his shoulder.

"You gotta wait for super training for that, I've only been through basic." We chuckle, but it's flat.

"I'm going to miss you, brother. It's been you, me, and Bug forever." His voice cracks at the end.

I press my arm against his in support. "You still have Bella."

"For how long?" He looks up at the brightening sky. "I realized this week she's all grown up. I can't keep her here, she's too good for this place. She's going to do such amazing things." He stares off, as if he's picturing everything she could accomplish.

My heart drops and my palms sweat. Am I holding her back?

"Thank you for taking care of Bella," Ace continues. Does he know? I might actually be sick. "She tries to hide it, but I can tell she's struggling. I'm worried one more blow and she'll crack completely. She needed that one night of normal. You know?" He wraps his arm around me in a rare side hug. "I'm so grateful you've always had my back, brother."

That final farewell from Ace plays on repeat in my mind. On the long flight to special training. Through weeks of classes.

Then her first letter arrives.

As I read her words, the color comes back to my world again. Confidence grows within me with each page I devour. I've never—would never—ask her to put her life on hold while I serve. If anything, this is my angel's time to spread her wings. I'll root for her from afar and once my contract is over, follow her anywhere.

Filled with renewed hope, I write to her and tell her everything in my heart. The future I see for us, from her days as a famous chef to my Friday nights coaching our son's football team. I tell her to go chase her dreams, and I'll find her when I'm on the other side, with a diamond ring in my hand.

I carefully tuck the letter in my trunk, safe until the next mail call, and head out on my mission. We're checking surveillance equipment behind enemy lines. Silently, we trek through the dunes in single file at night. My foot slips in the sand and grazes something metal. Time stills. I turn and see a flashing red light. As I squeeze my eyes and prepare for death, all I see is my Annabel. Her smile. The curve of her hip.

"Hey brother, you alright?" Another Marine slowly approaches, scanning the terrain around his feet before stepping.

"Not really. Seem to have found a mine. No idea why it hasn't gone off yet." Every muscle in my body tenses.

"You got one hell of a guardian angel." The man squats and gingerly uncovers the explosive.

My angel. An image of Bella sobbing over her mother's grave comes to me. Ace's voice echoes in my mind, "one more blow and she'll crack completely." What if I'd stepped further left? Would my death be the final blow?

"Good news. Looks like it's been here a while, and the sand damaged the sensor. On three, I'm going to cut this wire and we run like hell. Ok?" He peers up at me expectantly.

"Wait! What's your name?" I'm stalling, but it also doesn't feel right to potentially die next to a man without knowing his name.

His teeth glow in the moonlight against his dark skin. "Ronnie Smith. Now let's get you out of here before we braid each other's hair. One. Two. Three."

We dive and roll down the hill, but nothing happens, the bomb successfully neutralized. By the time we get back to camp after an exhausting but ultimately positive mission, Ronnie and I swap life stories.

When the next mail call comes, another letter arrives, but I don't post mine. That doesn't stop me from inhaling every word she writes.

I realize I *am* Bella's final blow. Maybe if I make her hate me, if I don't make it home, she'll crack but not completely shatter. Every month, I almost give in and mail my letter and beg her forgiveness. Every month, I remind myself this is to protect her.

Her letters are my drug. I love them and loathe them. They keep me going on my darkest days as I reread them. But as long as they arrive, I know she's not really living her life. When they finally stop, I grieve their loss and cheer my angel on her next adventure.

A month later, I get an envelope addressed to me in an unfamiliar hand. Out falls a wallet sized picture with a brief note.

D-

When you're ready to pull your head out of your ass and win her back, come see me. Until then, I'll take care of our girl.

In my hand is our prom photo. Bella is smiling at the camera, but I'm staring at her like she hung the moon. I kiss her face and tuck the image by my heart, where I carry her with me... my lucky charm.

CHAPTER THIRTY-SEVEN

Bitter Truth

DAVID - NOW

"All set. Here's the user manual. Username and temporary password are on a sticky note. Make sure you change it today." I hand Colin the booklet and start gathering my equipment up.

"Thanks a million. It's grand to have all this ready in time for the baby. Want a drink before you go?" Without waiting for an answer, Colin heads for the kitchen.

"Alright. Really appreciate your patience, and for not canceling the order after... well, you know." I squeeze the back of my neck, feeling awkward.

Colin hands me a beer and waves my gratitude off with his bottle in hand. "I know better than anyone that the road to love can be rocky." He takes a swig, acting so obviously casual that I tense. I can already tell I'm not going to like his next words. "Did you hear they caught the guy who broke into Pop?"

Yup, not liking where this conversation is going at all. "That's good." Raising the drink to my lips, I try to match Colin's easy stance.

"Deputy Ramirez is bragging around town that he cracked the case, something about new video evidence. You wouldn't happen to know anything about that, would you, David?" His green eyes are sharp as he stares me down over his bottle. Daring me to contradict what he's already worked out.

I like him. In another time and place, we would have been close friends. Hanging out while our better halves did their thing. Double dates. Sunday cookouts. Holiday parties.

It would have been a great life.

I pick at the label on my beer. "Pop is a customer of Smith and Hawthorne. *If* in our routine review of client data, we found evidence, snd *if* we then gave that surveillance to the authorities to aid an ongoing investigation, there'd be nothing wrong with that."

Colin continues to eye me over his drink. "Mmhmm. How about engaging suspects in self-incriminating conversations in locations perfectly visible on security cameras? The only ones which happen to have a microphone."

I run my tongue over my teeth as I debate my response. "That's not the only camera with a microphone at Pop."

His eyes widen, and he points at me with the mouth of his bottle. "Ha! So it was you! Why doesn't Anna know? Why weren't you there that night?"

Actually, I was there, just out of sight until I was sure she was ok. With a heavy sigh, I lean against the counter behind me and place my drink down. This isn't going to be a quick beer between guys. "Because I don't want her to know." Like I don't want Bella to know that I texted Asher to watch for her after I broke up with her.

"Why the fuck not? You are so obviously in love with her." I open my mouth, but he waves to shut me up. "Don't even deny it. She's fucking crazy about you, too. So what happened? Why does she think you walked away?"

"Because I did." Unable to take the tension from Colin's gaze, I break eye contact, hiding behind my beer. I chug the entire bottle.

"Are you a *fecking eejit*, man?" Colin collapses against the counter opposite.

"Look. Family is everything to Annabel. Her brother made it clear he does not approve of us. If we stayed together, it would be years of tense gatherings. The rest of the siblings would need to pick sides. Do we invite Atticus or Annabel to Christmas this year? What about weddings? Baby showers? Until eventually they break all contact because it's easier, and she loses more of her family."

Swallowing around the tightness in my throat, I stare Colin down. "That path just leads to resentment, and us apart anyway. She doesn't see it yet, but Bells will be grateful some day I saved us both the heartache."

"Great plan, *boyo*. One problem. Her brother is still being a dick even with you out of the picture. So you didn't actually accomplish anything."

The skin on my face suddenly feels too tight. My pulse drums in my ears as I hold myself up on the counter. "What?"

Colin's eyes brighten with victory. "Anna came by yesterday with frozen meals for when the baby comes. Girl looked a wreck, told me all about how big brother Atticus still isn't really talking to her." He studies my face for a beat, then grabs two more beers for us.

"What about the rest of her brothers?"

"They've all taken her side, the fiancée too. Seems Atticus is in the doghouse all around. Doesn't stop Anna from feeling guilty as hell, though."

I nod. That sounds like my angel, always too busy taking care of everyone else to look out for herself. That's where I've always come in.

If I walked away, who's putting Bella first? Not saying the girl is incapable. She built a successful business and has made a great life here. But when she goes into full caregiver mode, who's going to baby her? Rub her feet and run her bath?

Guess it'll be some other lucky bastard.

"If it's only one brother, what's really stopping you?"

I take a deep breath and blow it out. "If it was any brother except Atticus, I might not have walked away."

"You mean because he was your friend? You honestly think you two loving each other is a betrayal?"

Pressing my lips into a thin line, I shake my head. "Ace is her fucking hero. The two of them grew up attached at the hip. When their mom got sick, it was the two of them holding everyone together. That's not a bond that breaks clean. It festers."

"Well, I still think you're an *eejit*. But I don't know the brother like you do. I said my peace, I'll drop it," Colin points his bottle at me, "for now."

I finish my drink and bring both bottles to the sink. "Thanks for the beer. I need to get going, though."

Sitting in the cab of my truck, I fidget with my cell. My thumb hovers over the call button, but I sit indecisive. With a growl, I stab the screen and raise the phone to my ear. On the second ring, it connects.

Grace's bright tone rings through the line. "Hey, Holly. What's up?"

"Uh, it's David, not Holly."

"You don't say. Not much here. Ace surprised me with lunch. Isn't that sweet?"

My shoulders slump. Guess I won't get a productive conversation today. "I heard Ace isn't talking to Bella. Can you get him to pull his head out of his ass?"

"Hmmm, I'm not sure that will work. How about Saturday? Ace has to help at his dad's place most of the afternoon, so I'll be alone."

Freaking brilliant! How Atticus landed her, I'll never know. "Thanks, Gracie. I'll just have to get through to him myself."

"Good luck. I'll see you this weekend. Bye."

Now what the hell am I going to say to Atticus? If he wants to be a dick to me, fine. I probably deserve it. But he can't do this to Bella.

CHAPTER THIRTY-EIGHT

Missing Pieces

In the days following the attack, my depression has given way to rage. The bustle of the kitchen should be comforting, but it's not. Instead of acting as a nice hum of background noise, the constant buzz feels like sandpaper on my skin. I'm wound tighter than a pageant girl in spandex after a burrito. Seriously, if someone drops a pan, I might explode. I already made Heather cry—feel kind of bad about that.

Especially since we haven't even opened yet.

Bree gave me the number for her therapist. That's been helping me cope after the attacks. When something brings my mind back to that night, she told me to use the 3-3-3 rule, and it grounds me back to the present. I name three objects I can see, sounds I hear, then move three parts of my body. It helps.

Working where I've been attacked twice is challenging, but I remind myself this is *my* kitchen. Some hateful bigot will *not* ruin it for me. I've fought too hard to get here. The fact Ryan's going away for a long time doesn't hurt either.

The drama at work has settled, but the rest of my life is still a wreck. I can't shake the feeling that I've destroyed everything. Atty says he's not *not* talking to me, but we've barely spoken. When we do, he shuts down like he can't think of me the same. So Grace is still pissed at him—exactly what you want days before a wedding, right?

They say when you lose one sense, the remaining five grow stronger to compensate. Must also be true of brothers. One brother is ghosting me, and the other three won't leave me alone.

Rhett FaceTimes me more often, which is nice, but the pity in his eyes hurts too much. Huck keeps blowing up my phone with funny memes and videos. He calls it "dopamine hunting"—whatever that means. After his visit, Tommy sent me an entire pitch deck on how to launch 401Ks for the restaurant employees. Like I have the time to undertake that right now. Though I saved it for after Brianna's maternity leave. That's way more her expertise, anyway.

I have seen neither hide nor hair of David since he dumped me. Kind of confirms my early suspicion that he was running into me on purpose. It's a small town, but not *that* small.

He blasts into my life after a decade of no contact. Blows it to hell in a handbasket. Then ditches me.

Again.

I should be mad, but I miss him too damn much. Plus, something isn't sitting right about the whole situation. Why did he end things? Did he think I was going to choose Atty over him and broke ties before he got hurt?

I wasn't, though.

Guess he didn't feel the same way.

"Um, Chef?" Chrissy calls me from the other side of the pass. She's tugging at the bottom of her dress.

I take a deep breath. I don't need a lawsuit from making another employee cry today. "Yea, Chrissy. What's up?"

"There's a guy here. He says he needs to speak to you urgently, but won't give his name. He has a Marine tattoo on his arm. Do you want me to..." Before she can finish, I'm out the double doors leading to the dining room.

He's here!

I can just make out the silhouette of a man standing by the windows, tall and broad, as I rush towards the front. My feet halt as a man I've never met steps into the light. My stomach drops. What is going on here? "Can I help you?"

His dark eyes look conflicted as he searches my face. He gives a single nod, coming to some conclusion. "I recognize you from your picture. I'm sorry this is the first we're meeting, though. Name's Ronnie. I served with David." He holds out a hand and I shake it on autopilot.

"Is he ok?" My voice trembles. Oh God, please don't be here to tell me something happened to David. Did he re-enlist or something?

His lips twist into a humorless smile. "He's being an insufferable ass, but he's alive. Look, he doesn't know I'm here. Probably wouldn't like it." He scrapes a dark hand through his cropped hair.

Seriously, what is going on here? "Alright. Why are you here then, Ronnie?"

"I've watched that man carry a torch for you for a decade. Did you know he keeps your prom picture in his wallet? Calls it his lucky charm. Still carries it, by the way."

My lips quirk a little at the idea, but I only shake my head no.

"He suggested we start our business here to be close to you. That first day in town, he brought this to give you." He holds up a tattered and stained envelope. "Idiot thought you were dating that Irish guy and threw it out, but I grabbed it out of the bin when he wasn't looking. Figured you deserved to know the whole truth before you decided to walk away."

He shoves it at me, almost aggressively. My hands shake as I take it. The paper was once white but has yellowed with age, the edges frayed. On the front, I find my name and address in Hitchcock.

"I don't understand. What do you mean 'walk away'? David ended things, not me." I meet his dark eyes and watch them widen.

"He did?"

I tilt my head as I study the man. Looks like my gut was right. There's more going on than I know, and Ronnie might have the answers I need. "Can I get you some sweet tea or water or something?"

At his nod, I lead him to the bar area. I wave off the bartender who is prepping fruit slices and grab two glasses of ice. Reaching to the back of the mini-fridge, I take the pitcher of sweet tea I hide there for me and Asher. "You thought I walked away?"

He has the decency to wince as he takes the glass from me. "He was rather tight-lipped, and I made an assumption. Sorry about that."

"Don't apologize for being loyal. How is he really?"

Ronnie blows a breath out forcefully. "A mess. Haven't seen him this lost since your last letter to him on deployment." I start to argue, but he holds up a hand to stop me. "I know he stopped writing first, but he never stopped reading. Must have read those letters a thousand times."

The iced tea is refreshing, but can't keep my temper from flaring. "He didn't *stop* writing. He *never* wrote."

"He wrote." Ronnie nods at the envelope on the bar between us. "He just never sent it. I bet he doesn't talk much about what went down over there. After you see shit like we did, it's easy to push people away. You feel... tainted. And you don't want to spread it to your loved ones."

My glass clinks against the surface. "I can see how that could make sense."

"David almost died the day I met him. He says I saved his life, but it was dumb luck we didn't both meet our maker that day. He wrote that letter right before the mission, but he never sent it. Once when he was drunk, I asked him why not. He said something about how he wouldn't be the reason his Bella shattered. That you were meant for so much more."

My face goes cold and my hair tingles. My whole axis shifts as the missing pieces fall into place. As the rushing sound builds in my ears, I brace my hands on the bar top. Ronnie stands from the stool and reaches out as if to steady me.

"Son of a biscuit. David wasn't worried I'd choose Atty." I meet Ronnie's confused stare with wide eyes that burn with building tears. "He was worried I wouldn't."

That selfless, stupid, infuriating, wonderful, stubborn man. As I cuss him out in my head, I grab two shot glasses and the bottle of Fireball, filling them to the brim.

"I'm going to tan his hide." I shoot one back and push the other towards Ronnie, who only shakes his head with cautious eyes. Shrugging, I throw back his shot, too. "I'll remind him why he started calling me 'Hell's Bells' in the first place."

A slow, understanding grin spreads across Ronnie's face. "I like you. Ok, what's the plan?"

We sit and discuss strategy for a bit as the restaurant prepares to open around us. When I can avoid my responsibilities no longer, I thank Ronnie and send him on his way with a hug and promises of dinner soon. Letter safely stored in my office, I get to work until I can take the time to consume David's words.

CHAPTER THIRTY-NINE

Confrontations

I look out the window of my truck at the Bennet residence. For the first time in twenty years, I feel out of place here. Unwelcome. Anxious.

Blowing out a breath, I squeeze my neck hard as I give myself a pep talk. This is for Bella. If Ace can never forgive me for loving his sister, so be it, but he needs to stop hurting her. Mind made up, I exit the cab and stride up the front walk.

The storm door slams open before I reach the porch steps. A furious Atticus stands on the top step, glaring down at me. "What do you think you're doing here, asshole? You must be lost." The muscle in his jaw bulges and he clenches his fists at his side. Don't think I've ever seen him this mad.

"I'm here to tell you to stop being a dick to your sister." I stand my ground and meet his glare without flinching.

He stomps down two stairs, face red. "Oh, you mean my baby sister that you fucked?" Spit flies from his mouth.

I close the distance between us. Even though I'm one step below, we're nearly nose to nose. "Why don't you yell that shit a bit louder, Atticus?

Don't think all of Hitchcock heard you. You show your sister some goddamn respect."

"Why should I? She didn't respect me. Neither of you did!"

"This isn't about you! Did you ever stop to think that?"

"How is my best friend and my sister screwing around behind my back have nothing to do with me?"

"I swear to god, Atticus. I love you like a brother, but if you talk about your sister that way again, you're going to find my fist in your mouth. It wouldn't have been behind your back if you hadn't made Bella so scared of your reaction. Seems she was right to be worried after all."

Atticus rocks back on his heels. "So that's it? Twenty years of friendship gone because you decided to get your dick wet?" His eyes shine with suppressed emotion. "You were my brother, too. Why her? You could have any girl you wanted. Why did it have to be Bella?"

I wipe my hand over my face roughly and turn my head up to the sky. "Don't you get it?" My voice breaks, I clear my throat and try again. "It's *always* been Bella. She's the fucking love of my life. But it doesn't matter anymore."

Atticus flinches back as if I hit him. "What? Why not?"

"Family is everything to Bella. I would never take that away from her. So I removed myself from the picture."

Confusion replaces the rage in his eyes. "You did what?"

"I walked away. Bella's happiness comes first. Always has. Always will. So get your head out of your ass and call your sister!"

He hesitates, then closes the gap between us. "You broke up with my sister?" Ace's eyes narrow. "You hurt my sister? I'll fucking kill you."

"Go ahead. I gave her up once before, don't particularly look forward to doing it again. Just quit being a dick to her."

Ace squints as he studies my eyes. "You really love her?"

"More than anything."

We're standing chest to chest. Ace's hands fisted in my shirt, mine by my sides. The sound of squealing brakes draws our attention. In unison, we turn our heads to the street as a car slams to a stop and the driver's door flies open.

Like an avenging angel, Bella storms up the walkway.

Her blond hair is in a messy bun on top of her head. She's wearing leggings and a food-splotched tee. With her eyes full of fire, and fury crackling around her, I don't think she's ever looked more beautiful.

"Atticus Finch, I have a bone to pick with you. How dare you think you have a say in my love life? I'm a grown adult and deserve to be treated as such."

Her rib cage heaves with her anger. In a moment, her fiery gaze lands on me. She pulls something out of her back pocket and slaps it against my chest. Instinctively, I catch it and look down, shocked to see the letter I wrote to her a decade ago. But how? I threw it out.

"You, Mr. Hawthorne, I'll get to in a minute. You don't get to run away again because you think you know what's best for me. Guess you both could use a reminder that I'm a grown-ass woman and can make my own decisions. Are we clear?"

My lips quiver and I bite my cheek to stop from grinning. God, I love this woman. "Yes, Bella. I'm sorry." Her eyes soften slightly as she nods at me once. There may be hope yet.

As Bella turns back to Atticus, her face regains some anger. "How dare you stick yourself in our relationship? Do you honestly think that little of us?" Her eyes turn glassy. "You know, Atty, I think you forget Davy was *my* friend first. It was always the three of us, together, and now you demand we choose? What gives you that right?"

A single tear glistens down her cheek. My fingers itch to dry her eyes and hold her close.

Atticus's shoulders drop. Any lingering anger gives way to guilt and remorse. "Bella Bug..." His voice is full of pain.

The front door opens again. Mr. Bennet stands in the doorway and holds a hand out to Annabel. "Baby girl, why don't you come in here and let these two work their shit out? I've been hankering for your pecan cookies. Can you come in and whip me up a batch?"

As Bella passes him, he squeezes her shoulder, then meets my eyes. "David, be sure to come in when you boys finish your stupid fight." With barely a backward glance, he disappears into the house as the door slams behind him.

Ace and I blow out our breaths and slowly sit on the top step, hip to hip, in complete silence.

The minutes tick by, then Atticus speaks again. "How long?"

I could be a dick and say the bachelor weekend, but I know that's not what he means. "Probably since she showed up with that damn grilled cheese and Coke to share. Didn't quite realize it until high school."

Ace's eyebrows pinch, his eyes distant, like he's replaying old memories. "Prom?"

I shake my head no. "I knew before that, didn't think it was mutual until that night, though."

He nods absently. "That's why you and Holly broke up? And why you didn't date anyone after that?"

"That was a major part of it, yeah." I lean back on my elbows and watch the clouds.

Ace's eyes widen, and he turns to me, smacking my shoulder. "That's why Bella hasn't talked to you since you shipped out. What did you do?"

I hand him the envelope Bella shoved at me. "The day I wrote that, I stepped on a landmine. They say your life flashes before your eyes, but all I saw was Bella. How she wouldn't move past it. It was too soon after your mom, and I couldn't let her waste her dreams on me." I shrug. "So I made her hate me, to protect her. Even if it meant I'd lose her."

As he scans the letter, his eyes soften. "That is the sweetest, and the fucking dumbest, thing I've ever heard. You're an idiot."

A humorless chuckle shakes my chest. "Yea, Grace said pretty much the same."

"Wait... Grace knew?"

I wince. Shit, didn't mean to throw her under the bus. "Uh, yeah. I love you, man, but you're the most oblivious person I've met. I think everyone noticed but you."

He melts onto the top step, looking completely shell-shocked. As he turns to me, his expression is serious. "You really love her?"

"More than anything."

Ace nods. "Take care of my baby sister." He holds out his hand for me to shake, then pulls me in for a one-armed hug.

"Always." I stand up and use our clasped hands to pull Ace up beside me. "We good?"

"Yea. Sorry, I was an ass."

I shrug. "We both could'a handled it better."

"Guess I owe Bella an apology." He winces. "You don't think she'll give me a black eye for the wedding, do you?"

I bump his shoulder with mine. "Naw. You're lucky she loves Grace too much to ruin the photos. You might want to protect your balls, though." Ace's Adam's apple bobs as he gulps. With the look of a man facing enemy fire, he enters the house, leaving me alone on the porch.

Not ready to face the music quite yet, I sit back down to watch the clouds. The boards squeak as someone sits next to me. "So, it all worked out then?"

I turn, smiling down at Grace. "Almost, Sunshine. Still need to get Bella to forgive me, but, yea, me and Ace are good."

"She will. You two were made for each other." Her small head leans on my larger frame.

"Thank you for all the help." I swallow around the lump in my throat, thinking back on all the letters and packages, especially that first one with my lucky charm. "But I got it from here."

"Glad you finally got your head out of your ass." She stands and brushes the dust off her shorts. "Come on, let's make sure there's still a groom for the wedding after Bella gets done."

Now to sort out what to say to a very pissed Bella.

CHAPTER FORTY

Apologies

Daddy gives me a hug and a "give them hell, baby girl" before disappearing into his study. My anger is still simmering as I spread the ingredients across Momma's kitchen island. I don't have to wait long before the rusty screen squeals and footsteps echo down the hallway.

I throw the bag of pecans at Atty, not bothering to watch if he catches them or not. "If you're going to talk in this kitchen, you're going to work in this kitchen. Get to chopping." Pushing a cutting board and knife to the left, I measure out the dry elements from memory.

"Look, Bug, I'm sorry. You're right, you're all grown up. You don't need me looking over your shoulder."

I gnaw at my lip, dump a cup of flour into the bowl, and turn on my big brother. How can I expect him to treat me like an adult if I'm not honest with him? The truth is, I've hidden a lot more than Davy from him. "I was attacked twice this summer at Pop."

The blade clatters on the counter as Atty turns to me, his eyes the size of dinner plates. "What? Are you ok? Did they catch the bastard?"

"The first time, I hit him with a frying pan. The second, I swung a bottle of vodka before I lit him on fire. I don't need a white knight."

"Holy shit, Annabel," Atty stumbles back, "I didn't know."

"Of course not, because I didn't tell you. You had enough going on with the wedding and then with us not talking." I wave him off, trying to get ahead of the guilt shining in his eyes. "The point is, I took care of myself until the police came. And David."

Atty's forehead wrinkles. "David was there?"

"Yea. I was strong when I needed to be, but with David, I can also be vulnerable when I need to be." I search Atty's blue eyes, hoping my message is getting through. "It was never a casual hookup."

"I'm starting to realize that. I'm so sorry I freaked out and made it about me. Guess I just don't like change. Can you forgive me?"

In answer, I step forward and wrap my arms around his waist. His bigger frame engulfs mine in an instant. I've missed his hugs. "Love you, Bug."

"Love you too, Atty. Now get to chopping."

One down, one to go.

We chat as we bake. The awkwardness is finally gone, and we're Atty and Bella Bug again. We catch up on everything. How his new practice is doing. All about the pending expansion. My attention drifts to the hallway periodically, but the front door is frustratingly silent.

What feels like an hour later but is more likely only minutes, heavy footsteps echo in the hall and two familiar faces appear in the kitchen.

Davy stands by the counter, gripping the back of a stool, knuckles white. "Hey, Bells. Care to go for a walk?"

My eyes dart to Grace, but she just gives me a wink. In answer, I take off my apron and head for the back door.

Davy catches up before I hit the top porch step. His hand captures my hip as we descend the old, warped steps. I should make him sweat a little, but the truth is I missed him more than I want to admit. The innocent touch feels too good to reject.

We walk in silence, his hand still on my hip. Our feet take us down a familiar path, still worn from years of use. As the clearing opens, we see the time-beaten clubhouse, but Davy leads me to a fallen tree that provides a convenient seat. The birds call around us, and still we sit in silence. I'm content to wait for him to break the tension. Until then, I'll breathe in his comforting scent and the soothing sounds of nature.

When he speaks, it's low and gravelly. "You were right."

"About?" Yea, not going to make this easy.

"I'm not helping you if I'm smothering you in the process. I should have talked to you instead of deciding for you."

"Thank you." I weigh the questions in my mind before picking one to say out loud. "Did you mean what you wrote in the letter?"

"Every word." His voice breaks and rings with sincerity.

I swallow past the lump in my throat. "Why didn't you think we were worth fighting for?"

David jerks towards me, eyes wide. "What? Bella, no."

"Then explain it to me. If you love me, how could you walk away? Again."

"It's *because* I love you so much." With a harsh sigh, Davy combs his fingers through his hair. "Watching you lose Momma and being powerless to help was the hardest thing I've ever done, and I hadn't even realized I loved you yet. Harder than bootcamp or missions or staying away the first time."

Davy's hand cups my knee. "So when you were losing Atticus, and there *was* something I could do to make it go away. It was as easy as breathing. I'd do anything for you, Bells, even if it means I'm miserable the rest of my life."

My eyes sting with unshed tears. I wrinkle my nose against the building wetness. This amazing, infuriatingly stupid man.

Davy grunts as my open palm connects with the back of his head. "Ow, what was that for?"

"Just tryin' to smack some sense into you. No more being a martyr. For either of us. We're in this together, and from now on we talk things through. No more runnin'"

The smile spreading across his handsome face takes my breath away. In a nimble move, David turns to pull me until I'm straddling him. With a squeal, I settle myself more firmly against him, with my hands resting on his shoulders.

His eyes are intense and dark with need as they meet mine. And so much love. His hand cups the side of my jaw and pulls me even closer to capture my lips. His motions are swift but gentle—a man starved, with the patience of a saint. It's a combination that leaves my core wet and achy.

My fingers dig into his hair, holding him close as I match his frenzied kisses with my own. I rock against his hardening length beneath me, desperate for relief. His name is a whispered plea against his lips.

His fingers dig into my butt as he surges upward with a powerful push of his legs. Without encouragement, I lock my limbs around him. I feel weightless as David takes purposeful steps towards the old clubhouse. He struggles with the door—carrying, kissing, and door opening, evidently too much to juggle. An exasperated growl escapes me, wringing a throaty chuckle from Davy.

Reaching behind me, I slap at the door until I find the handle, and it swings open. Davy breaks our embrace to survey the shabby interior. "Not here. You deserve better."

The mattresses are stained and flat, leaves and discarded cans litter the floor. Rhett's obviously been having a blast in our old fort.

My hands cup his cheeks to force his gaze on me. "It was fine the first time. I don't want to wait any longer."

His eyes heat moments before his mouth descends again in a bruising kiss. It doesn't matter how many times we come together like this, each time is as consuming as the last.

My back gently bumps against the wall. Fingers stroke down my thigh, encouraging my legs to let go. I whimper as Davy's lips leave mine. Hot kisses trail along my jaw and neck above my shirt. Those fingers find my waist and slip under the band as electrical shocks spread from the contact points.

Davy lowers himself to his knees. His eyes heat as he looks up at me, commanding me to stay still and watch. My leggings slide down my body. Each inch of exposed skin treated to a kiss before the downward assault continues in a pathway of tingles.

The fabric is finally clear of my foot, the shoe carelessly thrown aside. Davy draws my leg over his shoulder, opening my throbbing center to him.

I watch with hooded eyes as Davy takes a first tentative lick. My eyes close as my head falls back with a moan. His tongue sets a steady rhythm as he circles the sensitive nub.

Taking my moans for encouragement, Davy uses both hands to open me wider as he eats with abandon. I grip his shoulder for support as desperate sounds catch in my throat. The pulse in my core strengthens as it desperately clutches on nothing. Reading my mind, Davy teases my entrance with his finger, testing my wetness.

My first orgasm shocks me with its intensity. I cry his name as I clutch his shoulders, his hair, anything I can touch. He continues to pump into me, drawing out my release until it finally subsides in little quakes.

"I need you." My fingers fist in his shirt, pulling him to his feet. I fumble with his belt and jeans as he leaves teasing, nipping kisses on my lips. When his hard length springs into my hand, I stroke him slowly.

With a grunt, Davy's forehead drops to mine. "Hell's Bells. If you keep doing that, it's not going to end well."

I rub him again, wanting to hear him groan. "Then you'd better hurry up and take me."

A primal growl is all the warning I get before I find myself pinned up against the wall. My legs wrap around his waist, and I reach between us to notch him at my entrance. As he slowly lowers me onto his length, I cup his face and tenderly kiss his lips.

With one arm wrapped under my hips, and the other palming by spine, I feel secure. With the fire in Davy's eyes, I feel desirable.

I squeeze my thighs tighter and use my grip to ride him. Each glide back down, my clit rubs against his shaft, sending sparkles of pleasure through me. Together, we chase our release with furtive movements and whispers of love, then crash over the edge, gazes locked.

Gently, almost reluctantly, Davy lowers me back to the ground and helps me get my leggings back on. We share a grin, neither of us ready to pop this bubble. Reaching up, Davy tucks a last strand behind my ear. "Hell's Bells, I love you."

Cupping his hand, I turn my cheek into him. "Love you too, Davy."

With a new lightness, we walk back up to the house, arms wrapped around each other. As it always should have been.

CHAPTER FORTY-ONE

Full Circle

DAVID - NOW

The kitchen is noisy as we walk through the back door. All the Bennet brothers are now in attendance, arguing loudly in the small space. As we join the party, Bella moves as if to slip out from under my arm, but I hold her close.

I'm done hiding.

I drop a kiss to her temple to soothe her, and she melts against me. That's the best feeling. When this hellcat of a woman turns soft for me, I feel like the damn king of the world.

"Hey man, I see you two made up." Ace nods to me in greeting from his spot by the stove.

I nod back to him and Grace, who's similarly wrapped in his arms. "Could say the same to you."

"Yea, seems y'all got a two for one deal on rectal-craniotomies." The kitchen falls silent and five nearly identical sets of blue eyes turn on Grace in confusion. "What? They finally got their heads out of their asses..." Grace's eyes are wide as she looks around the room for support.

Bella snorts. I look at her with a raised brow, which only turns the giggles into a full belly laugh. She clutches my shirt and buries her face into the fabric as she continues to howl hysterically.

Rhett is the first to join her, but the twins and Mr. Bennet soon follow. The kitchen is full of warmth and laughter, and it feels like old times.

Huck wipes a watery eye as he walks over to grip my shoulder. "I hope she didn't call you a micro-dick fuckwad."

"Language. But what's a micro-dick fuckwad?" Mr. Bennet is smiling from the table as he looks at each of his children.

Next to me, Bella's face reddens, and she leaps at her brother. I catch her around the waist as Huck dances out of reach. "Gee, you should ask Bella, Dad," he calls.

"Huckleberry Finn Bennet! I'll get you for that." Bella yells after her brother, but doesn't fight my embrace. I pull her closer and smile into her hair.

"Come on, Bella. We need to blow this popsicle stand, anyway." Grace turns and kisses Ace's cheek before stepping out of his arms.

Ace's face crumples like a toddler. "What?"

"Yea, what?" God, do I sound as whiny as he does?

"I'm getting married tomorrow. You, sir, are sleeping here tonight with the boys and I'm stealing Bella for a sleepover at our place. I already put your bags by the stairs." She grips his chin and drops a kiss to his pout. "Don't be late. I'll be the one in white."

Bella's lips are a thin line as she stares up at me. She looks as disappointed as I feel. I lower my mouth to the shell of her ear, my words only for her. "Go have fun with your new sister. I'm not going anywhere, Bells. We have the rest of our lives."

As I pull back, her eyes glow with love and maybe tears. She stretches up on her toes to kiss me. It's a chaste peck as far as kisses go, but a warmth spreads in my chest knowing she kissed me openly. In front of her family.

"That is going to suck," Ace mutters from behind me.

Bella says goodbye to each of her brothers and gives her dad a hug and kiss. Grace squeezes my arm with a warm smile before dragging Bella out the door. My Bella's eyes stay locked with mine until the last moment.

Mr. Bennet claps his hands. "Ok, boys. What are we doing tonight?"

"Poker," Tom calls.

"Whiskey," Huck answers.

"Not too much whiskey. If we're all hungover for the wedding, Grace will kill me." Ace shudders at the thought of his bride being upset. She really has him by the balls.

We settle around the Bennet dining room table, a deck of cards, snack bowls, and glasses of Jack and Coke clutter the surface. As we play, the chips dwindle for all except Rhett. The boy is a natural card shark. Tommy tries to give him a run for his money, but we're all broke within a couple of hours.

The bottle of Jack passes around and we decide to switch to hearts and chat. Rhett comes back from the kitchen with the plate of cookies.

"Hey, those are mine." Mr. Bennet reaches for one, but Rhett moves the dish away.

"Says the man who lost all his money." A grin splits his face, and he puts the plate down by his father before pulling up the chair next to him.

"So Dad, any words of advice? How'd you and Momma stay so happy?" Ace leans back in his seat and swirls his drink.

Mr. Bennet's eyes turn dreamy and his lips tilt into a gentle smile as he thinks of his wife. "Son, you already got the first step, which is finding the right woman. Though how the hell you've convinced her to stick around for fifteen years, I'll never know."

I chuckle into my tumbler, feeling lighter than I have in years. "That's what I've been saying!" Ace tosses some popcorn at me and I laugh more.

"There is no secret to a happy marriage. It takes work. Communication. Patience." The corners of his eyes crinkle as they shift to me. "Don't try to solve her problems for her. Let her vent and really listen with your full attention. Don't ask how you can help. Use your eyes and take care of what needs doing. Flowers for no particular reason don't hurt, either."

We share smiles and swap stories late into the night. Gradually, each Bennet man excuses himself to his old bed upstairs until only Ace and I remain in the dim kitchen.

He dries dishes as I wash them. "Listen, I need to say again how sorry I am."

I wave a wet hand in his direction. "Don't. We're good. It's in the past."

"Just let me say this once, and then it's truly in the past."

I turn off the tap and wipe my hands on my jeans, giving Ace my full attention.

"You've been my best friend for most of my life, so I owed you the benefit of the doubt. I've been running it through my head since we talked, and memories are hitting differently. I can see it now. Especially after seeing you two actually together." Ace's eyes glimmer, and his voice cracks. "That's the real deal, and I'm sorry I fucked that up for you."

Ace pinches the bridge of his nose before blinking up at the sky. "I get a little nuts about Annabel. Maybe we all do. She's so much like Momma—like this little precious piece of her left behind." His eyes are wet and full of grief as he stands before me.

I pull him into a hug. Not one of those one-armed manly things, a full body hug. Ace's shoulders shake in my embrace. "Bella isn't the only thing your momma left behind. All of you are pieces of her. Your family is so beautiful and so strong."

Ace's arms tighten around me. "I wish she could be there tomorrow. I miss her so much."

"She'll be smiling down on you. And you know she adored Grace."

With a wet laugh, Ace pulls back. "She was pretty crazy about you, too."

Now I'm sniffing back tears. "Come on, you need your beauty rest."

Ace checks the locks and turns off the lights. "You can stay in my room like when we were kids. I'm not ready for you to sleep in Bella's room."

Bumping shoulders the whole way, we fall into the queen bed, like a thousand times before. A sense of peace fills me. Everything is going to be ok.

CHAPTER FORTY-TWO

Girls' Night

ANNA - NOW

I drive us over to Grace and Atty's house even though it's so close we could have walked. The old house has seen better days, the front porch sags and the ancient wallpaper is peeling in the living room. I know they'll fix it up together and make it into a home full of love.

Grace calls for a pizza while I find something to watch. The doorbell rings. Remote still in hand and eyes on the screen, I walk over to answer.

We made it. My deepest fears came true, but we fought through it and came out the other side. Everything is perfect.

"Oh." I jerk at the sound of her voice. The storm door opens and Holly's face appears.

Well, almost perfect. Though it shouldn't be a surprise that Grace's best friend is here. "Hey, Holly. Grace is ordering food. Why don't you pick a movie for all of us?" I hand her the controller.

Awkwardly, we take seats in the living room. Holly starts halfheartedly flipping through streaming services. For the first time, I try to look at her with fresh eyes. Forget that this is the same girl who made me so miserable in high school, and really look at her.

Her face is pale and her skin looks tight. The stress of the divorce must be wearing her down. Being in a wedding so soon after is probably torture, even before you throw an ex-boyfriend into the mix. She's got to be white-knuckling through this weekend.

Tinsley's words from the bachelorette haunt me as I try to see from Holly's perspective. "I owe you an apology," I say.

Holly's eyes widen as she freezes with the remote held out. "Pardon?" She lowers her arm and eyes me warily.

I take a steadying breath. This is going to hurt, but it's time. "Did you know Davy was my friend first?"

She holds her hand up and jerks to stand, eyeing the front door. "Oh, for Christ's sake. I'm not doing this."

"Wait," I place my hand on her, "please. Just let me try to explain, and I'll never mention it again."

Holly's eyes narrow and her lips press into a white line, but she stops trying to pull away. She crosses her arms over her chest and sits back down, glaring at me.

"Davy's been my best friend since I was nine. Up until high school, he and I were closer than he and Atty. David never cheated on you. But with time and age, I realize that emotionally, I took pieces of him that should have been yours."

She's closed off, but she's listening. "All those late nights and calls. You still want me to believe nothing was going on then? When I know you're sleeping together now?"

"I swear. Nothing sexual happened between us until long after you broke up." Tears tickle my throat. "You know my mom died when we were young, but you probably didn't know she was sick for years before that. I had to take care of Momma and Rhett a lot. It didn't really leave time for socializing, but Davy would come next door to help. Keep me company."

Sniffing, I peek at her to make sure she's still listening. "When Momma passed," my voice breaks and I swallow, "Rhett had dad. The twins had each other. Atty had Grace. I had my only friend."

Holly's eyes are red lined and her nose is pink as I finish. Her arms drop and she looks at me as if seeing me for the first time, too.

Blinking my own tears, I reach out and tentatively grip her hands. "When you came into the picture, we were being Davy and Bella, just like we'd always been. But that was wrong. Our relationship should have changed. We never meant to hurt you, but we did. And I'm so sorry for not understanding that before."

Holly sniffles and takes a watery breath. "Thank you. I didn't realize I still needed that closure." She squeezes me back. "I should apologize, too," her cheeks redden. "I said some pretty horrible things to you in high school. Things I'm not proud of."

"I'd like to start over. You're Grace's best friend. This is only the beginning—soon there'll be baby showers and birthday parties. I want to be friends."

Her lips spread into a smile as a tear trickles down her cheek. She looks younger and lighter. "I'd like that too."

We watch silly rom-coms and stuff our faces with junk food. It's wonderful. The night ends fairly early—Holly insists everyone needs beauty rest for tomorrow.

My bag vibrates against the bathroom counter as I get ready for bed. I finish washing my hands and dig my phone out. Seeing the name of the sender, I smile.

Davy:

Goodnight, Love. Miss you already.

Me:

Miss you too. How'd it go tonight?

Great. We're good, Bells. You?

I debate my response. Am I good? This new relationship with Holly still feels tentative, but I feel a peace I haven't felt in Hitchcock since before Momma died.

Same. See you tomorrow.

Can't wait. Love you.

Love you, too.

As I lay in bed next to Grace, my mind wanders. Was it really only a few months ago Davy waltzed back into my life? When I saw him standing on the other side of my bar, I never imagined we'd be here today. Well, I also couldn't have imagined all the hog slop we'd have to wade through to get here.

But I'm still here, and stronger for it. You never know what extra spice life is going to throw into the pot. You just need to roll with it, add some complementary flavors and find balance.

After a decade apart, I know I can live without David Hawthorne, that's a lesson I've learned twice. But I also know I don't want to. Life's sweeter together. Like pecans and caramel, or grilled cheese and Coke. With a smile on my face, I drift off to the sounds of cicadas singing in the trees.

CHAPTER FORTY-THREE

Wedding Bells

Sunday morning I rise early, as usual, but thankfully the nightmares stay away. I stealthily evacuate the room without stirring a snoring Ace and head down to the kitchen.

Mr. Bennet sits alone at the small table, a steaming mug in front of him. "Son, pour yourself a cup and have a seat. I want to talk to you."

As I perch on the edge of the wooden chair across the way, I can't help but squirm. In many ways, Mr. Bennet has been a father to me since mine split, so the idea that I've disappointed him? Well, it tears me up inside.

"Sir. I'm sorry for how y'all found out, but I'm not sorry for loving your daughter. She deserves all her dreams to come true, and I aim to help make sure they do. I'll spend the rest of my life making her happy—if she'll have me. It would mean a lot if I had your blessing, though."

His eyes sparkle as he leans back in his chair. His lips quirk into a crooked smile. "Well, it's about time."

My heart drops into my stomach. I couldn't have heard him right. "Sir?"

Shifting, he reaches into his pocket. He pulls out a simple black box and slides it across the table towards me, nodding for me to open it. "Is this...?" I look up at Mr. Bennet, lost for words.

"I still remember the day I came home and my Lizzie told me Bella had met the boy she was going to marry. I thought she had been reading too many books—our girl was only nine. For years, she'd say 'Clay, that boy would move the stars for our Annabel. Just you wait and see.'" Eyes bright, he sniffs as he thinks of his wife.

"It wasn't until the funeral I saw it for myself. After Rhett cried himself to sleep, I couldn't settle. Figured I'd bury my sorrows in a tumbler of bourbon." He pauses, clears his throat, and takes a sip of coffee.

"I saw you two in the study that night. I can still picture it clear as day all these years later. Even in sleep, you clutched each other. The way you held her like she was the most precious thing, like her pain was yours. I knew then that my Lizzie was wiser than I gave her credit for. You've always had our blessing."

"I... I..." Swallowing past the ball in my chest, I try again. "I don't know what to say."

Walking around the table, he places a warm hand on my shoulder. "Welcome home, son." With a last squeeze, he heads down the hall, leaving me alone with the box and my thoughts. "Get a move on, boys," he shouts up the stairs. "We got a wedding to get to."

The organ music fills the small church. Ace practically vibrates next to me as he stares at the back of the room. The Bennet brothers crack jokes behind me. One by one, girls I've known most of my life walk towards the altar.

When she passes through the double doors, the rest of the room fades away. The sun shines through the stained glass, lighting her in a golden glow.

My angel.

Her steps are sure as she walks towards me. A burning tingle starts in my eye. She's so beautiful. I can't wait for the day she's walking down this aisle to me in all white.

My cheeks ache and I realize I'm grinning. I can picture that day now—know it's a possibility. It's been a rocky path to get here, but we're where we belong.

Together.

And surrounded by family and friends. I'll never question myself again, never decide for her instead of talking it through. I'll always put Bella first, but I'll do that by her side from now on.

The priest drones on about love and loyalty. As he reads out the vows, I stare into her chocolate eyes. Silently, I make the same vows to her.

Before I know it, I'm grabbing her hand and walking with her back up the aisle. We grin at each other like it's us getting married. Through countless pictures, I keep a hand on her. I can't seem to hold back from touching her, still shocked that I have the right to. An arm around her waist. Linked pinkies. Like if I don't have some connection with her, I'll stop breathing.

CHAPTER FORTY-FOUR

Wedding Cake

The bistro lights twinkle overhead like starlight. A dance floor and speakers transform Daddy's backyard into a trendy club. Purple linens cover bar tables scattered across the grass. It's like something straight off a Pinterest board.

"Beautiful." A deep voice rumbles by my ear, sending tingles down my spine. I beam as I lean back into David's warm chest. His arms immediately tighten around me.

When I walked down that aisle this morning, the man who waited at the end was more like my old Davy than the man I've spent the last few months with. He looked a decade younger and as if an immense burden had been lifted off of his shoulders. His lips curved into a boyish smile as he tucked his hands into his tuxedo pockets. His eyes were only on me.

"It sure is. Can't believe Huck did all this. What a wonderful surprise." Grace and Atty didn't want to spend a lot of money on a fancy party when they have student loans and mortgage payments. Huck used his club connections to make the mini reception in the backyard a full-blown event. For a party animal, he can be surprisingly thoughtful.

Davy's lips brush my temple. "I was talking about you. Dance with me."

Grabbing my hand, he pulls me onto the dance floor. It doesn't take much convincing—I'd follow this man anywhere.

I skirt my hands up his broad chest, the silk lapel of his tux smooth under my touch. He circles my waist, fingers trace my spine and urge me closer. We sway to the music, content to just be together.

Huck winks at me from behind the DJ booth. As David and I turn to the beat, I search out more of my family. At the sweetheart's table, Atty and Grace are lost in their own world, their eyes locked on each other. They look so happy.

Daddy sits in a lawn chair next to David's mom. Both have bright smiles as I give them a wave over Davy's shoulder.

Tommy stands off to the side with a beer in one hand and the other typing away on his phone. Does the man ever stop working? As I debate if I should yell at him, Rhett sneaks up and pushes a cupcake into Tommy's nose. I laugh as the two chase each other around the yard.

I'm truly blessed to have this family.

My attention returns to the man in front of me. He watches my inattention with a half smirk on his face. As I smile up at him, his eyes heat. He lowers his head for a kiss and we stay that way until the song ends.

The embrace ends, pulling a disappointed whine from me. David chuckles and raises our joined hands for a kiss. "Come on."

"Where are you taking me?"

He darts between tables and heads for the side of the yard. "You'll see."

We make it to the edge of the porch before I see Holly against the wall. She looks beautiful as she smiles up at Ace's med school friend. He stands with his arm propped over her head, leaning close to talk. Noticing us, Holly glances over. "Oh, hey, Bella."

"Hey, Holly. Having fun?"

An endearing flush spreads across Holly's cheeks in the dim light. "James and I were debating who's worse—difficult homebuyers or patients." Her eyes sparkle with amusement as she peers up at him.

"I think that depends on if he's a surgeon or not. 'Cuz if they're unconscious, they're probably not that bad," I say.

Holly's tinkling laugh has James bending closer. You could cut the sexual tension here with a butter knife. "You're so funny, Bella. Better take good care of this one, David." There's no malice or sarcasm in her tone. Holly means it, and it feels good.

"Plan on it. Have fun, y'all." David grabs my hand and keeps pulling me around the house. I try to wave back, but they're already wrapped in each other.

We reach the driveway, and instead of going to his truck like I expect, Davy pulls me towards his mother's house. "Huh? What are you up to?"

"Hell's Bells, have some patience. Sit here." He points to the top step before slipping into the house. I tap my toe against the concrete as I wait.

Davy re-emerges with a plate in one hand and a can in the other. I frown at him in confusion as he hands me both. The smell of grease and bread tickles my nose. "Did you make me grilled cheese?"

"Yeah, and a Coke. Like the first day we met right here. Now go ahead, have a taste."

Chuckling and shaking my head, I take a bite of the salty, gooey goodness. The man is improving! Pretty soon he'll be making grilled cheese like a professional. Balancing the dish on my knees, I pivot to open the can and take a bubbling sip.

When I turn back, I find Davy down on one knee in front of me. "Oh my goodness, David?"

He smiles as he takes the plate from my hands and then clasps them. "Annabel Lee Bennet, I have loved you for twenty years. You are the literal love of my life and my reason for getting up every day. I know this may seem crazy fast, but we've wasted so much time, I don't want to waste another second." Davy reaches into his pocket and pulls out a box. "Will you marry me?"

"Davy... I..." Speechless is not a word that typically describes me, but it fits now. Am I sure this man is my future? Yes. Do I love him and am I ready to jump in with both feet? Also yes. But marriage? Especially after our relationship almost imploded my entire family?

I rip my eyes from his and actually look at the ring. My trembling fingers cover my lips as I gasp. Tears blur my sight, but I recognize the princess diamond ring with an entwined gold wire band. "Is that...?"

"Your Momma's ring. Turns out, she left it to me."

Right there, in his hands, is the proof of my family's approval. This is Momma's way of helping from heaven. A tear slips free of my lashes and trails down my cheek.

"Don't cry, Bells. I never want to make you cry again. So," his lips twist into a boyish smile, "let me spend the rest of my life making up for the last ten years?"

With trembling hands, I place the plate to the side before reaching for him. "Yes. I hear makeup sex is the best kind."

With a shout, David draws me to my feet and into his arms. He slips the ring onto my finger and dips me low for a kiss. I run my fingers through his trimmed beard as he plunders my mouth. How I've missed this man's hands on me—it's like coming home.

David pulls me upright with one last firm peck. "Does this mean you'll finally tell me the secret ingredient in your grilled cheese?"

I laugh and tap his nose. "I'll think about it."

"Come on. Let's tell everyone."

We don't actually get the chance to. We barely make it to the dance floor before Grace is running at us. "Did she say yes?"

My cheeks heat as I hold up my left hand. The entire Bennet bunch descends on us. I'm passed from brother to brother in a sea of hugs and well wishes. The most emotional congratulations come from our parents. The champagne flows again as the twins pop fresh bottles.

A sense of peace fills me as I sit tucked tightly against David's side, looking at my family around me. I can't believe we made it here. All together again and so very happy. I wish Momma could be here to join in this, but I know she's watching down on us. I know she helped us get here somehow.

I lay my head on Davy's shoulder and whisper, "I love you."

His arm tightens as his lips brush my temple. "Hell's Bells, I love you more."

That's probably not possible, but we have the rest of our lives to argue it out.

Epilogue

ANNABEL

Two Months Later

Since returning from Hitchcock, things have been amazing. We're back in our love bubble, but it's infinitely better not being a secret. We've grown even closer with Atty and Grace, meeting up for weekly video game nights.

Our days are spent building our separate businesses. Davy and Ronnie secured a huge contract with a local chain, and will be installing equipment around the state over the next few months. They're even talking about having to bring on more people. If they're not out of town on a job, Davy will wander in for lunch, more often than not. After the storefront officially closes, Davy always comes to Pop for a bite together before settling into the back office to finish up paperwork until I'm ready to go home.

Our home.

I moved into the little house off Main Street with Davy. Don't get me wrong, I loved my apartment, but it's nice actually leaving work. Room by room we've been decorating. I'm happy to say we even have furniture in the guest room. It came in handy when my brothers came for a visit.

The sound of Davy's baritone humming in the shower drifts down the hall of his—or should I say, our—house. My smile widens as the diamond of my mother's— my—ring sparkles on my finger, catching the light as I prep lunch. We've spent the day renovating in the new event space at Pop. It's really starting to take shape, and there's already a waiting list for when we open. The guys all pitched in painting walls, installing lights, and constructing a custom bar. Five shirtless men with tool belts and tight jeans were quite the sight. With the way the girls were sweating, I was half worried the fire alarm would go off.

I only had eyes for my man, though.

The water turns off and the humming stops. Carefully, I add the bread to the hot pan on my fancy Viking range and adjust my new apron. The edges of the bodice and skirt have a frilly lace edge, and it ties in a giant bow at the back. It reminds me of old magazine drawings of '50s housewives.

"Hell's Bells, I think I still have pink paint in my hair." As Davy's footsteps get louder, I flip the sandwiches. "Mmm, baby, it smells good. Whatcha cooking?"

He's almost to the kitchen now. In three. Two. One.

"Be—." Eyes wide and jaw hanging open, Davy freezes mid-step. His eyes darken as they sweep over me, drinking in every detail.

"Perfect timing. Lunch is ready." Biting my tongue to keep my expression innocent, I plate his surprise. When I turn my back to him and place the food on the island, Davy launches into motion.

Warm hands cup my bare shoulders then skate down my exposed sides until they land on the waist of my apron. "Fuck. Are you trying to kill me, woman?" He groans as he lowers his lips to my neck. As he cages me with his body, I can feel his hardness press against my bare Georgia peach. "You cooking naked has been an ultimate fantasy of mine."

I bite my lip as I drop my head onto his shoulder. "You've mentioned it once or twice."

"Whatever I've done to earn this, tell me so I can do it every day." He groans again as his hands slip to cup my hip bones.

A sense of feminine satisfaction unfurls in my center. The fact I can bring this strong Marine to his knees is such a heady sensation. I love this man so much. "I made you a grilled cheese."

The lazy kisses continue along my skin. "I'd rather eat you."

I force a pout into my tone. "I thought you loved my special grilled cheese."

"Baby, that sandwich is my ultimate comfort food, but nothing compares to you."

"Apples." I roll my head to see him better, as his hands and lips stall.

When he lifts his head, his eyes are glassy and confused. "What?"

I turn in the circle of his arms, leaning back against the stone countertop as I rest my fingertips on his impressive forearms. "The secret ingredient is thinly sliced apples for a touch of sweetness."

The confusion in his eyes fades as understanding dawns. Even more so than when I agreed to marry him, revealing this twenty-year mystery is me committing to a lifetime together. Me telling him he's my family now. A different fire ignites in his gaze, full of promise and love.

His thick fingers spear into my hair as he captures my lips in a shattering kiss. He dips his knees to scoop his other arm under my butt and lifts me to the counter.

I let loose a very undignified squeal and jump back down. "Dang, that stone's freezing cold!" Maybe I didn't think this naked cooking in an apron thing through. My tongue runs across my teeth as I try to think of a solution.

Davy's lip curls in a wolfish smile, sending heat straight to my core. He raises one hand behind his neck and fists the back of his polo. I watch, mesmerized, as his biceps bunch and dance as he pulls his shirt off in a fluid motion.

Why is it so hot when guys do that? Are they taught that in high school? Or are all men just born knowing how to do that?

His hands cup my butt and lift me back to the counter before settling me on the warm material. Way better.

"No offense to the chef, but I think I'll start with dessert first." I watch him through my lashes, eager for a repeat of our night in the cabin.

This isn't the life I planned a decade ago, but it's so much richer. Sometimes in life, like in the kitchen, adding extra spice creates something more meaningful than if you simply stick to the recipe.

Stick to the Deal

Want more Friendship Falls? Nic's story is up next, in *Stick to the Deal*, as she deals with the family drama and "Grandmama Dearest."

She is escaping society's expectations. He is conforming to them. Their marriage might just lead to unexpected love.

Nicolette: Rules governed my childhood. I escaped that world as soon as possible, capturing the world through my lens and living life on my terms. The cost? I agreed to marry a man who meets my grandmother's standards by thirty—and time's up. It's not all bad being an heiress, and a deal's a deal after all. If only I could fulfill my obligation without losing the life I've fought to build.

Reginald: Duty dictates my life. I've always toed the line, but secretly dreamed of building something truly my own. Just as my vision takes shape, my father orders me to marry for the good of the family, and I must comply. Broken dreams are just the price of being heir to an earldom.

After a chance encounter, Nicolette and Reginald strike a bargain that just might solve all their problems. Pretending to be a happy couple blurs the lines of reality. With a ruthless gossip column closing in, they must confront their deepest fears and decide if independence is worth the cost of a deeper connection.

Available Late 2024

About the Author

R.S. Barry, a resident of Central Florida, shares her life with her loving husband, her two kids, and their faithful canine companion. A dedicated and passionate reader for many years, R.S. Barry now makes the voices in her head work for her.

Drawing inspiration from life's experiences, R.S. Barry weaves contemporary tales of love, connection, and self-discovery. As a long-time reader and working professional, she brings a unique perspective to her writing, infusing her work with a genuine understanding of the complexities of human emotions.

When she isn't writing, you'll find her running around the local theme parks, reading by the pool, or making magic in the kitchen.

Find out more and see her complete book list at www.RSBarry.com

And find her on Facebook, Instagram, and TikTok

f facebook.com/authorrsbarry

⬡ instagram.com/authorrsbarry

♪ tiktok.com/@authorrsbarry

𝓟 pinterest.com/authorrsbarry

Acknowledgements

This was a very personal story for me. When my mom passed unexpectedly last year, I was still at the airport trying to get back home and I missed my chance to say goodbye. Through Bella, I could have the closure I didn't get in real life.

I wasn't originally sure if the chapter would make it into the final draft—I accidentally read too many books with death and grief that triggered me in those early days and didn't want to do that to someone else. I turned to friends and family with similar life experiences and asked for their thoughts—unanimously, the vote was to include it. One even said it inspired them to write their own chapter for closure.

Huge thank you to my developmental editor and alpha readers. You encouraged me to be vulnerable, which made the story so much deeper. You entertained my dozens of texts and in-line comments as I was refining drafts. I even appreciate you checking my football logic.

All my love to my husband, Jay, who spent three hours sorting index cards on the living room floor with me, to fit in the flashbacks appropriately. I'm sorry you don't like cinnamon roll heroes! Thank you for all your support. You have coined this my grief arc, but you have been there every step of the way over this hellish year, supporting me.

To my family and friends who cheered so hard after *Stick to the Plan.* When the doubts creep in, you keep me going. You didn't need to recommend my book to friends, book clubs, and anyone who would listen, but the fact you did warms my heart. I'm sorry I forgot how strong my support system truly is.

To my author tribe on Threads and TikTok. Your advice, friendship, and encouragement have been invaluable. I appreciate you sharing resources and support. The community literally saved this book when I was spiraling at the 11th hour!

And of course to the readers who found *Stick to the Plan* and have connected with me on social media. This book loving section of the internet is a beautiful place and I love engaging with you all. Though my TBR is bursting at the seems thanks to y'all!

Also by

Stick With It Series:

Stick to the Plan: A Forced Proximity, Workplace Romance

Stick to the Recipe: A Second Chance, Brother's Best Friend Romance

Stick to the Deal: A Marriage of Convenience Romance (Late 2024)